# The Girl in the Ice

Jason Vail

A Hawk Publishing book.

Cover illustration copyright Can Stock Photo Inc.
Cover design by Ashley Barber

ISBN-13: 978-1492794691
ISBN-10: 1492794694

Hawk Publishing
Tallahassee, FL 32312

# The Girl in the Ice

# The Girl in the Ice

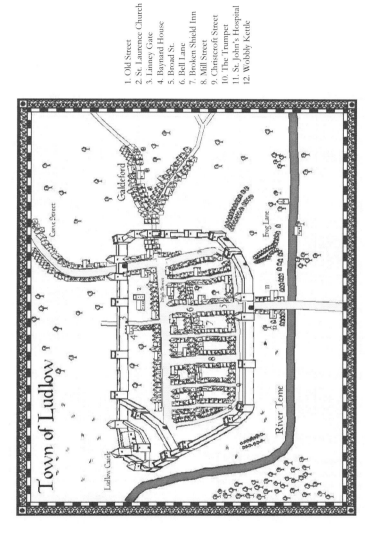

Town of Ludlow

1. Old Street
2. St. Laurence Church
3. Linney Gate
4. Baynard House
5. Broad St.
6. Bell Lane
7. Broken Shield Inn
8. Mill Street
9. Christcroft Street
10. The Trumpet
11. St. John's Hospital
12. Wobbly Kettle

Galdeford

Cove Street

High Street

Frog Lane

Ludlow Castle

River Teme

# The Girl in the Ice

# DECEMBER 1262
## to
# FEBRUARY 1263

# The Girl in the Ice

# Chapter 1

If Edith Wistwode hadn't made everyone in the household go to Christmas Day Mass, the dead girl might not have been found until spring.

That December was as cold and wet and deadly a month as you could ever hope for. Snow came unseasonably early, the day after the feast of Saint Andrew on the last day of November. The snowfall gave a light picturesque dusting to the town, and its quick melting was welcomed, especially the fact that it resulted in very little mud, Ludlow's bane. But a bone-chilling cold followed immediately, which froze the melt, and a sheen of ice covered the ground. The long incline of Broad Street became so treacherous that two horses broke legs in falls and had to be put down, one of them by Stephen Attebrook, who happened to be passing at the time. An old woman fell in the street and broke her hip, a mishap from which she eventually died. Three beggars were found frozen to death outside the town around the remains of their fire. Mistress Bartelott, the widow of late middle-age who lived across the street from the Broken Shield Inn and who had nothing to keep her company but her faith, took a tumble on her way to Mass one Tuesday and broke her wrist. She repaired to her bed and was not seen by anyone throughout the month, to the relief of more than one of the residents on Bell Lane, who were spared her lectures on correct deportment, which she was often keen to dispense from her upper window at no charge.

At the end of the first week, it snowed again, partly melted, and froze once more, leaving another dangerous crust of ice. On Corve Street outside town, a fire left burning too high for warmth during the night threw out sparks that caught the straw on the floor and burned up the house and six of the family inside it; only a child of seven survived by jumping out an upstairs window.

# The Girl in the Ice

This second freeze had no sooner hit than it snowed yet again, this time even more heavily. The third storm left a fall more than knee-high in the streets. In some places the wind sculpted drifts to waist high, and across Saint Laurence's churchyard there was a monstrous drift as tall as a man's head. Most of the roofs of the houses were steep enough that the snow could not find a grip, except along the very peaks. Whenever Stephen threw open his window in the morning, which he still often did despite the cold, he had a glorious view of the town, with brilliant white bars of snow capping every roof clear down the slope to the walls and beyond to the river.

The scene at dawn on Christmas morning was much the same, although the air, which had taken on an almost spring-like tang, was warm enough to leave the shutters open. It was amazing, after so many days of cold, to have a day when you could not see the mist of your breath. How did weather happen? What caused it? Stephen wished he knew.

He paused before closing the shutters. He loved this view, which he took in very morning, even when it rained. Below, movement at the stables caught his eye. Harry the legless beggar sat in the open doorway. It was hard to read Harry's expressions, given the great tangled mass of hair and beard that concealed his face like a mask. But Stephen had come to know him pretty well, and Harry was giving every sign of distress. It was harder for Harry to get around than most people. He sat on a board that had cunning rockers nailed to the bottom, on which he propelled himself with his hands, which were protected by thick leather gloves. He was on his board now and had on his gloves. And he rocked back and forth in the doorway as if about to launch himself into the sodden snow that covered the yard. He had sat like this every morning since the weather had turned bad. In the early part of the month, he had defied the weather and clumped down to his licensed position at Broad Gate. But when the snow got really thick, he had been trapped in the stable like other people were in their houses. Stephen doubted that he had collected more than three pence in the last two weeks. He was probably close to starving. It was a miracle Harry had survived at all.

"Harry!" Stephen called.

Harry looked up. "Don't be taking a piss out of that window, hear? You'll fall and break your neck!"

"Lovely day!" Stephen called back, ignoring the insult. It was best to ignore Harry's insults.

"The damned sun's shining, that's all I have to say about it."

"You're not thinking about going to work, are you?"

"The thought crossed my mind."

"On Christmas Day? It's a day of rest, of rejoicing."

"For you maybe. What do I got to rejoice about? My stump's got frostbite and my purse's empty. Wistwode's charity will only extend so far." Gilbert and Edith Wistwode owned the Broken Shield. They rented Harry his space in the stable; he had fallen behind because of the storms. They had even allowed him some meals for free.

Stephen sighed. He could see Harry's dilemma. One had no right to exist on another's charity. Harry had to go out, despite the hardship. "Wait there!" he called. "I'll be down in a few moments."

"What?" Harry spat. "You're going to give me your blessing?"

But Stephen had already left the window.


He hurried down the stairs, limping because of the pain in his bad left foot, which was missing from the arch forward, the dying gift of a Moorish warrior on the walls of a Spanish castle. It ached so terribly this morning that he could barely stand on it. Sometimes it itched. Sometimes he even thought he could feel the toes that were no longer there. He could hear thumping as people moved around. There were fewer thumps and voices than usual. The deep snows and treacherous conditions on the roads had brought travel to a halt. There were only two guests now, the fewest number in the four months he had lived here. Business had been bad because of the weather for more than just beggars.

The stairway emptied into the hall by the great fireplace. Stephen found Jennifer, the oldest of the Wistwode children, on her hands and knees blowing on the coals to restart the fire. Her mother, Edith, stood behind her, wearing an angry expression. It was evident that Jennie had let it go out, a major sin.

Gilbert the Younger, a boy of seven, suddenly appeared, racing from the back rooms in the inn, which held the pantries and led to the kitchen, a separate building out back. He darted across the hall, weaving between the tables — or attempted to, anyway.

Edith whirled with speed remarkable in so short and stout a woman — for she was shaped, Harry had once remarked in one of his more uncharitable moments, like an ale keg — and snared him by the collar.

"Gillie!" his mother said stonily, "behave yourself! Or I'll have you thrashed!"

The threat was a real one, because Edith's temper had been growing shorter since the first of the month, as business at the inn went from bad to almost non-existent. But Gillie was not the sort of boy to be intimidated. "Yes, mamma," he said with apparent sincerity, and working loose from Edith's grip, he slunk away to the front of the hall, where he began poking his younger brother, Horace, in the ribs with a finger.

Edith did not see this, however, because her attention had turned to Stephen. Her eyes traveled from his head to his feet, and had that measuring cast that he had seen her use on prospective guests when gauging their ability to pay. He became acutely aware of the threadbare state of his clothes — battered and rather shapeless maroon hat, faded with wear; his tatty green coat with the frayed collar and cuffs; the outer shirt, half blue and half white, needing the attention of a laundress, its hem dangling several loose threads; the red stockings that had once been so bright they were almost festive, and now seemed tired; the scuffed and worn shoes. Although he was, or had been, a member of the gentry and had been knighted in Spain, for what little that was worth, his present position paid neither well nor regularly, and this was the best he could do.

In contrast, Edith, Stephen suddenly noticed, was arrayed in her best: a brilliantly white and starched wimple adorned her round head, the veil trailing like a waterfall down her back; a checkered green and yellow traveling cloak joined at the neck with a silver broach; an outer gown of embroidered yellow linen; sleeves so long on the underdress that they almost touched the ground; and her best shoes of delicate calf skin. For a member of the merchant class, she looked quite elegant.

"Sir, you'll be accompanying us, of course," Edith said in a tone that did not invite dissent.

Stephen, who had been expecting this, said, "Yes, of course."

"Do you good," Edith nodded decisively. "You don't get to church half as often as you should." Her attention swung back to Jennie. "Leave it. We have to go, if we're going to get a good spot up close."

"Yes, Mum," Jennie said with some relief.

"Where is your father?" Edith asked. Moving to the bottom of the stairs, she called out, "Gilbert! What's keeping you?"

"Coming, dear!" Gilbert Wistwode's voice came from the depths of the stairwell. "Coming!"

Within moments, Gilbert clumped into view on the landing and descended to the hall. He was no taller than his wife and just as round, as if they had been poured from the same mold. But where Edith's face was often pinched with concern as if on the brink of being overwhelmed by the myriad details involved in running the inn, his pug-nosed visage was genial and relaxed. Like Edith, Gilbert was arrayed in his best for Christmas Mass: a black coat with embroidery in silver thread, a stark white linen shirt underneath and black and white stockings. On his round head, looking as if a breeze could knock it off, was a round red cap that Edith had bought only the week before, venturing out into the cold and snow to do so.

"I'm here, dear," Gilbert said taking Edith's arm affectionately. "There's no rush. It's early yet."

"Jennie let the fire go out," Edith said. "And it is not early. The sun's up and they could have already started."

"Oh, dear," Gilbert allowed, unmoved. "Well, we'll get it started again. No harm done."

"It will be freezing when we get back."

"But there'll be no one to tend to it while we're gone. You've made everyone go to church, including the guests. It's not safe to leave a fire unattended." His eyes swept the room, where the only two guests, a pair of soap sellers, were finishing their platters of bread and cheese that Jennie had set out for them earlier. "We could come back to find a pile of cinders instead of an inn."

"I suppose," Edith said fretfully. She had high standards for the inn, and it pained her when they were not met. A frigid hall was not acceptable.

"There we go," Gilbert said. "Shall we be off?"

The Wistwode family turned toward the door, as Edith called to the family servants in the back to come along.

Stephen headed toward the side door to the yard.

"Sir!" Edith called to him. "Saint Laurence's is this way."

"I've got to see about Harry. I'll be right along."

"Harry," Edith said, as if she had forgotten about him.

She followed Stephen into the yard, where he saw that Harry had not attempted to move from his dry spot in the stable door into the slushy yard.

Edith regarded Harry with her hands on her hips while Stephen disappeared around the stable. He returned a few moments later with a small two-wheeled handcart. Normally it was used for hauling wood from the enormous woodpile that stood in three rows behind the stable.

"What on earth is that for?" Edith asked.

"Harry needs a ride to work," Stephen said. "I thought that, this being Christmas Day, you wouldn't mind if he borrowed it."

"I do in fact mind," Edith said indignantly. "No work should be done on Christmas day."

"The cooks have to cook and the servants have to serve, otherwise we won't have a feast today."

"That's different. That's allowed. Begging is not." Her eyes narrowed as a thought crossed her mind. "He shall come along with us. He needs communion as well as we do."

Harry looked startled to see his fate so quickly decided, and without any effort to consult him. "Now wait a minute," he began.

"Don't say a word," Edith snapped, "or I'll take you for a heathen and you can find another place to spend your nights. You can go to Mass just one day a year. Beg forgiveness for your sins, and pray for salvation. I'm sure that will take most of the day." She looked into the distance and added less harshly, "And pray the weather has truly broken and business gets better. God knows, we need both."

"You can't fight it, Harry," Stephen said. "She'll wear you down."

Harry got a cunning look. "All right then. I'll go. But how am I supposed to move that thing?" He gestured to the cart.

"I'll have to pull you," Stephen said.

"Really!" Edith said, surprised and shocked at the idea.

"Penance for my sins of the year," Stephen said. "There are certainly many." Many that Edith did not know anything about, and with luck she never would: like the dead man in the old latrine not more than thirty yards away and a man he had killed in the lane outside just last October. "Or you could look at it as Boxing Day come early."

"Boxing Day indeed! It's about time that someone recognized my importance," Harry said, cheered at the notion of a role reversal, the comic theme that ran through the heart of Boxing Day, when the low switched places with the high. "Well, what are you waiting for? Set me aboard! I can't climb up there by myself."

Stephen bent to lift Harry. The legless man was heavier than he looked, and, crossing his massive arms in a lordly fashion, did nothing to assist. With a grunt, Stephen heaved him over the side of the cart. Harry landed with a thump and a bitten-off curse. He smoothed his hair and beard. "And I'll have my board, too, lad."

Stephen gritted his teeth at Harry's tone. "It isn't Boxing Day yet." He put the board behind Harry and got between the traces of the cart, regretting his impulse to volunteer.

It didn't help his pride that Gilbert and the servants were staring at him with gap-mouthed astonishment as he struggled across the yard, and Gillie and Horace were openly snickering. "Wipe that smile off your face," Stephen snapped at Gillie, who tried without success to appear solemn.

Stephen continued without pause to the gate and went through to the street, hoping he wouldn't meet anyone he knew.

"Come along!" he heard Edith command behind him and everyone headed into Bell Lane toward Broad Street in procession, with Stephen leading the way.

Stephen's hope that he might remain invisible was dashed at Broad Street. When he turned the corner, he found there were gaggles of people heading uphill to Saint Laurence's Church for Terce Mass, which was the most popular Mass on Christmas day. He knew they were looking at the spectacle with the same degree of amazement as Gilbert and the servants had shown. Some even looked as though they might say something. Stephen's face burned and he kept his head down and pulled. The more quickly he got this humiliation over, the better.

Harry, however, was enjoying his ride. He waved and called greetings to everyone in earshot, and since he knew everyone on Broad Street, he was able to do so by name.

"If you don't stop that," Stephen grated, "you're going to walk back yourself."

"It'll be worth it, your honor," Harry laughed. "Best ride I've ever had in my life."

"I hope you freeze to death, then."

"Not likely. God, what a day! What a beautiful day!"

On good days, a crowd often gathered in the churchyard before the start of a Mass, but not today. Because of the wet, everyone was going straight inside. Stephen manhandled the cart to the edge the path that had been dug through the snow outside the door. Gilbert, Edith, and their family procession flowed inside. Stephen was a bit stung that Gilbert hadn't paused to help him unload Harry.

Harry, for his part, was still waving at those who passed, with a broad smirk on his face.

"I ought to tip you out," Stephen said.

"Don't be churlish, especially at church. Not the Christian thing to do."

Trouble was, Harry was right, and it was this exact impulse that had originally driven Stephen, although his humiliation had overridden his sense of charity. Feeling equally shamed by his public humiliation and by his ugly thoughts, Stephen dropped Harry's board in the snow and deposited Harry upon it.

The smirk vanished from Harry's face as he buckled himself onto the board. "Thank you, Steve," he said softly.

"You're welcome, Harry."

Harry did not pay much attention to the Mass or take part in communion, although he had no doubt that Edith Wistwode intended that he benefit from it. He stayed in the rear of the church by the main, west-facing doors, where the children played and made too much noise for him to hear even the sermon let alone the service. He came in late anyway, having taken the opportunity to hold out his begging cup at the doors to the church. It wasn't his licensed spot, and beggars normally weren't allowed to beg at the doors to the church, but no one had objected.

He had been to enough Masses, though not lately, to know when the end was nearing. He levered himself toward the big double doors. "Be a good lad and open the doors for me, will ya," he called to a boy of about ten who was loitering with his friends against the walls. He had expected they'd refuse and that he'd have to scoot through when the first parishioners left, but the boy and his friends took the request as a sign that they might escape from the confines of the church, and he was able to slip out as they fled.

Harry swung down the path dug in the snow for about thirty feet to be clear of the doors, which he expected to put him outside the cluster that would form there. His plan was to catch the stream as parishioners headed toward the gate. He hoped he'd do even better business than before because he stood to be the tollman for the entire congregation rather than only part of it, as he had earlier in the morning.

The diggers of the path had thrown up the snow into two mounds running from the doors to the gate. The mounds were between knee- and waist-high, except in spots where they had been trampled down, and the thaw was reducing their size so that you could almost see them melting. The spot Harry chose was one of those that children had trampled down in their games and he was able to get almost fully off the path without too much difficulty. He settled in and got out his cup, which was now empty, this morning's collections having gone into the purse which hung from a thong around his neck under his shirt where it was safe from thieves. It is hard to a cut a man's purse that is next to his heart.

He rubbed cold wet hands on his upper thighs, which were all that remained of his legs after his accident. A husband, wife and three young children emerged from the church and headed his way. He put on his best pathetic expression and held out his hand. The family ignored him.

He hawked in disgust and turned to spit.

But something in the snow caught his eye. It looked like a smooth, white pebble. But there were no such pebbles in the churchyard as far as Harry remembered. Perhaps it was a lost gem that a supplicant had carelessly dropped on his way into the church.

He leaned over, the prospect of riches on his mind, and smoothed snow away from the thing.

What he saw made him swallow the hawk.

He smoothed away more snow until there could be no doubt what the thing was.

It was a hand. The slender fingers — which had to belong to a woman — were relaxed and curled as if she was merely asleep, although the palm was covered in crystalline, icy snow. The hand was attached to an arm the disappeared under the mound beside him.

Harry swallowed again. He called to the boys who had preceded him out the church door. They were engaged in a snowball fight and it took several shouts to get their attention.

"Hey!" Harry said. "Come here. I want to show you something."

"What — you want to show us your stumps?" one of the boys mocked.

"No. Something else, you jackass. Something you won't see every day."

You can't go broke betting on the curiosity of young boys, and true to type they swaggered over to see the alleged mystery.

Harry pointed to the hand in the snow.

"Jesus the merciful!" one of the boys gasped. "Is that real?"

"You can bet your soul it's real. Do any of you know the deputy coroner?"

"No." There was a round of head shaking in the group. Young boys and crown officials, well, the employee of a crown official to be exact, do not generally run in the same circles.

"He's inside. Tall fellow, well set up. Black hair. Green coat, blue and white shirt, red stockings. Carries himself like a soldier. Name of Attebrook. Go fetch him right now."

## Chapter 2

Stephen knelt by the hand. He did not touch it. For a few moments, he just looked at it, as what seemed like the entire church congregation drew into a circle around him.

Impulsively, he said a silent prayer for the soul of the dead person. He had never been especially religious, and had become even less so since Taresa died and taken his happiness with her. But there were moments these days when he unaccountably felt the need to call out to God. This woman was surely beyond his help, but not beyond God's. At least, he hoped so.

Then he started clearing the snow away from the body. He began at the hand itself and scooped snow away from the arm. When the snow had first fallen, it had been light and fluffy, but the succession of thaws and freezes had turned it into a blanket consisting of little granules of ice, which made crunching sounds that seemed louder in the silence as he dug, and cut his fingers.

It took a considerable time to dig out the arm, for it lay under the mound bordering the path, which was about two feet high at this spot. It was a slender and shapely arm, although hard as wood. The smooth texture of the skin, which was as white as ivory, gave the impression that it belonged to a young girl. From what he could see so far of her clothing, she had been a working girl: the sleeve of her gown was brown wool, unfashionably short, and utterly undecorated. Underneath, the hem of a linen undergarment was visible.

A church servant jostled his way through the crowd. He had a shovel with a wooden blade, which he held out to Stephen. "You might want to use this, sir," the servant said. "The work'll go faster."

Stephen stood up. The thought of digging down through the snow with the same abandon that one used in digging in the dirt, made him hesitate. He thought about the violence it could do to the poor girl's body.

"I'll do it, sir," a voice said behind him.

Stephen turned to see Thomas Tanner's blunt and homely face. Relieved that he would not have to dig himself, he gave Thomas the shovel. He indicated where he thought the remainder of the girl's body lay. "Be careful. It's not like digging out roots."

"I understand," Thomas said.

It was doubtful that Thomas had ever dug a body out of a snow drift before, but he acted as if he knew exactly what to do. He shaved off layers of snow over the area Stephen had indicated so that an oval flat patch rapidly appeared in the mound which gradually got deeper as Thomas methodically progressed.

Meanwhile, the crowd did not dissipate. The inner circle, which had the best view, stood quietly and watched. But beyond that thin band, the crowd was turbulent and noisy. If anything, it seemed to be getting larger. Death in the street always seemed to attract a crowd the way dung attracts flies. Here it was Christmas Day. They had Yule feasts to prepare and attend. Stephen wished they would just go away.

He spotted the undersheriff's stocky figure in the front row to his left. "My lord!"

Walter Henle was watching Thomas dig. He had the same mixture of horror and fascination on his mallet-shaped face as almost everyone else. It seemed to take a moment for him to register that Stephen had spoken to him. "What is it . . . uh, Attebrook?"

The English gentry had honed the practice of insult to a high art. A nonchalant tone, a carefully composed and subtle arch of the brows or turn of the mouth, were designed to cut as well as any sword. Henle had more than enough reason to hate Stephen. Three months ago, Stephen had saved a man that Henle had been intent on hanging. That the man had been innocent of the crime that had sent him to the gallows did not seem to matter much to Henle. Such flouting of authority was hard for a man like Henle to forgive, but it was surprising and distressing that he would let his feelings show publicly.

Public insults were not to be ignored. Stephen considered how to respond. "Please clear away the rabble, sir," he said evenly.

Henle looked around. Beyond the close ring of rather sober onlookers, the part of the crowd making the most disturbance consisted of younger men and boys and not a few girls. Several snowball fights were going on between various sides whose membership it was impossible to determine. One of the snowballs, which must have been more ice than snow, flew astray and shattered a clay pitcher one man had brought into the yard, spilling ale on him and the woman next to him. Someone had broken out a flute and was playing a saucy tune Stephen recognized. It was a good thing nobody had tried singing along yet, because the verses were very bawdy. At least a dozen men and girls were dancing to the tune. A fistfight had erupted for some unknown reason and the two boys involved rolled on the ground, the bigger of the pair obtaining the command position on the other's chest, from which vantage he proceeded to pound the other boy in the head until a third boy grabbed him by the hair and pulled him off.

"I don't see that they're doing any harm," Henle said. "People must be allowed to have their fun."

"Someone has died by the church door," Stephen said, "and lain here for many weeks. People don't just drop dead at church doors."

"Are you saying you think this was murder? You seem awfully quick to suspect the worse."

"The possibility must be taken seriously."

"I suppose," Henle said in a tone that said in fact he supposed not.

"There may be clues under the snow that will tell us how this girl died."

"Over such a wide area as this? I hardly think so."

Stephen had to admit that Henle was probably right about that. If this was murder and there were clues hidden in the snow, they were probably close around the body. But his temper had taken control of his tongue. "As the crown's representative in this matter, I request that you have the crowd cleared away."

Henle's eyes glinted at Stephen's invocation of his authority. At first, it seemed that he might refuse, which he could very well do. Stephen's real authority was as threadbare as his clothes. But then Henle said, "Very well. If you insist." He turned to the church prior, who also was standing nearby. "My lord prior, if you would kindly lend me the use of some of your servants?"

"Of course, sir," the prior said with some relief. He was no more comfortable with the disturbances than Stephen.

Henle gave terse instructions to one of his deputies, who relayed them to the servants, several castle soldiers who were in the vicinity, and two deacons whose curiosity had led them to linger nearby. They formed a cordon that, with some difficulty, began moving the crowd out of the yard. Those in the quiet circle did not think themselves included in the evacuation order, and remained where they were. Stephen would rather they had gone, too, but he said nothing. Many were leading citizens of the town and although in theory Stephen could order them around, in practice is was not a wise thing to do so.

Gilbert pulled on Stephen's sleeve until he bent over. "Have you lost your mind?" Gilbert hissed in Stephen's ear.

"No, I haven't."

"What do you want to antagonize Henle for?"

"How could such a simple request have made him angry?" Stephen said blandly. "It's his job to keep the peace."

"Humph!" Gilbert crossed his arms and glanced at Stephen, who wore an expression of stony determination. "Well, Christmas dinner will be cold and late — for us, at least."

"Yes, I'm afraid it will be."

Thomas had dug down the depth of a man's forearm when he came upon the first signs of the body: folds of a brown woolen dress.

"I think that's enough, Thomas," Stephen said, kneeling beside him. "We'll clear the rest by hand, if you don't mind."

"Right, sir," Thomas said, putting aside the shovel.

Stephen and Thomas scraped the remaining layer of icy snow from the body with their hands down to ground level, or what passed for the ground, because underneath the body was a layer of solid ice.

When they were done, Stephen rocked back on his heels. Despite the cold, he found he was sweating under his woolen jacket.

The body was indeed that of a young girl just entering her womanhood, fifteen or sixteen years old. She lay on her back as if casually flung down. Her left hand rested beside her head; the right, which Harry had discovered, was thrown out straight to the side. Her left leg was cocked, as if it had been drawn up at the time of her death and then, as life escaped, had subsided to the ground. The other leg lay straight. As Stephen had suspected, she wore a simple brown woolen dress, the sort favored by the poorer maids and servant girls. Beneath the body, lodged in the ice, was a cloak of faded green. Her shoes matched the dress: simple, battered from wear, and cheaply made. Had that been all, there would have been nothing exceptional about her. But that was not all. Even in death, her face still partly covered with snow, it was evident that she had been strikingly beautiful. Gingerly, feeling as if he was trespassing, Stephen smoothed the remaining snow from the girl's face, including the puddles that had formed on her eyes. The face was almost triangular in shape, the chin sharply pointed. Above it was a small, thin-lipped mouth that was now filled with snow and which Stephen did not disturb. Above that was a nose which was narrow but rather jutting and sharply defined but which went well with her prominent cheekbones. Her eyes, which were slightly open, were green, which formed an odd combination with her hair, a thick, lustrous auburn that seemed to glow in the morning light. It made Stephen's heart lurch to look at her: so young, so beautiful, and so dead.

Stephen looked up at the assembly around him. Most of the town's prominent citizens were in the ring, leaning forward to get a better look.

"Does anyone know her?" Stephen asked them.

Nobody did.

## Chapter 3

When Stephen asked the town jurymen to move the body inside the church, they found it was frozen fast in the underlying layer of ice and could not be budged. Stephen asked the prior to have water heated and brought in buckets to melt the ice. This, he was told, would take the remainder of the morning.

The pinnacle of excitement having passed with the uncovering of the body, the town luminaries disappeared home. Stephen let the jurymen go as well. There was no point in forcing them to forego the pleasure of their Yule feasts. Even Gilbert, Edith, and their children hurried away, since Gilbert was not needed at the moment. Soon there was no one in the churchyard but Stephen, Harry, and a few starlings, which pecked at the thawing, exposed ground.

Stephen maneuvered the handcart closer so he could sit on it. He hopped up, his legs dangling. He rested his chin in his hand and regarded the dead girl's face. A gust of wind carried down College Lane from the north, which made him shiver; at least he thought it was the wind, which was cold here in the western shadow of the stone church. A servant poked his head out the church door, but jerked it back when Stephen glanced at him.

"How'd you do, Harry," Stephen asked, not taking his eyes from the girl's face.

"How'd I what?" Harry jerked his head around. He had trouble looking anywhere but the girl's face too. "Oh, how'd I do!" He rummaged with a finger in his begging cup, where there were quarters and eighths of pennies. His mouth moved silently as he counted. "Five and a half pence," he announced finally.

"It was a good morning, then," Stephen said.

Harry grinned. Somehow he had retained all his teeth. Stephen wondered how he had managed that, given the hard life he led. Harry said, "I've told you, you should get yourself a crutch and let 'em see that sundered foot of yours. Pays better than doing that coroner work."

"Sometimes I don't doubt it," Stephen sighed. His superior, Sir Geoffrey Randall, the actual coroner, was late as usual with his month's salary. He had hardly any money, and payment on his stabling fee was over due again for his three horses, the finest things he owned. He looked back at the girl. "I wonder what her name was."

"Doubt we'll ever know," Harry said.

"You don't know her either?"

Harry snorted. "I'd never forget a face like that. Nobody in the county would. Serving girl or no, every man in the shire would be swarming about her and her name would be on the lips of every gossip. I'm surprised she wasn't married already. Girl like her has the means to marry herself into the best of families."

"So she's probably not from Herefordshire."

"Nor Shropshire either, or at least the south of it." Ludlow lay at the northern edge of Herefordshire, and many in southern Shropshire did their business here because it was the closest market town.

"Someone will miss her though."

"I'd say so."

"But she must be from a long way off, because she's been lost for a long time and no one's come here asking after her," Stephen said.

"How do you know?"

"How do I know what?"

"That she's been missing for a long time?"

"Well, three weeks at least — since the last big snow." Stephen said. "Look there. She's stuck in the ice from the last melt, which was three weeks ago. The last snowfall was right after that. Or is your head so addled that you've forgotten already?"

"You're the one who's addled. Three weeks ain't a long time. Two months is a long time."

"All right. Not a long time. But three weeks. She's been dead three weeks. She has to have died just before the last snow. Otherwise she'd have been discovered."

Harry shook his head. "Fancy that. People walked right by her not even knowing she was there." He suddenly laughed, a short bark. "Old Mistress Bartelott took her fall right here — right where I'm sitting! Close enough to touch the lass! Do you think we ought to tell her?"

"I reckon she'll find out soon enough, if she doesn't know it already. The crows speak to her. I don't know how she finds out about things. She never seems to leave her window."

"Aye, she's a witch."

"What do you know about witches? I've met real witches, and she ain't one."

Harry's eyes narrowed. "In Ludlow you've met witches?"

"I didn't say that. But as a matter of fact, yes."

"Who?"

"Never you mind. It's none of your business."

Harry crossed his arms and pouted. "Give over."

"No. Met her on crown business. Sworn to secrecy, I am."

"Lying bastard. You've not met any witches in Ludlow."

"Have too."

Harry was silent for a while. Then he said, "This witch you claim to know, there isn't any chance you'll be coming across her anytime soon, is there?"

"I doubt it. Why?"

"Nothing. No reason."

"What is it? What do you want?"

"Don't want nothing. Oh, all right. Witches, they're supposed to be good at brews. You know, cure you of stuff."

"What ails you, Harry?"

"Nothing." But Harry was blushing furiously above his deep brown beard, which covered his face like a mask and hung as far as his stomach, as if he had suddenly had second thoughts about speaking. "Nothing ails me."

Stephen wondered what could make Harry blush so fiercely. "If you don't tell me what to ask for, I won't be able to get it."

"Forget it. It's not important. Lovely weather we're having today."

"Right. Nice day for finding corpses in the churchyard."

The morning wore on as they waited. The air warmed and puddles began to form in the path. Droplets of melt from flecks of snow Stephen had not cleared away appeared here and there on the dead girl's face and dripped down like tears. Children, released by their parents at the conclusion of their Christmas feasts, drifted into the churchyard. Stephen glared at them and they skittered out of harm's away. Stephen gave the corpse a pull on the leg, hoping that the warming weather had loosened it, but it was still stuck fast.

Gilbert, followed by Jennie, waddled through the churchyard gate.

"Still here?" he asked.

"It takes forever to boil water," Stephen said.

"I'll go check on it," Gilbert said and disappeared round back of the church.

He returned a few minutes later, lugging a pair of buckets. Steam wafted from the mouths of the buckets, like trailing fog. He said in disgust, "They all went to dinner, it seems."

"I'd have gone too, but Stephen appropriated my cart for a chair," Harry said.

"Be quiet and get out of the way," Gilbert said, putting the buckets down beside the body. "Or you'll get wet."

"Come to think of it," Stephen said, "he could use the bath. Have you ever seen or smelled anything so foul?"

Gilbert wrinkled his nose. "Now that you mention it, it smells like dead horse here."

"I had a bath in July," Harry said indignantly. "That's good enough for any man." Nonetheless, Harry moved a safe distance away.

"Shall I do the honors?" Gilbert asked with a touch of weariness.

"If you please," Stephen said, resuming his seat on the cart.

"I don't please. I just had a feeling you'd insist on it."

"Quite so. At some point you need to remember my rank and pay proper respect. You're wearing your clerk's hat now."

"Humph," Gilbert said. "Clerks are paid for writing, not for this." He tested the water in one of the buckets with a finger. Then he began to pour out a small stream around the edge of the body. When he had emptied the first bucket, he took up the second and pour out its contents, too.

When he was done, Stephen tried moving the corpse. It was still stuck. "You'll need to go for more," he said.

"Damn," Gilbert said. "And I've a bad back."

"This is the first I've heard of it."

"You haven't been paying attention." But Gilbert clumped back round the church with his empty buckets.

After he had gone, Harry swung close to the body. He tried moving a leg. "Why don't you give a heave at the shoulders, while I tug here," he said to Stephen. "I think she'll come loose."

Stephen made a face. The thought of jerking the poor girl free like so much frozen wood was deeply distasteful. He had hoped that the hot water would make it possible to lift her without effort. "No thanks," he said. "I'll wait."

Harry did not comment for a change. Instead, he took hold of the girl's legs with his powerful arms, which had grown incredibly strong since he'd lost his legs in that cart accident a couple of years ago, and heaved. To Stephen's surprise, the body came free rather easily.

"There you go," Harry said airily. "You just have to have the right touch."

"You're a wonder, Harry," Stephen said.

"That ought to be worth a penny," Harry said.

"We'll see about that."

Just then, Gilbert appeared with two more buckets of steaming hot water. He saw with some dismay that the girl had been loosened from her icy prison. He put down the buckets and groaned, holding his back.

"Stop your faking," Harry said.

"How'd you like to sleep in the snow tonight," Gilbert shot back.

"You wouldn't. It'd be un-Christian, and this being Christmas Day."

"Enough of that," Stephen said, kneeling at the girl's head. "Help me lift her."

"Where are the servants when you need them?" Gilbert grumbled.

"Same place they were when you went to fetch water," Harry said reasonably.

Gilbert shot him another hard look but did not respond. He took the girl's feet, while Stephen lifted her at the shoulders, and together they placed her on the cart.

The green cloak remained snagged in the ice, however, and threatened to tip over the cart. Stephen knelt and freed the girl's skirt and cloak. Her clothing was stiff and still partly frozen.

"Where should we take her?" Gilbert asked.

"Into the church," Stephen said.

He was about to take up one of the traces of the cart when a shiny object on the ground caught his eye. It lay in the puddle formed by the hot water in the place where the girl's body had sprawled, but was still partly frozen in the ice. Stephen pried it loose with the point of his dagger. He held it up to examine it closely. It was a ring, gold with a green stone. The wide band was molded with sinuous shapes, Irish in appearance, that could have been mistaken for serpents, but which were something at once both ordinary and sinister. The sinuous shapes were not snakes but the stalks of a flower, the heads of which blossomed below the stone. Stephen had seen the like of those flowers before, a dandelion, as an owner's mark burned into side sides of stolen kegs of salt taken from a party of merchants he and Gilbert had discovered murdered on the Shrewsbury road in the autumn before the recent war with the Welsh began. He remembered the vivid sight of seven naked bodies lying in the grass beside a beautiful stream, the peace of the morning disturbed only by the buzzing of the flies about the corpses. He wanted to say something, but his mouth had gone unexpectedly dry and his throat contracted so that he could not speak.

He showed the ring to Gilbert, who bent over to examine it in Stephen's palm. "A lovely piece of work," Gilbert murmured.

"A coincidence?" Stephen asked.

"It must be so," Gilbert said. "Perhaps she's from the same family. Or frequented the same goldsmith."

"Perhaps."

"We mustn't jump to conclusions," Gilbert said.

"I'm not jumping to anything."

"Hmm. I know you well enough by now to see a leap coming."

"What do you have there?" Harry said, clumping close, irritated that they would talking about something and did not include him. Since Stephen was kneeling down, they were at eye-to-eye level. "Somebody lost something?" He gaped at the ring, which must have cost a great deal of money. "Aren't you the lucky one! Don't need your salary now, do ya! That'll fetch well!"

"I don't think I'll be fetching anything with this," Stephen said, closing his fist around the ring and standing up.

"What do you mean?" Harry asked.

"Means I won't be selling it."

"Why not?"

"It's evidence," Gilbert said.

"Oh," Harry said, deflated, as if he had expected to share in the wealth of the find. Unexpected treasure usually was at least worth a round of drinks. "Evidence of what?"

"Of, of — of something," Gilbert said. "Now stop with your questions. We've work yet to do."

Stephen nodded agreement with Gilbert. The ring was evidence, although about what was not clear as yet. He slipped the ring in his pouch and took up one of the traces. Gilbert groaned and lifted the other trace. Together they balanced the frozen body, which was in danger of slipping off as they moved, and wheeled the tragic assembly into the church.

"Do you think she was a thief?" Harry asked. His words echoed in the cavernous interior of the church, which was empty except for him, Gilbert, and Stephen. They were at the mouth of the south transept, just down from the great stone block of the altar, which stood behind its wooden screen in the chancel, or far eastern end. The body still lay upon the cart. Stephen and Gilbert leaned against a wall, waiting for church servants, who had finally turned up, to return with a table.

"What makes you think she was a thief?" Stephen asked.

"Don't know," Harry said. "But that ring looks like too much a bauble for a girl like her."

"We don't know if she was carrying it when she died," Stephen said. "Someone from town — or even a visitor — could have dropped it, and she fell on it."

"The chance that she died on top of someone's lost trinket is too remote to merit contemplation," Gilbert said. "You can't think that, do you?"

"I don't know what to think right now," Stephen said.

"At least you're not leaping to conclusions," Gilbert muttered. "Shows you've learned something these last few months."

"What did you say?" Stephen asked sharply.

"Nothing, nothing," Gilbert said, no apology in his voice.

"You know," Harry said, "if it was hers you'd think she'd be wearing it."

"Wearing what?" Gilbert asked.

"The ring, you dolt."

"I'm losing my patience with you, you legless idiot," Gilbert said.

"You have such a charitable heart," Harry sneered. He waved at Stephen who wanted no part of this dispute. "That ring, it ought to've left a mark if it was hers."

"He's right about that," Stephen murmured. He examined the girl's hands. On the third finger of the left hand, where a woman wore only a wedding ring, were faint impressions that could have been formed by a ring. He held the ring he had found up to the girl's finger while Gilbert bent over his shoulder to watch.

"What did I tell you," Harry said with triumph. "A match."

"It could be," Gilbert said. "But why would she take it off?"

"That's easy," Harry said. "She had an argument with her husband, she gave him back the ring, and he couldn't take no for an answer and killed her. A story that's as old as snot."

"I hope that's all there was to it," Stephen said, thinking that if that was the case the death would be easy to account for once they found out who she was. "Or maybe the marks are nothing and maybe she stole it and the owner caught up with her." It was still too much of a bauble for a simple peasant girl, even if it was a wedding ring. Yet he had noticed something else about her hands when he had examined them. They were unchapped and uncalloused; not the hands of a peasant or serving girl at all. None of this made any sense.

"Oh, yeah," Harry said. "But you don't believe that."

Voices sounded at the western end of the nave. There was a barked curse, followed promptly by a sharp rebuke. The three turned to see who it was: two servants wielding a table through the door. One of them had banged his knuckles on the door frame, which explained the curse. The rebuke had come from the church prior, who was behind them. A third servant carrying the sawhorses on which the table top would rest trailed the prior.

The servants set up the table in the south transept and lay the body upon it.

"Must she remain here?" the prior asked, wringing his hands.

"Why not?" Stephen said. "The light's good in here." The light in the south transept was in fact the best in the entire church. There were stained glass windows on three sides, which gave access to the southern sun. Stephen noticed that high up, one of the panes had broken. A tall ladder leaned against the wall as if left there by a workman to fix the break. As he watched, a sparrow flew out the break in the pane. It was astonishing how it could streak through such a small opening at speed. He wondered how they did that. There were families of sparrows who lived year round in the church, nesting high up in the rafters. How they got in and out of the church had always puzzled Stephen, for somehow they found a way even with the massive doors closed.

"What has the light got to do with anything?" the prior asked.

"I want the people of the town to see her. Someone might know who she is. I'm sure her family will want to hear what's become of her."

"I see. Yes. A sad business."

"Also," Stephen coughed as he broached an uncomfortable subject, "it's warmer here and she'll thaw quicker."

The prior looked startled. "Thaw quicker?"

"She won't fit in a coffin with her arm stuck out like a tree branch."

"It can't wait 'til spring?"

When people died during the winter, it was not uncommon for them to be put in storage until the ground thawed out enough to dig a grave. Stephen grimaced. "She deserves better than to be left out in a shed like so much firewood."

"I suppose you're right," the prior said, although no doubt he was considering the cost of burying her now and who would have to foot the bill, the parish most likely. "What a lovely girl she was." He brightened. "We'll ask for contributions on Sunday."

"Good," Stephen said.

"Have you any idea how she died?" the prior asked.

"We were just about to find out. We'll need blankets — two if you can spare that many. Or sheets."

"Two? What for?"

"To cover her."

"But — but — she is clothed!"

"Not for long!" Harry cackled.

"Shut up, Harry!" Stephen said.

The prior looked shocked. "You're not going to . . ."

"We always do," Stephen said grimly.

"Almost always," Gilbert interjected. "That is, we must if the cause of death is not obvious." He added, "As it is not obvious here."

"Oh, dear," the prior said. "She'll be . . ."

"Naked," Harry put in.

"Get out, Harry," Stephen said.

"I can't stay and watch?"

"No. No one's to come in until we're done. It isn't fitting."

The prior had recovered from his shock. "Quite right. Out you go, all of you." He turned and addressed both Harry, who was close by, and the three servants, who had lingered by the altar curtain in hopes of learning something worth putting on the gossip circuit. The servants moved off obediently but Harry was slow in his clumping toward the main door.

"Leave off!" Gilbert and Stephen heard Harry protest. "You can't herd a man like he was cattle! I'm going — I'm going!"

"Don't think about trying to sneak back in, Harry," the prior said as they went out the door.

"Yeah! As if I can jump and reach the latch!" they heard Harry say as the door closed and a thick silence settled on the interior of the church.

Stephen and Gilbert turned back to the dead girl.

"Must we?" Gilbert asked.

"I don't see any other alternative. She didn't just freeze to death. People who freeze to death don't lie like that, as if they've been knocked over. Remember those beggars, curled up as if they had just fallen asleep."

"Yes," Gilbert said reluctantly. "I know."

"I'm not looking forward to this any more than you are," Stephen said. "But we must know. We must!"

Gilbert blinked, taken aback at the strength of Stephen's declaration. "She's just a girl, Stephen, who died in the snow. There is no need to become so agitated."

"Just a girl . . ." Stephen's voice trailed off. Gilbert had attended to hundreds of dead people as Sir Geoff's clerk. Stephen had attended only a few. It was easier being indifferent to death on the battlefield than it was to this. And though she was not the first woman he had attended — there had been two in the fire and one of the beggars — this death affected him as if she were the first. But he said, "Sorry. I'm still getting used to this."

"Of course." Gilbert nodded.

The first step was to cut off the girl's clothes to see if there were any marks on her body that gave any indication of the cause of her death. Gilbert drew his knife and leaned over her, as if to begin. But he hesitated, as he stared at that beautiful face, which even death could not diminish.

"That's odd," he said.

"What's odd?"

"I hadn't noticed it before," he said as if to himself rather than in answer to Stephen's question.

"Hadn't noticed what?"

"The marks."

"What marks?"

"There." Gilbert pointed to the girl's eyes.

"I don't see any marks."

"Look more closely. Those little red spots just below the eyes." Gilbert put his thumb on the edge of the girl's right eye. Remarkably, he was able to pull back the skin below the eye. "There are more."

Stephen saw the spots now — little red pinpoints, some of them looking faintly star-shaped on the cheek around the eye, on the flesh of the socket and on the eyeball itself. Like some kind of faint rash.

"What do they mean?" Stephen asked.

"We'll see. It could be nothing." Gilbert flicked the snow out of the girl's mouth. Stephen had expected her mouth to be full of snow. But instead, beneath a surprisingly thin sheen of snow there was dark, greenish ice behind her teeth. The lips and jaws were still frozen and could not be prized apart, but even Stephen could see, as he leaned his head close to Gilbert's for a better look, that she had bruises on the insides of her lips.

"Stephen," Gilbert said softly, "would you go fetch Harry's cup?"

"Harry's cup?"

"That's right. We've need of it, more than he does now, I think."

Bewildered, Stephen went outside, where as expected, Harry was waiting on the path. "I need your cup, Harry."

"What for?"

"Would you like me to send Gilbert after it? He'll not be as polite about it as I am."

Harry handed over the cup. "I want it back. And no spitting in it, or anything like that!"

Stephen went back into the church and gave the cup to Gilbert, who set it on the table beside the girl's head.

"Oh, dear Lord, forgive me," Gilbert sighed. He put the point of his knife in the girl's mouth and prized out a spoonful of greenish ice, which he put in the cup. When he was done, he sniffed the contents of the cup.

"What is it?" Stephen asked, as bursting with curiosity as Harry must be, marooned outside.

"I'm not sure," Gilbert said. "I don't recognize the odor, but then I am not very good with herbs."

"You think it's a potion?"

"I can't think of what else it might be."

"What about the marks? What do they mean?"

Gilbert put his knife away and folded his hands into his sleeves. "Sometimes they are found on the drowned. But more often on the smothered. I don't know what causes them, but I've seen them more than once. The marks on the lips, now. Those are common and their cause is immediately apparent — someone pressed her lips closed, violently. And from that, I imagine she probably died."

"Smothered! Then she really was killed."

"It would appear so. I'm satisfied with this evidence. I'm not cutting her clothes off. You can if you like."

Stephen had had little enthusiasm for such a violation to begin with. He had none at all now and welcomed any excuse not to go any further. Stephen picked up the cup and sniffed the contents himself. The odor was faint, a musty sharpness that he could not identify. "Someone tried to make her drink something she didn't want to."

Gilbert sighed again. "I assume so."

"The question is who — and why."

"Sadly, I doubt we will ever know."

# Chapter 4

The girl lay in the south transept for three days, her body covered to the chin with a linen sheet, which made it look even more like she was just sleeping. Everyone in town had a chance to see her. In fact, the church was crowded every day with onlookers. As news of her lying in state spread, she drew visitors from the surrounding countryside. Some came at least twenty miles for the spectacle. From this viewing it became ever more clear that she didn't come from the town or any of the surrounding lands. More oddly still, no one could remember how or when she had gotten through the gates.

Not even the gate wardens recalled her. "I'd not forget a face like that," the one-toothed warden Gip said, gazing down at her alabaster face. "And neither would you."

By Saint Innocent's Day, Thursday the 28th, the girl had thawed enough for burial. The priest had taken up a collection to cover the cost, and when Stephen arrived that afternoon at the conclusion of the noon Mass, he found a carpenter at work in the transept making the coffin. It was a pauper's coffin, a plain and simple box. No peaked top for her, just a flat rectangle of wood nailed down. She'd go into pauper's ground too, without anything to mark the spot where she had been planted. Grass would grow over the grave and within a few years she'd be forgotten, other than as a story to be told at Christmas. And before too many years doubtless even that story would be lost.

There was another craftsman at work in the transept, a stained-glass maker at the top of the ladder repairing the broken window. People did not normally work during the week following Christmas unless they were servants or there was some urgent business. This master was not from town. Stained-glass-making was a special skill and he had been brought in from outside by the prior. It must be that his holiday idleness was costing the parish too much money. Or perhaps the priest intended to plug one of the holes used by the sparrows, which often left gifts on the heads of parishioners, to the annoyance of all.

Since news that the girl was to be buried that afternoon had spread, a great crowd had gathered, with some jostling, at the mouth of the transept. There were leers on some faces, which irritated Stephen, and he drew the hem of the sheet over the girl's face.

"Hey," said a boy, who had been sitting on the ground by the foot of the ladder. He got up and pulled down the sheet to expose the face. "I'm not finished."

"I think you are," Stephen said, taking hold of the sheet and returning it.

"What's the problem, Bertie?" called the man on the ladder.

"He won't let me finish, Dad."

"He's your boy?" Stephen asked the craftsman.

"Yes," the craftsman said. He climbed down the ladder. He put down a green triangle of glass encased in a lead frame. He rested his hands on his hips in an unmistakably aggressive manner. "What, exactly, is the problem? Who are you?"

"I'm the deputy coroner," Stephen said, "and I wish that this woman be treated with a minimum of respect, which means she is not to be the object of gawking."

"I'm not gawking," Bertie said, unmoved by what little eminence Stephen's position might provide him. "I'm working."

"What do you mean, you're working?" Stephen asked, taken aback.

"Here," Bertie said.

He held out a sheet of Italian paper. That alone was startling enough. Italian paper was exceedingly rare and expensive, and Stephen had only seen examples of it three times in his life. But what was on the paper made his mouth fall open. It was a drawing of a face. In ink. He took the paper from the boy's hands and compared it to the face of the dead girl on the table.

"Looks right like her, don't it?" the glassmaker said proudly. "Don't he do a good job? Bertie's really got the touch."

"It's amazing," Stephen said. The resemblance between the face and the drawing was uncanny, magical even. It was the girl, as she must have been in life. Instead of the slack look borne by the corpse, her eyes were open and lively, and she wore a slight smile. It almost seemed as if she was smiling at him.

"Bertie does all me drawings for the glass," the glassmaker said. "He's got such a better hand than I have, and so young. Just eight, you know."

"You're not going to put her in the window, are you?" Stephen asked.

"I might. That's not a bad idea." The glassmaker's fingers drummed on his lips as he considered this thought. "Provided that old fussbudget doesn't notice. I could put her high up. There." He pointed. "You won't say anything about this, will you?"

Stephen shook his head. A mere coroner's deputy had no warrant to interfere with art, even if he might be inclined to express an opinion or two, politely, of course.

Bertie held out his hand. His fingers, Stephen noticed, were stained with ink. "Can I have it back now?"

"I'd like to keep it."

"It's mine," Bertie protested. "We need it now, see?"

"I've need of it, too," Stephen said. "More than you. You can make another."

Bertie's father looked as though he might protest but the look on Stephen's face stopped him. He said, "There isn't time. They're about to plant her. The box is almost finished."

"We'll wait."

"On whose authority?"

"On mine."

"Wonder what the prior will have to say about that?"

"She's lain here three days. Half an hour more won't make a difference."

## The Girl in the Ice

"It'll take more than half a hour to get it right," Bertie said.

"Better get to work, then." To stifle further protest, he tossed Bertie two pence, enough to buy four pounds of cheese, acutely aware of how empty his purse was now.

The glassmaker smiled at the gesture. "All right. Bertie, there's another piece of paper in the box behind the circle cutter."

"Thank you." Stephen blew on the ink to make sure it was dry. He carefully folded the paper and put it in his belt pouch beside the ring.

It took a full hour for Bertie to get his drawing done to his and his father's satisfaction. During the course of his work, the prior himself appeared. He observed Bertie's work with a frown, asked if things were ready, received the reply that they were not, and departed.

When Bertie was done, Stephen asked who would prepare the body for burial. The girl, being a stranger and lacking relatives to wash and to shroud her, had to depend on volunteers for this final service. Several women from the town had agreed to do this solemn work. Indeed, they had already performed part of this service, for earlier in the morning, when no one was about, they had removed the girl's clothes, which were in a neatly folded stack on the ground beneath the table, and washed her body. Two of the women were still in the crowd and they came forward to wrap the girl in the sheet, which would serve as her shroud. Then, one of the women at the girl's head and one at her feet, they lifted her with surprising ease down into her coffin. The carpenter nailed the lid shut with swift efficiency.

A boy was sent to fetch the prior, who for some reason wanted to be present. No special burial ceremony was planned, for one usually never was. The required ceremonies had already taken place: One of the priests of the church had conducted the required vigil and a Mass had been said as her funeral. All that remained was to give her to the earth.

During all this, people in the crowd began moaning and praying out loud. Suddenly, a woman cried out and stumbled forward. Her head was wrapped in a scarf so that only her eyes showed. She fell to her knees before the small stack of clothes, and unwound the scarf to reveal a face marked by a dozen seeping, awful sores. Before anyone could stop her, she lifted the girl's gown to her hideously marred face.

"What are you doing, woman?" cried the prior, who yanked the woman up by the shoulder and pried the dress from her hands. "Behave yourself!"

"I — I — I ask only that the lady bless me, lord!" the woman stammered. "To heal me!

"She was just a girl and had no power to heal anyone!" the prior shouted. "Get back, you!"

"You saw her face!" the woman cried. "She was a saint!"

"There may be saints, but that girl wasn't one!" the prior said adamantly, shoving the woman into the arms of the crowd.

Whether or not there had been any shortage of volunteers to prepare the girl's body, there were none now to carrying her coffin. The crowd surged into the transept, shoving Stephen against a wall and nearly trampling Bertie, who would have fallen underfoot if Stephen hadn't grasped his collar and pulled him to safety. A multitude of hands grasped the coffin and lifted it high and many other arms strained for a simple touch. The prior found himself in a tug of war as some people sought just for a touch of the garments while others tried to tear them from his hands, and if not accomplishing that, at least to get a fragment to take home.

Hands even reached for the paper in Bertie's grip, but Stephen batted them away. He felt a plucking at his belt pouch and hacked at the offender with the edge of his hand. Those grasping hands were so persistent that he had to draw his wicked, foot-long dagger to discourage them and to save Bertie's picture.

As the crowd surged away to the west door, Stephen handed Bertie back to his father. "You'd better guard that thing well," Stephen said, indicating the portrait. "Blink an eye and it'll be stolen."

"Aye, sir," the glassmaker said, pulling his forelock in his first sign of respect, "we'll keep proper care of it."

With the last of the crowd struggling through the west door, the only figure in the nave now belonged to Gilbert, who had come in without Stephen noticing. Gilbert looked sadly at the dagger in Stephen's hand, as he returned it to its scabbard on his right hip. Gilbert glanced at the prior. "Forgive him, father, for baring steel in a house of God."

The prior looked rattled. He clutched the girl's dress to his chest. Although it was rumpled and torn in a few places, the garments seemed intact. He gulped. "I didn't see anything, my son. And if something untoward happened out of my sight, God will deal with it in His due time."

"Let me help you, then, father," Gilbert said and assisted the priest in refolding the dress and undergarments.

"Thank you," the prior said, and hurried away to the exit in the chancel that led to the priest's dwelling house.

Somewhat dazed by this commotion, Stephen and Gilbert followed what was left of the crowd into the churchyard. It was still cool enough that there were large piles of snow everywhere, but they were much trampled down. Gilbert took the lead and forced their way through the press, calling out, "Make way, make way for the deputy coroner!" He seemed to get grim enjoyment out of this for some reason.

When they reached the center, they found the coffin set beside a hole that had been hacked in the ground. Although the top of the ground had been frozen, which required cutting with an ax, the soil beneath was soft, and in fact the snow melt had filled the grave with water which a half dozen men were removing with buckets on the ends of ropes.

When the bucket men had spilled out all they could, a gang of men lowered the coffin into the grave.

A call went up, "A prayer, father! A prayer for Our Lady!"

The prior pursed his lips in exasperation. Like most men in his position, he came from a gentry family, and only the women of the gentry or higher were entitled to be called lady. The swift promotion of the poor, unknown servant girl who had died at his church door ran against the grain. But the demand for a prayer could never be denied. "Be still then!" the prior ordered.

He put his palms together, bowed his head, and began speaking loudly in English so that the people in the crowd could understand, "Oh, Father, a poor innocent soul comes to you before her time, seeking succor . . ." All round, everyone went to their knees. It was unusual for people to do so at a funeral in the open like this with the ground wet and snowy. Only Stephen and a few figures watching from the street remained standing. Gilbert tugged at the hem of his shirt. Stephen looked down. Gilbert mouthed, "Get down." Stephen sank to his knees. The snow, mostly trodden to slush now, was cold and wet, and sent a shiver through him.

During the prayer, Stephen heard some schoolboys in a clump not far away hissing to themselves, and the words "Nostra Domina Nixae, that's how you say it," filtered through the bowed heads to his ears. Followed by, "Are you sure?" Answered by, "Yes, of course, I'm sure, you idiot."

Nostra Domina Nixae.

Stephen struggled to dredge up what remained of his Latin. Nostra Domina caused him no trouble, but he stumbled over Nixae for a moment until the meaning of the phrase finally came to him: Our Lady of the Snow. A murmur spread through the crowd like the rushing of the wind through a forest as the name she had been given leapt from one set of lips to another: the Snow Lady. Even Gilbert had taken it up. When Stephen glanced at him his lips were moving with the name and when Gilbert became aware of Stephen's eyes on him he said, "It seems fitting, doesn't it? She has to have a name, after all."

If the prior was aware of what was transpiring among the crowd, he gave no indication and continued with his prayer with blind determination to reach the end.

"Amen!" the prior pronounced with more authority than probably was necessary.

The crowd climbed to its feet.

The ceremony, such as there would be one, was completed.

The men who had carried the poor girl to her grave now took up wooden spades and began shoveling earth on top of the coffin. The first falls of earth landed with a hollow thump.

The crowd watched silently.

A woman bent over and threw a sprig of ivy, probably plucked from a Christmas display on one of the houses of the town, into the grave.

The woman with the sores on her face threw herself on the ground at the lip of the pit and cried out for help in healing her disease. Friends bent to her aid. People began to shout as the crowd packed around the grave so that the gravediggers were pushed aside. The tumult grew.

The prior, and probably even the bishop of this diocese, would have his hands full with this one. Ludlow had no native saint — not even the relic of one. Perhaps they had found one now. Only time would tell.

Stephen and Gilbert backed out of the crowd. He had done all that he could do for the girl. He had seen her to her final rest. This near riot seemed the wrong way to send the girl off, and he wanted no part of it.

The churchyard gate was jammed with people and there was no way out of the yard except to hop the fence. This posed no obstacle for Stephen, but Gilbert would have fallen if Stephen had not caught his arm.

"I say," Gilbert panted when they had gained the street, "I feared we might be trampled."

"They are a bit riotous," Stephen said.

He turned toward the Broken Shield, thinking of the warmth of the fire and the pot of ale that awaited him. He tried to push out of his mind the sense that he should do something to give the girl a name and determine the manner of her death.

But a half dozen people stood across his path: a short man dressed in the blues, reds and yellows of a successful merchant, a woman a head taller shrouded by a blue cloak, and three other men behind them, and last, a young blonde girl of marriageable age. They all wore solemn expressions.

"You're Stephen Attebrook, aren't you, sir?" The short man asked in a Gloucestershire accent. "Folk hereabout said you were."

"Why do you want to know?" Stephen asked, a little more harshly than common courtesy required, but he didn't feel in the mood to talk with anyone.

Then Stephen noticed the little silver badge the man wore on his coat — a dandelion with a drooping flower. The sight of that flower caused Stephen's heart to miss a beat and he felt Gilbert's hand upon his arm.

The stout man said, "Some of my family have gone missing. We wish you to find them for us."

## Chapter 5

"I believe the people you seek are dead," Stephen said.

The woman and the girl covered their mouths with their hands. The men all said at once, "Dead? Dead?" as if they did not want to believe it.

The stout man asked finally, "How would you know?"

"My friend and I," Stephen said, indicating Gilbert at his side, "found the bodies of five men, a young woman, and a small child on the road to Shrewsbury last month. They had been murdered and robbed." He pointed to the dandelion medallion. "They were carrying a cargo of salt. The barrels were marked with that same flower."

The older woman flung her arms around the stout man and buried her face in his chest. Her shoulders wracked with sobs. The stout man gazed at Stephen over her shoulder, his face grim. "Seven, you say."

Stephen nodded.

"The baby too?" the young girl cried.

Stephen noticed now that she was older than she first appeared, probably seventeen or eighteen. She was so small and slender that she looked younger. And she was so pretty that his mouth went dry at the sight of her. He said, "I am afraid so. A boy of about four. Would that be right?"

The girl nodded, her eyes squeezed shut and tears flowing down her cheeks. "Poor little Thomas."

"Who were they?" Stephen asked the stout man.

"My brother and his family, three cousins, and a carter. What happened to the bodies?"

"Buried in the churchyard at Stokesay. Do you know it?"

The man nodded. "I have seen it from the road many times since I was a boy. But I have never been there. Murdered," he added, as if he could still not believe it.

"Let us not stand here in the street discussing such terrible matters," Gilbert said. "Come to my house so that we can talk."

The stout man's name was Adam Saltehus. The family was from a place called Worlebury in Gloucestershire. The older woman was his wife, Mary, and the girl, his daughter, Agnes. The two men, Nichol and Benedict, were his brothers. Together they owned a saltworks on the bay of the Severn across from Cardiff. They stared at the fire in the fireplace at the Broken Shield with faraway looks in their eyes, taking no warmth from the blaze.

Stephen sat not far away with a cup on his lap. His skill at comforting the bereaved extended only as far as a clumsy "I'm sorry," accompanied by awkward shifts of weight from one foot to another, punctuated by nodding and overseen by a glum face. He had used all that up in the first few moments before they had repaired to the Shield.

Gilbert and Edith were much more able in this capacity. Edith made everyone comfortable and welcome, and she and Jennifer bustled about getting drinks and food and blankets for people to put over their laps, as it was cold in the inn's hall despite the fire. Normally the blankets cost a visitor extra, but Edith made no mention of this. For his part, Gilbert spoke soft condolences to each of the visitors, as if he was their parish priest, which to Stephen's surprise they seemed to appreciate a great deal.

"How did it happen?" Saltehus asked harshly. His hands shook and some ale spilled onto his leg.

Stephen and Gilbert exchanged glances. The memory of the horror was not something either of them liked to dwell on, for it had been worse in its way than any of the others they had attended — more terrible even than the corpse of a drowning victim they been forced to view or the bodies of people burned to death in their house, the flames having charred them black and shrunk the adults to the size of children. And the only time they had spoken openly about it was in their report to Sir Geoffrey Randall, Stephen's superior and the coroner in these parts of the county. Randall had received the news with no comment, since hearing about death was his job, but he had looked alarmed when they had given him their opinion about who was responsible and had ordered them not to speak of the matter to anyone.

"This is delicate," Sir Geoff had said anxiously. "Very delicate. The possible repercussions! We cannot make accusations without more proof. Until we learn more, I order you both to say nothing to anyone. Do you understand?"

"We can't just leave it lie," Stephen had said.

"You'll leave it lie if I tell you to! I must think about how to handle this. We can't simply accuse an earl — and a Marcher earl at that — of robbery and murder. We must be careful. We must be certain."

Stephen must have looked sulky at this order, for Sir Geoff had said, "Look, you. Know you nothing of politics? FitzAllan teeters on the edge of loyalty to the crown. If we accuse him, we risk pushing him into the baron's camp."

Stephen sloshed the remains of the ale in his cup, remembering that conversation.

"How did it happen?" Saltehus said relentlessly, his voice a monotone.

Stephen sighed. He did not wish to speak about the matter any more than he cared to remember it. But these people had a right to know. So, he said, "We were on our way to the Augustine priory at Clun. We found them about a mile north of Onibury on the Shrewsbury road." He went to describe where he and Gilbert had found the bodies: in a pleasant, unmowed pasture by the river; how he concluded they had been shot down from ambush from the high ground on the right of the road and then killed as they lay wounded by perhaps eight or more robbers. He left out how he had concluded that the woman had fled with the child only to be captured and killed, or about how the bodies had all been stripped and left naked, covered with flies when he had seen them. He told them also about the cart which had been emptied of its contents and left overturned in the middle of the stream; and how the tracks of the killers had led off to the west.

"Who did this?" Saltehus grated. "Do you know?"

Stephen hesitated. He and Gilbert had a firm suspicion that the man ultimately responsible was the Earl of Owestry and Clun and lord of Arundel, Lord Perceival FitzAllan. But in truth, as Sir Geoff had said, they hadn't any real proof. Stephen had guessed at the man's guilt after spotting a barrel of salt bearing the same dandelion mark in the possession of a Welshman known to trade in stolen goods, and one of the Welshman's drovers had let slip that the barrel had come from FitzAllan. Stephen had leapt to the conclusion that it was FitzAllan behind the robbery, even though he knew that leaping to conclusions was a dangerous business and that one was as likely to fall into error as collide with the truth.

"No," Stephen said at last. "I don't know." He looked up from the fire into Saltehus' eyes. It was hard meeting them. "No one knows who's responsible for the robberies on the highway."

"There have been many these last few months," Gilbert murmured. "The road to Shrewsbury is not safe."

"The sheriff should do something about it," Mary Saltehus said.

"Too busy collecting taxes to spend on his own comfort and hiding from the Welsh," Benedict said.

"Aye," the others agreed.

"We can expect no help from the authorities," Saltehus said. "If we're to have justice, we must make it ourselves."

Stephen nodded, holding his cup out for Nan to refill on her way to the kitchen at the rear of the inn. Saltehus was right. You couldn't depend on anyone but yourself in the end. But he dreaded what he knew would come next.

"The folk here say you're good at finding things," Saltehus said to Stephen.

"It's just a rumor," Stephen said. He waved at Gilbert. "Started by him."

Saltehus glanced at Gilbert, who stared at the fire with a rueful curl on his lips. Saltehus said, "More than a rumor, I've heard."

"People do exaggerate."

"We can pay you."

"We are expensive."

"We?" Gilbert said.

Stephen smiled humorlessly, without looking at Gilbert. "We," he said with some emphasis. At Saltehus' puzzled expression, Stephen added, "He is the smart one. I just get in fights."

Gilbert snorted and almost lost a mouthful of ale. "That's true."

"I'm sure we'll need both before the end," Saltehus said.

## Chapter 6

The purse that Saltehus had put on the table before he departed sat heavily on Stephen's lap. He was a good judge of the weight of money and it felt like five shillings — a quarter the cost of an average horse. He owed three shillings for the stabling of the three horses he possessed and the stableman had been around several times during the last week to badger him for the arrears. He loosened the drawstrings and poured some of the silver pennies into his hand. Most were tarnished and dull, but a few were shiny.

He had taken the money against his better judgment, half now and half when the robbers were found. He did not expect to see the other half. It seemed impossible that they would find enough evidence to condemn FitzAllan. But the money was hard to resist. Now the only problem was how to make his inquiries without Sir Geoff finding out. After the warning to lay off pursuing FitzAllan, he would not be pleased to be disobeyed.

"I do not wish to traipse about the country on a fool's errand like this," Gilbert said, eyeing the coins in Stephen's palm. "It's the middle of winter. Haven't you noticed?"

"Winter is hard to miss," Stephen said. He dumped the remainder of the contents of the pouch onto the table and began dividing it into to equal piles.

"It will mean riding," Gilbert said more to the fire than to Stephen. Gilbert disliked few things more than getting onto the back of the horse, or in his case, a mule.

"Riding?" asked Edith, who was passing by with a tray of cheeses. "Riding where?" She paused, her eyes flitting suspiciously from Gilbert to Stephen, then to the piles of money on the table. She had the ability to sense trouble at forty paces and her senses were screaming.

"Nowhere, my dear," Gilbert said.

"I should hope not," she said emphatically, giving Stephen a stern look. "You have not yet recovered from your last misadventure. It is too soon for another."

"Easter would be soon enough," Gilbert murmured as his wife strode off, dispensing cheeses to the patrons who had demanded them. "If ever."

"We can't let him get away with it," Stephen said, disbelieving that such words issued from his mouth. As much as he wanted to see FitzAllan get his just reward, he desired someone else to do it. FitzAllan had suspected they discovered what he was up to while they were in Clun, and had thrown them in his gaol to silence them. The memory of their stay there was too fresh, and he did not wish for a repeat of the experience.

"We can't afford to go into the Honor of Clun," Gilbert said, referring to the great swath of land surrounding the village and castle of Clun which was Perceival FitzAllan's principal domain, as if he had read Stephen's thoughts. The truth lay somewhere deep within the honor, and undoubtedly the only way to get it was to enter that land.

"No."

"Or anywhere near it."

"Well, we shall probably have to go near it."

"You're sure I must go?"

"You're my conscience. I can't do without you. Think of the trouble that will ensue in your absence."

Gilbert sighed. "God knows, you need one. Since you haven't one of your own, I suppose I shall have to do." He waved at Nan to refill his cup, and said, "Being a conscience is hard and dangerous work. I will cost you a lot of money." He eyed the piles with some surprise that one was not smaller than the other.

Stephen smiled thinly. "You will cost a lot of Saltehus' money."

"It's good to know that someone thinks I'm worth a lot of money."

After training with the castle guard the next morning, Stephen stopped at the Ludlow guildhall, a tall half-timber building across Castle Street from the Wattepas' goldsmithery. The hall's upper floors projected into the street and were held up by posts, giving the impression of a porch, where people could, and often did, shelter from the weather. Benches had been put up by the front door for that very purpose, and three of the town's deputy bailiffs occupied them.

"It's a bit early to see you up and about, sir," one of the bailiffs said as Stephen reached for the door latch. Even though Stephen had his shield on his back, his helmet under one arm and a wooden and real sword under the other, and it was perfectly clear what he had been doing, the bailiff asked, "Somebody die?"

The other bailiffs seemed to think this was very funny.

"Not yet," Stephen said. "Is Tarbent about?"

There was some creaking on the boards above their heads, followed by shouting. A muffled voice answered the shouting and was answered by more shouting. The bailiff who had spoken pointed in that direction. "The scribbler's up in his hole, as usual."

"Watch yourself," another bailiff said. "He's in a foul temper this morning. His clerks were slow in getting his fire going."

"He's always in a foul mood," Stephen said.

"Shake that pointy thing in his face, your honor," another bailiff said. "That might improve his temper."

"Make him more polite, at least," the first bailiff said.

"Until your back's turned," the second bailiff said.

"Aye, there's that."

"Sir Geoff says I'm not to make him mad," Stephen said.

"Sir Geoff knows best," the first bailiff said.

"I always say that as well," the third bailiff said.

"Shouldn't you be out collecting taxes or rents or something?" Stephen asked.

"It's too early for that," the first bailiff said.

"Most people are still at breakfast," the second bailiff said.

"People don't like being bothered at breakfast," the third bailiff said.

"Why aren't you at breakfast?" Stephen asked.

"We're waiting for Wattepas to open up. He feeds us every morning."

"Good fellow, Wattepas," the third bailiff said. "Knows how to treat people, well Master Wattepas does, anyway."

"Right," said the first bailiff. "Can't say that the wife is as charitable."

"They're late today," the second bailiff said. "Problem with their fires as well."

"Wet wood," the first bailiff said. "It's the thaw. The wood piles got wet and the wood's damp."

"Say," the second bailiff said, "any word on who the girl in the ice is?"

Stephen shook his head. He still had the folded piece of Italian paper with her portrait drawn on it in his belt pouch. There was no need to show them the paper. They had been among the throng who had seen her laid out in the church.

"Yeah," said the third bailiff. "I'm not sure I believe this saint business. She was a pretty thing, but hardly a saint."

"Don't you go talking like that," the first bailiff said. "She could be a saint."

"Saint or no," the second bailiff said, "she died just the same. Seems to me that she must have had lodgings in the town. I doubt she got in one of the gates after dark. The wardens would have said something. Girl like that is hard to forget. Have you thought to ask around?"

It embarrassed Stephen that he had not thought of this. "The town was full of refugees. People threw their houses open to them. She could have stayed anywhere. And as you said, she was memorable. Someone would have spoken up. Besides, it's not really my business who she is. It's the sheriff's."

"Aye, that's true," the second bailiff said. "Though I don't think any of those fellows are likely to pull a muscle in trying to find out anything about her," he said referring to the deputies under Walter Henle. "Well, it's just too bad that we'll never know her name." He glanced at the first bailiff. "Saint's got to have a name. You can't just call her Saint Somebody." He fixed his eyes on Stephen again. "You'd be doing the town a service if you could put a name on her. We've been experiencing a rush of pilgrims since she was found. Gate tolls are up from it, not to mention donations at the church."

The first bailiff nodded. "And tomorrow's a market day. You'll see what she's doing for the town."

Edmund Tarbent, the town's chief clerk, was beating one of his scribes when Stephen entered his office at the front of the guildhall. The scribe lay curled into a ball on the floor as Tarbent rained blows on him with a cane. Tarbent, a short and muscular man with a blunt face and long brown hair that surrounded his bald head like a shawl, wielded the slender wand with great vigor. It made an audible thump at each stroke, which the scribe endured without a whimper. Another scribe hunched over parchments on a desk, pretending not to notice.

Tarbent paused and wiped his brow, as if taking a break from heavy work. Irritation passed over his face at the interruption. The scribe looked through his fingers at the pause and scuttled behind a table.

"Attebrook," Tarbent said, setting the cane in a corner by his chair where it would be handy and acting as if the unpleasant scene had not occurred, "what brings you here?"

"A favor," Stephen said carefully, pretending that he had not seen the beating. He had endured similar treatment from Ademar de Valence long ago when he had been Valence's clerk, but the memories and hatred of the experience were still fresh.

"Ah, what sort of favor?" Tarbent said. He glanced at the two scribes as if to question whether they should remain. Some favors should not be discussed with others about.

"I need a beggar's license for the market," Stephen said.

"Oh." Tarbent's eyebrows rose in surprise. "Not for you, of course."

"No."

"That fellow who lives in your stable?"

"Yes.

"For the market."

"That's what I said."

"Well, there is a problem with that."

"Oh?"

"All beggar's licenses for the market have been given out."

"Have they really?"

"Yes. We carefully regulate the number we grant. Helps maintain public order, you know. The beggars don't get in as many fights over the choice territory and the people aren't bothered as much."

"Sensible. I am sure that you can help me, though."

Tarbent glanced again at the scribes. The one who had been beaten by now had climbed to his feet and resumed his place at a table, where he avoided eye contact with Tarbent.

Tarbent barked, "Richard! Clarence! Go fetch some wood! Dry wood, understand!"

"Right, sir," both scribes said in unison as they went out.

"If I grant this license," Tarbent said when the door had closed and they were alone, "there will have to be an accommodation."

"Of course."

"I will require one quarter of the earnings. Paid promptly at the end of the day, before this fellow leaves the square."

"A quarter!" Stephen had been expecting to pay a bribe, although nothing as large as this. "That will leave me with practically nothing."

Tarbent smiled thinly. "I suspect it will leave your fellow with practically nothing."

"A tenth. Not a penny more. He always does well. People are always generous because of his injury. He will yield you plenty at that fraction."

"His personality offsets any sympathy he might receive due to his injury. A fifth. I shall go no lower."

"An eighth. You are taking advantage, sir."

Tarbent almost laughed because they both knew who was getting robbed and it wasn't either of them. He said after a pause meant to indicate a desperate internal struggle, "I suppose that in this one case I can make do with an eighth — besides the fee, of course."

"You are a gentleman, sir."

Tarbent nodded, pleased at the courtesies Stephen had shown. He was from a gentry family, but a lesser son with few talents who had found no other place for himself but as town clerk of Ludlow. "You will have to straighten things out with the other license-holders by tomorrow. The bailiff will tolerate no disturbances among them."

"I will speak to them personally."

"Very good," Tarbent said, as he gathered a blank piece of parchment and reached for a pen. "Oh, and there is a charge that must be paid immediately."

"You surprise me, sir. I thought we had concluded our business."

"Only just," Tarbent said as he held out his hand.


A chill wind whipped through Broad Gate, where Harry sat on the ground wrapped in a blanket. Whenever someone came through the gate, he pulled the blanket back to reveal his stumps and held out his cup with a miserable, suffering expression. How he was able to convey suffering with his face so covered by matted hair and beard was a mystery to Stephen. He must have managed to convince many a traveler, for he usually did all right at the gate, even with the regulars. Perhaps they enjoyed the show he put on.

Other than for Harry, the gate was empty when Stephen arrived. Even Gip, the gate warden, could not be seen, as he was sheltering in the tower. He would not come out until a traveler arrived, depending on Harry to give the warning.

"Ah," Harry said as Stephen stooped beside him, "you wouldn't by chance have brought me something to nibble on, have you? Edith wasn't generous with breakfast this morning."

"Not exactly," Stephen said. He held out a folded scrap of parchment.

Harry's hand snaked from under his blanket and accepted the scrap. He opened it and held it upside down. The ostentatious way he did this implied that he knew which way the letters ran, although he could not read. "Parchment's hard on the digestion. What is this?"

"A license to beg in the market," Stephen said.

"You're going to beg at the market?"

"No, you are."

"I am?" Harry squinted suspiciously. "What is this going to cost?"

"An eighth to Tarbent after the fee."

"He always gets his cut, the robber. What's yours?"

"I want you to ask around about the robberies on the Shrewsbury road. Learn everything you can. I'm especially interested in anyone who has been robbed on the road within the last month or two and lived to tell the tale. If you find anyone like that, ask them to stop by the Shield."

"That's it?" Harry asked, astonished.

Stephen nodded.

"Why can't you do this yourself?"

"I would rather not be connected with the inquiry, openly at least."

Harry grinned. "You don't want FitzAllan finding out that you're on his tail, eh?" He had heard the story about how Stephen and Gilbert suspected FitzAllan and had been arrested and gaoled by him as a consequence.

"Something like that."

"He's the vengeful sort, that's true."

"And rather lacking in scruples."

"Same as all lords. Out for themselves alone, and the rights of the little people be damned."

"They're not all that way."

"When you find a decent one, you let me know." Harry drew the scrap under his blanket. "Give a man a little power and what does he do? Enriches himself at others' expense. Look at Tarbent. He'd be a pauper if it wasn't for the graft."

He rubbed his hands together. "You won't mind if I make a few pennies in the effort?"

Stephen shook his head. "I expect that."

"Oooo," Harry cooed in anticipation of his profits. Being able to work High Street on a market day was the most coveted beggar's license in town. His brow curled in sudden concern. "One-eyed Mary, Toothless Dick and the Walnut won't be happy about this." These were among the other beggars licensed to beg the weekly market.

"I'll take care of them," Stephen said.

Harry pulled his beard. "How long's this thing good for? Just the day?"

"Forever," Stephen said, "if you live that long."

## Chapter 7

Harry paused at the threshold of the stable and gazed with distaste at the churned up slush in the Broken Shield's yard: nasty, cold and damp, puddles everywhere with a sheen of ice upon them. Once the sun got properly up, all would melt and the yard would become a pond. The market, broad and open as it was, would only be worse.

"You're going to make me sit in this wet?" he asked.

"I'm not making you do anything," Stephen replied with some impatience. "I'm offering you an opportunity."

"My normal working conditions are better than this," Harry complained. "It's dry under the gate. Although," he conceded, "it does get windy and cold this time of year."

"So what? Sacrifices must be made. Think of your profits, man."

"If my stumps get frost bitten, there's nothing left to amputate." He added with some slyness, remembering his trip to church on Christmas, "There is our little cart."

"You can make it go yourself now?" Stephen asked.

"No, but you could help."

"I will not." Hauling Harry to church on Christmas had been humiliating for a person in Stephen's position. He had been able to justify it as charity on the holiday and as an early Boxing Day. But those times were long past now. He had sunk pretty far since the heady days in Spain when it looked like he might become a lord with a manor of his own, but he was damned if he was going to sink any lower than Sir Geoffrey's hired helper. There was some dignity in that, but not much.

"Then I guess I'm not going."

"Damn it, Harry!" Stephen fumed. Why was it so hard to make people do even the simplest things? Then he realized, Harry was trying to manipulate *him*. It was working pretty well, too.

Stephen spotted one of the stable boys on his way from the woodpile to the kitchen. "Mark!" he called. "How would you like to earn a farthing."

"Sir!" the boy called back. "Would I! Just a moment!"

Mark rushed into the house and returned to them. "Who do I have to beat up?"

"You couldn't beat up a bale of straw," Harry said.

"Be polite, Harry," Stephen said. "Mark's going to be your helper. Mark, Harry needs to go to the market this morning, and he would like some assistance. Namely, he is borrowing the handcart and he needs someone to pull him up the hill."

"That's it?" Mark asked with distaste.

"And Harry will pay you the farthing," Stephen said. "From his earnings."

"Damn you, sir!" Harry protested.

"Thank you, Harry," Stephen said, charitably bringing over the cart.

Neither Stephen nor Mark made a move to help Harry onto the bed of the cart. Harry gazed up at it, as if he expected such assistance. But when it did not come, he pulled himself up with surprising ease. "All right, then," he said. "I'll need some straw. This bed's rock hard."

"Fetch some straw, will you Mark?" Stephen asked.

"A farthing, you said," Mark said.

"A whole farthing, payable at the end of the day. After you fetch him back."

Mark pursed his lips and disappeared into the stable, returning with an armload of straw which he dumped beside Harry. "You can make your own bed," he said.

"Thank you, Mark, my boy," Harry said with exaggerated courtesy. "You are too kind." When, of course, he had not meant to be kind at all. Like most people, Mark looked down on the deformed and crippled as lesser people.

Stephen handed Harry his blanket. "Off you go now."

Despite his misgivings, Mark got between the traces and dragged the cart toward the gate, as Harry waved his good-bye to Stephen. "And careful not to stick yourself with that thing!" he called out, meaning the arrow thrust into Stephen's belt. Then he also waved to Edith, who regarded him from the side doorway with some suspicion since the cart belonged to the inn and no one had asked permission to take it.

"It's just for the day!" Stephen called to Edith as he entered the stable to saddle one of his horses.

"Carts cost money!" she shouted at his back. "Make sure it returns in one piece and unfouled."

"Harry!" Stephen said when he passed the cart just before it reached Broad Street. "Edith says you may not piss in the cart."

"Well, damn," Harry said. "That's really going to ruin my day. There's nothing like a piss in an old cart to make a man feel better."


Ludlow had four main gates and three smaller ones. Only locals who were absolved of the toll were allowed to use the smaller ones, which opened onto lanes outside of town where the town's suburbs lay. Everyone else had to use the main gates. Since the girl in the ice was not a local, she had to have come in one of the main gates. It couldn't have been the one at Broad Street, for Harry's usual spot was within the Broad Gate tower. He was a sharp observer and he would have remembered a girl as striking as she had been. So that left the Dinham, Corve and Galdeford Gates.

Stephen climbed Broad Street, wishing for better weather: warmer or colder, it didn't matter. But this in between, with slush and ice everywhere was torture. Because of the muck and the danger the mare might fall, he led the horse up the hill on foot. His boots were immediately soaked through and his remaining toes had begun to complain before he even reached the top of the hill despite the fact he had stayed at the edges of the road and out of the stream that had already begun to flow down its middle. The only people in view were a half dozen small boys who had launched twigs and blocks of wood into the stream and were chasing them down hill, followed by three barking dogs.

"Careful you don't fall in!" Stephen called to the boys. "You could be swept to your death!" The tendency of Broad Street to develop a torrent down its middle during winter melts and storms was a subject of jokes that were very old and often repeated, although most people never got tired of them.

"Not bloody likely!" one of the boys shouted back.

At the corner he had a view all the way along High Street to the castle. Normally this early on a market day, there was a good mob of vendors in the middle of the street. But today there might have been only a dozen or so, most of them standing about clutching their arms against the chill in puddles of water, looking miserable. They seemed to be local people with surplus grain hoping to sell to people from the countryside whose stocks had been destroyed or carried off. There were in fact more sellers than buyers picking among the offerings and the air was oddly quiet, without the usual calls from sellers about the extraordinary value of their wares. It was altogether a very sad spectacle. But then there was really little to be happy about in any winter, and with the Welsh having despoiled a good bit of the country about the town, there was even less. And there was still February and March to look forward to, when food really got scarce.

Stephen did not linger here, but continued eastward past Draper's Row where a certain draper's establishment lay empty and as yet without a tenant as a result of the owner's untimely death last fall to the crossroads where High, Old Street, and Galdeford Road came together. This was the Beast Market on another day, but there were no beasts in sight. Nor, apparently was anyone interested in commerce. The windows of the cooks, bakers, tailors, and smiths whose shops occupied this place were down and the shops open, but there were no customers in sight.

Stephen felt so sorry for one baker, who sat alone at his window with his head in his hands, that he bought a bun he could not afford, as he had a weakness for honeyed sweet buns. On impulse, he showed the girl's picture to the baker. The fellow marveled at the picture, and at how accurate a likeness it was, but he denied having seen the girl before she had been displayed in the church.

"I'll tell you," the baker said as Stephen returned the picture to his pouch, "I'd sure remember a girl like that."

"You'd think so," Stephen said. "But nobody seems to."

"It's as if she just popped out of the ground — or out of the sky," the baker corrected himself, as the reference to the ground suggested she had come from an unsavory place.

"Yes, but girls can't fly."

"Well, she's a saint, after all."

"I think that has yet to be determined."

"I wish they'd hurry up."

"The Pope has something to do with that. I hear he takes his time about it. Centuries, even."

"That isn't going to help the town. Anyway, the girl doesn't need the Pope's permission to work her miracles."

"If only she really could," Stephen said, turning away and finishing his sweet bun, wishing he had a whole tray of them. "I need one now."

As he trudged up toward the Galdeford Gate contemplating the possibility of miracles, he reflected that he had in fact given himself an impossible task — no, two impossible tasks. It was bad enough that he felt compelled to give the girl a name, but it was far worse that he had taken someone's money for a job that he never would be able to fulfill. It was dishonest. There was no getting around that. I am as bad as those killers on the road, he admitted bitterly, hating himself for his weakness.


None of the wardens at Galdeford Gate had seen anyone resembling the girl in the drawing, so Stephen continued to Corve Gate. It was the oldest in town, distinguished by its square towers rather than the rounded ones found at the other gates. The gates stood open and the two wardens on duty were warming themselves by a fire set in a metal grate that rose above the sodden ground just inside the gate. They shared a bench while the beggar licensed for this spot, Clemmie Paddlefoot, squatted on a stone with one of her children.

Stephen showed the drawing of the girl in the ice to the two wardens, who shook their heads that they had not seen her except in the church.

"What about the boys upstairs?" Stephen gestured toward the towers looming overhead. Most of the wardens were bachelors who were given beds in the towers as partial payment for their service.

"They'da said something," said one of the wardens whose name was Tim.

Clemmie snorted. "The boys wouldn't notice if she had run up and kissed 'em. Let me see that thing."

"Would have," Tim the warden said.

"Bullshit."

"Watch your tongue."

Clemmie stuck out her tongue. "You watch it. I know you just want to suck on it."

"I wouldn't mind if you'd take a bath once in a while."

She cackled. "This from the man who likes to take sheep to bed!"

"Well," the warden said, laughing, "sheep are more fun than you anyway."

Clemmie winked at Stephen. "Look what I've got to put up with."

"You poor dear," Stephen said, handing over the drawning.

Clemmie studied the drawing. She handed the sheet of paper to Stephen, and only then did he notice for the first time that her middle finger was missing. "I seen her," Clemmie said.

"Have not!" It was Tim's turn to snort.

"Have so!"

"Why'd you never say nothing?"

"You wouldn't have believed it."

"I don't believe it now."

Clemmie looked slyly at Stephen as if she was considering demanding a contribution. Stephen waited with crossed arms. Evidently concluding that there was no reward, nonetheless, she said, "It weren't here. I seen her down by the Trumpet. Just a glimpse, mind you. But I think it was her."

"Not bloody likely," Tim said.

"It could've been."

"What were you doing down there anyway?" Tim wanted to know. The Trumpet was a modest inn in Dinham Lane, which was on the other side of town just below the castle.

"None of yer damned business," Clemmie said.

"When was this?" Stephen asked, returning the drawing to his pouch.

"A month ago, maybe."

"During the troubles." When the town had filled to overflowing with refugees from the countryside fleeing the Welsh. All the inns had been so full that people had opened their houses and those not fortunate to find a bed with a roof had been forced to sleep in the streets.

"Yes."

"What was she doing there?" Stephen asked.

"Trying to get a bed," Clemmie said. "Well, the girl who was with her was, anyway."

"The girl who was with her?" Stephen asked, startled.

"Yeah, she was trying to sweet talk Jacky." Jacky was the owner of the Trumpet.

"The other girl was trying to sweet talk Jacky," Stephen said, still struggling to digest that the girl in the ice had not been alone. That meant that someone, this other girl, had abandoned her, could even have played a role in her death. If he could find that girl, he would know the dead girl's name.

"That's what I said. You deaf?"

"And you saw the girl in the ice?" Stephen asked.

"Just a glimpse, mind you."

"How did you get this glimpse?"

Clemmie hesitated, glancing at Tim and the other warden, who were following this exchange closely, for it would make excellent gossip that they could parlay into free drinks. Clemmie rose, "Can we talk privately, governor? In confidence?"

"All right."

The two of them withdrew to the middle of the street. Clemmie said, "I approached her."

This explained her need for secrecy. She had begged outside the Trumpet, where she had no license to do so. If the wardens found out about it, they were bound to report the transgression, which could mean a fine.

"You won't tell on me, will you, governor? On account of the help I've given you?"

"No," Stephen said. "So you asked for a contribution and at that point you saw her face?"

"As close as I am to you. But she turned away and drew her hood about her. Never said a word. Then Jacky chased me off."

"So you left them at the Trumpet."

"Aye."

"You're sure it was her?"

"Well, it all happened real quick like. And it was evening, so the light was bad, you know."

Evening: so Clemmie was begging within the town after dark, when the gates were shut and curfew had fallen. The town beggars were supposed to stop work at sundown and be off the streets like everyone else. But early December had been a time of tumult, when the usual rules had been set aside, for the streets had been filled with people even after curfew.

Clemmie continued, "But it's always stuck in my mind why such a highborn girl would be trying to find room at the Trumpet. You know, rather than at a better place. Like the Broken Shield."

"Highborn?" Stephen asked, startled again, although he had already had suspicions about this.

"Yeah, it was pretty clear she weren't no peasant or serving girl. She smelled too good for that. All perfumy."

Stephen nodded, ruminating on this information, hoping it was true. "Was this before the big storm, or after?"

"Before."

"You're sure."

"As sure as I'm missing a finger."

"Thank you, Clemmie."

"Yer servant, governor," she said, beaming at the courtesy. It probably wasn't often that anyone thanked her for anything.

She strode back to her stone.

Tim asked, "What'd you tell him?"

"Nothing."

"What'd she tell you?" Tim called to Stephen, who was still standing in the middle of the road, staring into space, mind churning.

"Nothing that would interest you," Stephen said finally.

"Shit it don't!" Tim called to his back, as Stephen passed through the gate and left the town proper. He said to Clemmie, "Come on, what'd you tell him?"

"Crown business," Clemmie said. "I ain't allowed to say."

The argument continued as Stephen passed out of earshot.

## Chapter 8

Ludlow was so small a town that it could support only two fletchers. Both had shops on Corve Street down the hill from Corve Gate which lay within shouting distance of each other. Since the two men were brothers, this was probably not a coincidence. Since they did not get along, there were frequent complaints from their neighbors about their arguments in the street.

The shops were small, as in ordinary times there was not a great need for arrows. But with the recent troubles and the expectation of more fighting in the spring, demand for replacements had overwhelmed the proprietors, and at the first shop Stephen came to, the apprentices said the owner was off buying wood for arrow shafts and would not be back until the end of the week.

At the second shop, the owner and one apprentice were hard at it trimming goose feathers while the second was heating glue in a pot over a small fire at the rear. Only a single bundle of sticks that would be shaped into shafts stood against a rear door. Normally, bundles hung from the ceiling to cure, but now there were none, although there were as many as twenty bundles of finished arrows waiting only to have heads applied to them stacked by a rear door.

"Could I speak to you for a moment?" Stephen called to the proprietor.

"Go see what he wants," the shop owner ordered the apprentice hovering over the fire without looking up. "And be quick. Don't let the pot get too hot."

The apprentice removed the pot from the direct flame and came to the window. He looked apologetic. "Is there something I can help you with, sir?"

Stephen laid the arrow on the counter. It was yellow along the shaft except for red and yellow alternating stripes from the level of the fletching to the nock. Stephen asked, "Have you ever seen this sort of work before?"

The boy regarded it politely. He shook his head.

Stephen didn't expect that the boy would be able to answer the question. "Will you ask Master Farwell?"

"Pa! He wants to talk to you."

"Is he ordering?" Master Farwell asked. "Or is he selling?"

"No, I don't think so. It's that coroner fellow. The one who solved the draper's murder, and the one up the road at Webbere's."

"Tell him to go away. We're busy."

"He's busy," the boy said to Stephen.

"I gathered that."

"I have to get back," the boy said. "The glue will overheat. Then it goes bad." He hurried back to the fire. But he hesitated, as he prepared to move the pot back over the flames. "This isn't about a murder or anything, is it, sir?"

"Yes," Stephen said. "It is."

Master Farwell glanced at Stephen. "I don't know nothing about no murder, and I've got a thousand shafts to make by the end of the month, or I lose the contract to that pissant of a brother of mine. Can't get enough good birch wood, the smith is behind on the heads, and there's a shortage of good feathers. So go away."

"I will not," Stephen said. "This is crown business." Although it most definitely was not. There was always the chance that Farwell would gossip about the visit, but he thought it unlikely that it would get back to Sir Geoffrey.

Farwell put down the feather and knife in his hand and came to the window. He glanced at the red and yellow arrow on the counter. "What's this?"

"The killers left it behind."

"What killers?"

"There've been robberies and murders on the Shrewsbury road." Stephen hoped that the fletcher would not apprehend that fell outside his jurisdiction.

Apparently, the fletcher did not think of this, for he said, "These are bad times. There are murders all over the place. I cannot keep up with all of them."

"Well, I am interested in a particular murder."

"Why?"

"None of your business. I want to know about this arrow. Can you tell who made it?"

"That depends," Farwell said, bending over the arrow. He took it up and flexed it, sighted along the shaft, fingered the fletches, ran his fingertips along the wood and laid the point of the slightly barbed head to the pad of his index finger. "Made of alder," he said dismissively. "Whippy, too, even for that miserable wood. I don't use alder. Too light and weak even for hunting arrows, in my opinion." He returned the arrow to the counter. "Utterly unremarkable. You say this was used in a murder?"

"You heard me right"

Farwell sniffed. "Well, it's a hunting arrow, of course."

"I thought it might be. From the markings and the head." War arrows were sometimes painted, but since they were often produced en mass, decoration frequently was neglected. Hunting arrows, however, usually were painted so that they could more easily be found in the brush if the arrow happened to miss its target.

"Ha! It's the wood gives it away. No one uses alder for anything but hunting arrows." Farwell sniffed at the arrow. "It's decently fletched, I'll give him that. But its cheap: cheap wood, cheap hunting head. It's too whippy for a longbow, as well. Why, it hasn't even got horn on the nock. It would tend to shoot wide." He reached for a length of string on the table behind him. There were black marks along the string at one-inch intervals. Farwell laid the string beside the arrow and counted out the inches. "Thirty and a quarter," he said when he finished. "Made for a big man with a long draw. Still, I doubt it was meant for a longbow. Flatbow more likely."

"But can you tell who made it?" Stephen was counting on the fact that craftsmen in a region knew each other, even if they lived in separate towns, and could spot each other's work.

"Wasn't me, I'll tell you that. Or my brother."

"I did not think so."

"So, it killed somebody, this arrow?"

"It shot wide."

"You don't say." Farwell smiled at his prediction being proved right.

"You have no idea then? This work is foreign to you?"

"I didn't say that. I may have seen its like before."

"Yet you seem reluctant to share your opinion. It makes me wonder if you have one. Perhaps I should consult your brother."

"My brother is an idiot."

"Not everyone thinks so."

Farwell drummed his fingers on the counter. "There are fellows who make arrows of this like."

"You are no closer to satisfying me than before."

"Fellows in Shrewsbury."

"That is helpful. A name. Give me a name."

"I would ask Edmund Tomkys. I have seen him peddling such inferior work at the Hereford fair."

"Hereford. That's far afield for a fellow from Shrewsbury."

"People there don't know him, or the poverty of his skill. He profits from the unsuspecting."

Stephen took up the arrow. "Still, shot from the right bow it should serve."

Farwell shrugged. "I suppose so. I know that I would not make its companion. I am an honest man, unlike some."

"Edmund Tomkys," Stephen repeated.

"A tall fellow. Brown beard mixed with gray. Very morose."

"You know him better than you let on."

"We've met. That's all I care to say about it."

"Thank you, Master Farwell. Good day to you."

## Chapter 9

Stephen mounted the mare and turned back toward town. At the bridge to Corve Gate, he directed the mare into the ditch circumventing the town. Since the houses in the suburbs did not overflow into the ditch, it was one of the more popular short cuts around the town.

The ditch was so deep that even on the back of a horse Stephen's head did not reach above ground level, and his only views were of the tops of houses and the town wall, where one of the watch looked down with bored eyes as he passed by. "Watch yer step there, governor!" the watchman called, as the mare swerved around a pile of trash that someone had thrown into the ditch in defiance of the law, and then a woman squatting on the slope by a folded patch of canvas that had been a tent. It had been pitched at the bottom of the ditch, but with the melt it was too soggy for good camping. The woman watched him suspiciously as if she feared that he had come to run her off, since strictly speaking, squatters were not allowed to populate the ditch any more than people were supposed to use it as a repository for their trash. But Stephen merely nodded as he passed, and then turned the corner as the walls led southward.

At Galdeford Gate, he dismounted and walked up the slope to the road, as the incline was so steep that he feared the mare could not make the climb with him on her back.

He passed another bun shop on the road, which made his mouth water, but he had spent his quota on buns for the day, and though the proprietor called to him, he could only wave at her.

He went left at the fork onto the Upper Galdeford Road, keeping to the edges of the street as much as possible, for the mud was less pernicious there.

Shortly, he passed a little stone chapel on the left and the houses began to peter out, with the yards becoming larger and the houses more separated from each other, until he finally reached the house which sat under a large spreading oak.

Beth Makepeese was in the yard with her oldest daughter Sally raking up acorns. The poor often ate boiled acorns and acorn bread when food got scarce. Beth leaned on her rake, and said, "Well, governor, come to visit, have you? It's been a while. I thought you might have forgotten about us."

"Do you know if Julia is home?" he asked nodding toward the stand of wood beyond the field at the back of the house.

"She might be," Beth said. "There's a fire going there. She usually banks it when she's out. Don't want to leave it going, you know, and burn down the house."

Calling Julia's hut a house was overly generous, but Beth was right about the fire, because now that Stephen looked more closely, he could see smoke rising from among the trees. "Mind if I cut through?"

"Suit yourself. Say, you wouldn't mind delivering a satchel for me, would you, if you're going that way? It'll save us a trip."

"All right."

Beth waved at Sally, who ran into the house and emerged with a wool satchel. She handed the satchel up to Stephen, who saw it contained a loaf of bread — real bread, too, not the acorn variety. Beth had been badly beaten in the autumn by a fellow who turned out to be twice a murderer, and Julia, who had a way with herbs and healing, had tended to her injuries. This must be part of the payment. It moved Stephen to realize that Beth and her children were eating acorn bread so they could pay the debt.

"Good day to you, mistress," Stephen said as he rounded the corner of the house.

"Good day to you, governor," Beth said, resuming her search for acorns.

Stephen crossed the field to the stand of trees. About forty yards inside the wood stood Julia's hut, a thing so small that five or six people could not sleep comfortably within it, as Stephen himself had learned last autumn, when he had spent a night here.

Julia stepped out of the hut as he dismounted and tied the mare to a sapling. "Well, look who's here." She was old and bent, with a face as wrinkled as a well-traveled roadbed.

Stephen handed her the satchel. "From Beth Makepeese."

Julia accepted the satchel. "What trouble is brewing now?"

"Enough to keep me busy." Stephen drew a clay vial from his belt pouch and held it out to Julia.

"What's this?" Julia fingered the vial.

"I was hoping you could tell me. You're the herb expert."

Julia pulled the leather stopper from the vial and sniffed the contents. She looked sharply at Stephen, then upended the vial over an index finger. Some of the contents, a greenish sludge, oozed onto the finger. Julia tasted it gingerly. She spat into the snow and flicked the sludge off her finger.

"What are you doing with this?"

"What is it?"

"A potion."

"I know it's a potion. What's it a potion of?"

"An herb, a simple vine. You'd just think it was a nuisance if you didn't know any better, though it's a pretty thing when it flowers in summer." She gestured to her garden by the hut which was barely visible in the snow. "I had some growing there. It's useful to treat many illnesses: rheumatism, gout —"

"Gout!"

"Yes," Julia laughed, "if taken carefully. Sir Geoff sends a man around every few months for the syrup I make."

Julia walked to a stub nearby that was used for splitting firewood and sat down, favoring her back. "It has other uses. It can intoxicate, give people trances, still the shakes in old people, relieve pains in the chest. Take enough and it will make you mad."

Stephen shook his head, bewildered why they had found such a potion in the girl's mouth.

"Why are you interested?" Julia peered upward at him.

"We found it in a dead girl's mouth. Someone clamped her lips shut as if trying to force her to take it."

"Ah," Julia nodded. "What girl would this be?"

"I'd rather not say."

She chuckled. "As well you might, if you don't want to tarnish her reputation, whoever she is."

"What do you mean?"

Julia stirred the slush with a foot. "It has other uses, more sinister uses."

"It kills?"

"In large amounts, yes. But in smaller ones, it will cause a woman to lose a child. There are those who come here, secretly, asking after the syrup of the nightshade, because they have got with a child they do not want."

"And you let people have it for that purpose?"

"I do not ask. I am not responsible for what they do. They pay. That is all that counts." She fixed him with a sharp eye. "Forced to drink, you say?"

"Yes."

"Perhaps by someone who did not want her to have the child."

"Could be," Stephen said, trying to digest this possibility. He remembered vividly how shapely the girl had been. She had shown no sign that she might have been pregnant.

"You sure you don't want to tell me who she is? Was?"

"No." Stephen recovered the vial and replaced the stopper. "That's best kept a secret." Already, people visiting the girl's grave were claiming miraculous cures simply from lying upon the spot where she had been laid to rest. Would their trust in her diminish if this truth got out?

"It's not hard to guess who she is, you know," Julia said slyly.

"If you do, keep it to yourself. If I hear the slightest rumor, I'll be back to visit you."

Julia opened her mouth to make some smart retort, but she reconsidered. She nodded.

"Good. Thank you for your help."

## Chapter 10

The Trumpet lay at the foot of Dinham Lane where that narrow alley running downhill from the castle struck Mill Lane, which ran along the south wall of the town. The plot it occupied was triangular in shape, and thus so was the building, a small intimate thing of blue-painted timber and white plaster, and the jaunty sign of a jester playing a trumpet that promised more comfort than it actually delivered. Among innkeepers it was known for its sparse food and sparse rooms, but travelers lacking means found it just a left turn from Broad Gate and perhaps a hundred yards farther on their journey, a much easier pull than the climb uphill to the Broken Shield with its greater comforts and greater prices.

Stephen paused at the prow of the building, where a rain barrel caught runoff from the roof. The mare nuzzled the contents of the barrel as he slid off. There was still a film of ice on the water, which Stephen broke with a fist so she could drink. He tied her to the handle of the barrel, and went into the common room.

The room was small and as triangular as the building that embraced it, with only half a dozen tables arranged to catch the heat from the fireplace within the far wall. Whoever was in charge of the fire had let it burn to embers that were in danger of expiring, not that it mattered at the moment, since the room was empty. Stephen wondered if it was always so at this time of day, even though the dinner hour was approaching. Perhaps such a modest establishment made its money on supper as people came in for the night.

He heard voices from the rear, in the rooms behind the fireplace. He pushed open the door by the fireplace. It opened into a kitchen, where a woman with a very broad behind was bent over a skillet of onions and sausage on the fire, and a stout man had thick forearms thrust into a barrel of dirty dishes.

"Have a seat there," the stout man said. "I'll be right with you."

"I didn't come for the custom," Stephen said. "Sorry."

The stout man dried his hands and arms on a towel. "I know you. You're that coroner fellow."

"I have that honor. You're Jacky Triplett?"

"You've coronered me!" Jacky said, laughing at his pun.

"Stop that!" the woman said without turning around from her skillet. "Sweet Jesus, and the man's not even drunk yet. Forgive him, yer honor, he's got things loose upstairs."

"I think we all have things a little loose up there," Stephen said. "We just try not to show it."

"I hope yer speaking for yerself, sir," the woman said.

Jacky poured ale into a wooden cup, which he extended to Stephen. "Whatever's loose upstairs, I know how to treat distinguished visitors. You've come on business, I take it?"

"Unfortunately." Stephen sipped from the cup, wishing he could have some of the sausages and onions instead, as his stomach had begun to rumble at the aroma. The worst thing about being poor, aside from the lack of steady women, was the bad food, if there was any food at all.

Jacky settled against a table and crossed his arms. "Nobody's died hereabouts lately. We'd have heard about that."

"This isn't about a recent death."

"Ah," Jacky said, waiting for Stephen to go on.

"During the recent troubles, before the big storm, two women came to stay here. Do you remember them?"

"Two women?" Jacky frowned. "Governor, we were overflowing, like everyone in town. All our rooms were packed wall to wall. I even had people camping in the back garden. You'll have to give me more."

"They would have been alone, without men."

"It may be that I recall such. Why?"

Stephen removed the drawing of the girl in the ice from his belt pouch. Jacky bent over it, with the woman peering over his shoulder. Stephen asked, "Was she one of them?"

"Good Lord!" the woman burst out. "You think *she* was here?"

"You didn't see her, though," Stephen said, disappointed.

Both of them shook there heads.

Jacky said, "There was a pair, though. You remember, Abby. They kept to themselves. I don't remember ever seeing the face of one of them. The other did all the talking."

"We thought she was sick," Abby said. "I don't know. It's hard to keep them all straight. There were so many."

"There was one thing about them that's hard to forget," Jacky said. "The night of the storm. As I recall, the two had gone out for the day. In the evening, just as the storm broke upon us, they returned. They met someone at our doorstep, several men it seemed like. There was an argument, quite a lot of shouting. They never came in, and they never came back. Left all their belongings, too."

"What became of their things? Do you still have them?" Stephen was eager to see what they had left behind. Perhaps there might be clues about the women's identity. Most innkeepers would have sold the lot without delay.

"I held on to them, in case someone should come to reclaim them. A week or so ago, a fellow did come. Described perfectly what was there, paid us for our trouble, quite handsomely too, and carried them off."

"You didn't happen to get a name in any of all this, did you?"

"Funny," Jacky frowned, "the girls never did give us their names that I remember. The fellow, though, he called himself Bill Sharp."

"That's not very helpful. England has almost as many Sharps as Smiths."

"Well, this one said he was from Shrewsbury, if that's any help."

"It helps if it was the truth."

"He seemed an honest, simple fellow. I know how to spot a liar — you've got to be good at it in this business, as your friend Wistwode knows. I had no reason to suspect a lie."

Jacky added, "Do you think that the saint really lodged with us?"

"She could have," Stephen said guardedly. "But anyway, she wasn't a saint."

"So you say," Jacky said with a hint of slyness. "You'll let us know if it was her, won't you? It will be good for business, people knowing that she stayed here."

"I'll let you know," Stephen said.

"It's a pity she died on the steps of the church," Jacky said, although to be accurate, she had died on the walkway. "Any idea what happened?"

"No," Stephen said shortly. He returned the empty ale cup to Jacky. "Thanks for your help, and good day to you both."

As Stephen passed through the common room he heard Jacky remark to Abby, "I smell a lie there. Wonder what's going on?"

"Well, thank God you didn't call him out to his face. He looks like the kind what would cut your throat if you looked at him sideways."

# Chapter 11

Stephen climbed Dinham Lane to the broad street that ran along the spine of the ridge from the castle to Saint Laurence's and was variously known as Castle Street or High Street, depending where you stood upon it. In fact, exactly where Castle Street ended and High Street began was a matter of some confusion as nobody could agree on the exact place where one indistinguishable bit of road deserved a different name than the other bit. Merchants with houses along the way, particularly those located at the middle, sometimes gave their locations as being on Castle Street and at other times on High Street, depending on their mood or fancy. The usual demarcation point was reckoned to be about where the guildhall sat. As much as there was some confusion about it, the matter was not insignificant, since the difference reflected the fact that the town was held by two different families, both descended from Walter Lacy, who died in 1241, leaving two granddaughters. On one side of the meandering line the Geneviles were entitled to the rents, and on the other the Verduns. Only Edmund Tarbent, the town clerk, knew who was paying whom, as things had not yet settled out between the two branches.

Today, what there was of a market stood in front of the guildhall. Often boisterous and noisy, this corn market had not altered from the small, somber affair Stephen had seen earlier in the morning.

Stephen trudged through the mud to Harry's cart, which occupied a spot at the corner of the market. Harry sat on the bed, wrapped in his blanket, looking appropriately miserable.

"How're you doing?" Stephen asked.

Harry pulled his blanket tighter. "It's cold. I miss the gate. Oh, the days when gallant old Gip would light up the fire and we'd settle around it, bosom friends."

Stephen stirred the contents of the cup. There were a half dozen farthings here. "You're not doing so badly. Heard anything?"

"Only the gossip of strangers. Not about anyone you'd know."

"No word about any robberies, then," Stephen said, disappointed. He was sure that Harry would have heard something.

"Well, there might have been. A whisper or two."

When Harry didn't go on, Stephen picked up his cup and tilted it as if he intended to pour the contents into his palm, giving Harry the eye. Harry opened his mouth to demand the return of his money, when Mistress Wattepas, wife of the town's leading goldsmith, walked up, trailed by a string of maids as if she were a lady, a stern look on an already stern visage. Stephan hastily returned the cup to the bed of the cart. Mistress Wattepas waved at one of the maids, who dropped a half penny in Harry's bowl, while he sputtered his thanks and showered Mistress Wattepas with praise that she probably did not care to hear as she drew off toward her family's house and shop.

"That's a good Christian woman, unlike some folk I know," Harry said.

"You were saying," Stephen said.

"About what?"

"About whispers."

"Oh, that. I doubt you would be interested."

"Let me be the judge."

Harry sighed. "If you must know, there have been two robberies on the Shrewsbury road in the last month."

Stephen looked about at the crowd. "Are your informants still here?'

"Nah. They've gone."

"You let them get away?"

"They weren't anyone you'd be interested in."

"Damn it, Harry! I need to talk to them!"

"The bad folk used an axe in one case and a bill in the other. Not bows," Harry sneered. "Can't be those you're looking for. Beside, some's already been caught and hanged. A pair of fellows living in the woods outside Onibury, they were. Hounds tracked 'em to their hiding place."

"Oh," Stephen said.

"Yeah, oh. Take me for an idiot, do you? Don't trust me to use my judgment, eh?" Harry fumed. "Hire a man, and then you've got to manage his every twitch?"

"Sorry," Stephen said.

"There is one bit you might find interesting," Harry said offhandedly.

"What's that?"

"It don't have to do with robberies, strictly speaking."

"I'm waiting," Stephen said.

"There've been some barn burnings. Four altogether. All north of here, east of the Shrewbury road."

"That's unusual. Welsh raiders?"

"Well, that's what some say."

"What do you say?" Stephen asked, since it was clear that Harry had an opinion about this.

But Harry was not giving out opinions. Instead, he said, "One belonged to someone you know: the Bromptones of Wickley. Can't mean anything, though. It's too far off the road to Shrewsbury."

Wickley was a village about fifteen miles northeast of Ludlow, and at least the same distance east of the Ludlow-Shrewsbury road, quite a long way for Welsh raiders to travel in the middle of winter, though it had happened before. What made it a place of interest was the fact that Stephen had visited there last autumn when he had contracted to find Bromptone's son who had absconded on his apprentice contract with a Ludlow draper. It had not been a friendly visit.

"There, now," Harry said. "You satisfied?"

"I suppose I shall have to be. For now. Keep asking."

# Chapter 12

Suppers were generally a light meal of leftovers from dinner, but travelers wanted something more substantial in the evenings after a hard day on the road, so the suppers at inns were more elaborate. However, that was only for the visitors. Edith and the serving girls put down a supper of bread, butter, cheese and leftover pea soup before Stephen.

Stephen huddled over his soup bowl some distance from the fire owing to the fact that guests had appropriated his usual spot, cloak over his shoulders against the draft that seeped through the cracks around the side door. The arrow he had found in the bushes at the site of the murder on the Shrewsbury road rested on the table, and every now and then, he prodded it with a finger.

Gilbert's puttered about making conversation with the guests to ensure they were happy. The only way to make an inn known was by word of mouth, so it paid to have happy customers, who would come back or urge their friends to stop. Good service was only part of it. A convivial host added considerably and Gilbert was more suited to this role than Edith. As the room was only half full, and the inn's rooms only half let, he finished his first round of talking early and dropped to the bench beside Stephen.

"More ale there, my good fellow?" Gilbert asked.

"No," Stephen said.

Gilbert cocked an eyebrow at the sharp response. "What's got into you?"

"Harry learned nothing useful."

"That's too bad. It seemed like a good idea."

"So, I've got to go Shrewsbury."

"I thought you were fond of travel. You make it sound like a hardship."

Stephen shrugged.

Gilbert sipped ale from his tankard. "I've heard that Margaret de Thottenham has a townhouse in Shrewbury."

"Really," Stephen replied with more interest than to the previous question, although he tried to disguise it. During the autumn, he had . . . his mind formed the word "affair," but it really had been too brief for such a description: more like a night or two together, as they both schemed to acquire a valuable list of supporters of the barons plotting an uprising against King Henry.

"Yes," Gilbert said. "Fascinating woman. Quite beautiful."

"What of it?"

"I thought you liked her."

"She tried to have us killed, remember?"

"It was business. I didn't take it personally. Neither should you."

"You think I wish to see her?"

"Well, it would make the journey more enjoyable, knowing that such a supple reward lay at the end."

"You assume too much."

"Why do you have to go to Shrewsbury, anyway?" Gilbert asked. "Obviously it isn't for love."

Stephen told him about his conversations with the fletcher, Julia, and Jacky at the Trumpet.

Gilbert listened with his tankard balanced on his stomach. "An interesting, and perhaps useful coincidence. You might have all your questions answered in one swoop."

As Stephen considered a reply, the boy Mark entered through the side door. His appearance brought Harry to mind and, with that, curiosity about whether Harry had learned anything else. "Has Harry had his supper yet?" Stephen asked him.

"How would I know . . . sir," the boy scowled and stepped around Gilbert's outstretched legs.

Stephen turned and caught the boy's arm. "You brought him back, didn't you?"

Mark pulled his arm away. "I'll not be humiliated by that man. He is rude — and he smells!"

Heads swiveled in their direction at the outburst.

"Well, he does stink a bit," Gilbert allowed. "What's this about bringing him back? Where did he go?"

"Mark here contracted to take Harry to the market this morning and bring him back in the evening," Stephen said. "You didn't bring him back, I take it?"

"No."

"Have you accepted his coin?" Stephen asked quietly.

"No," the boy replied, subdued by the menace in that quiet tone. "And I will not."

"What happened?" Stephen asked.

"He insulted me when I went to get him. Called me a stupid prick just because I was a little late. I told him he could freeze his ass off if that was going to be his attitude."

"So you left him at the market."

"I did. And he can rot in hell as far as I'm concerned."

Stephen could have ordered the boy to go back for Harry, if he was still at the market, but instead he stood up. "Fine."

Stephen went out to the yard and crossed to the stable, where he checked Harry's stall, the last to the left, to see if he had come back on his own. The stall was empty. He did not often pause to look in the stall, and though he had seen it before he had never actually *looked* at it. Despite the dimming light, he could make out that it was oddly neat for someone whose person was so disheveled: a nest in a pile of hay lined with two folded blankets that gave signs of having been washed. Spare clothing hung from pegs within reach of a man with no legs. A little shelf above the nest with a candle that had never been lighted, a fragment of mirror, an empty wine bottle shaped like a naked woman, and a series of corks set up in a row like soldiers. There was so little, but Harry seemed to take great pride in it.

Stephen emerged from the stables and nearly ran into Gilbert. "What's Harry doing at the market?" Gilbert asked.

# The Girl in the Ice

"Checking on robberies on the Shrewsbury road. I got him a license to beg the market in return for his asking a few questions."

"Ah. Well, that was clever of you. Sir Geoff will never connect Harry's inquiry with either of us, should Harry's interest reach his ears."

"That was my thought. You think otherwise?"

"Oh, no," Gilbert said at Stephen's back as he hurried to catch up. "Far be it for me to question your judgment."

"You do it all the time. Why stop now?"

"I take it from your haste that Harry has not returned," Gilbert gasped, jogging at Stephen's side as his longer legs propelled him up Bell Lane toward Broad Street.

"My, you are quick this evening. Don't you have guests to take care of?"

"They can manage for a few moments. After all, this is duty —"

"— of a sort," Stephen finished for him, with a smile concealed by the twilight.

"Of a sort," Gilbert echoed.

They turned onto Broad Street and climbed toward the church spire at the top of the ridge. Stephen slowed his pace so that Gilbert did not have to jog to keep up, although the older man still puffed from his exertions.

At High Street, they saw in the gloam the dim outlines of a cart with a man's figure upon it in the empty street. They hurried up to the cart. Harry turned his head at the sound of their approach.

"How good of you to come," Harry said. "And I thought I had been forgotten."

"What are you still doing here?" Gilbert asked, still gasping from the rush.

"Guarding the cart, of course," Harry said. "It would have been stolen if I'd left it here."

"Quite right," Gilbert said.

"I know Edith thinks the cart is worth more than me," Harry said.

"Well," Gilbert said in defense of his wife, "carts do cost money."

"So," Stephen said, "the question is who will take the cart back. After all, it is your cart."

"You're not suggesting that I pull it," Gilbert said.

"It's more than a suggestion," Stephen said. "I am a crown officer. Crown officers cannot be seen to pull carts."

"You did once."

"That was Boxing Day. Almost, anyway."

Gilbert glanced about the deserted street. All the shop windows were closed, only candlelight visible behind a few of them as the residents finished their supper and prepared for an early bed. "No one will see."

"Get going before the cart falls apart from old age."

"And old Harry here doesn't freeze to death," Harry said. "It's getting cold. Don't forget about old Harry."

"I should make you walk, for that tongue of yours," Gilbert said. "It's what got you in this trouble in the first place."

"The boy was rude to me," Harry said archly. "I cannot suffer people's rudeness, especially from serving boys."

"When they're not *your* serving boy, it pays dividends to be polite," Gilbert said. "A lesson you should take to heart. It will improve all your commerce with others."

"Tell you what," Stephen said, "owing to the dark and your old age, I'll take one trace and you take the other. That way we share the humiliation."

"Done," Gilbert said.

"What humiliation?" Harry asked, as they picked up the traces of the cart and began pulling toward distant Broad Street.

"An acquaintanceship with you is more than enough humiliation for anyone," Stephen said.

"I shall remember that, next time you need a favor."

"Meanwhile," Stephen said, "you are in my employ. While we are on our way, you can tell us what you learned today.

That way, you don't have to strain your tongue by repeating yourself for Gilbert's benefit."


Stephen was morose when they arrived at the Broken Shield. "I was certain he would hear something," he said.

"It was too much to expect for one day's work," Gilbert said. "But look — you haven't done so badly yourself. You've learned something useful."

"Yes, but I'm not sure I can do anything about it."

"What are you talking about?"

"I can't afford to go."

"What? Why, you were rolling in money only a day ago. That advance!"

"It's gone, or nearly so."

"What?" Harry called from the back of the cart as they reached the doors of the stable. "How can that be? Probably hiding out in the Wobbly Kettle while the rest of us toil in the wet and cold!" The Wobbly Kettle was a bathhouse that offered other pleasures than warm water down by the bridge over the Teme.

"Hardly," Stephen said as he set Harry's board on the ground. "Your license took up a good part of it. And then there were the fees for my horses."

Harry swung down to the board. "Don't go blaming me, you spendthrift. I've been telling you for months you ought to sell those miserable beasts. You've a fortune walking on horseshoes, and you know it."

"Let's not talk about that," Stephen said.

"Quit clinging to your illusions and face reality," Harry snapped. "Poor men can't afford illusions. You're not rich enough for them." Harry swung into the stable. He stopped and looked over his shoulder, then turned part way around. "If you go there, Shrewsbury, you might learn something about the saint?"

"She's not a saint."

"That's your opinion. You're entitled to be wrong."

"The inquiry could be no more productive than yours today."

"Still, there's a chance you'll find out her name and how she died."

"There is that," Stephen said. "Possibly."

"Wait here. I'll be right back." Harry swung off into the dark. While Stephen waited, he and Gilbert rolled the cart back to its place by the side of the stables, and returned to the doorway. Presently, Harry reappeared. He had a sack on his lap. He held out the sack to Stephen, and said, "This ought to cover your expenses."

Stephen took the sack, amazed at the weight of it. It was too dark now to see what it contained, but when he put his hand inside, he found it had coins at the bottom. "Harry, where did you get this?"

"I saved it," Harry said. "It's not like I have the opportunity to drink or whore it away."

"You're giving this to me — or is this a loan?"

Harry rubbed his thighs. "I'll have it back, if you please, and something in return."

"What?"

"That picture you have of her — I want it. When you're done with it, that is."

## Chapter 13

Shrewsbury lay within a great loop of the River Severn, surrounded by brownstone walls that glowed a brilliant orange in the afternoon sun.

The road from Ludlow crossed a wooden bridge to Coleham Island, a narrow strip of land just below the bridge leading eastward across a boggy pond from the town to the Benedictine abbey. Houses lined the road there, potters mostly, the air foul with the smoke from their furnaces, and at the bridge connecting to the causeway, Stephen and Gilbert found an inexpensive inn. They created an alarm when they entered, Stephen wearing helmet, mail, shield, and sword, as it was unusual for anyone to go about in that fashion. The inn's proprietor took one look and fled out the back door as if he had a guilty conscience about something. A splash was heard from the rear garden as the proprietor threw himself into the pond behind the house.

"What got into him?" Stephen asked mildly.

"You're not from the sheriff?" the proprietor's wife asked, taking command in this moment of crisis.

"No, I'm from Ludlow."

"You'll be wanting a room then, I suppose?"

"That was our intent."

"You're willing to share? Or do you want your squire there to have his own place?" she asked, nodding at Gilbert, who had collapsed onto a bench and was looking with great desire at a servant girl with a large pitcher of what had to be ale. Despite the civility of the question, she managed to communicate both reproof and amusement at the aging and somewhat disheveled state of the alleged squire.

Stephen caught both the reproof and the amusement, but did not disown Gilbert. "The same room will be acceptable."

"We can manage that. You can see it now, if you please."

She turned toward the stairs. Stephen gestured to Gilbert to accompany them, but Gilbert, exhausted by a thirty mile ride which they had accomplished in a single day, shook his head as he held out a cup to the serving girl, who passed him by without charging the cup. Gilbert said, "You go. I am sure you can be trusted in the matter of beds."

"Then I don't want to hear you complain if I choose unwisely, or not to your satisfaction."

"I'd be happy with a pile of hay at the moment," Gilbert said, snagging the serving girl's skirt at last so that she could not get away.

Stephen followed the innkeeper's wife upstairs to a room at the rear of the house. "I'll let you have it all to yourself," she said as she pushed open the shutters to admit light so that he could inspect the premises. "You'll note that it has a lock and everything, so your valuables will be safe. And that's a real feather bed as well."

The proprietor was halfway across the pond, his head and shoulders just above the surface.

"I hope he'll be all right," Stephen said, as he prodded the bed to test the mattress and scout for bedbugs.

"Don't mind him. This is the third time this month that he's swum the pond." She shouted through the window, "Get back here, you dumbass! He ain't from the sheriff!"

She closed the shutters, returning the room to semi-darkness.

"He could catch his death in this cold," Stephen said sympathetically. Although the thaw had melted most of the ice and snow, it was still chilly enough that a swim was something to be avoided.

"He's got more blubber than a whale," the woman said. "He'll be all right. Supper's half an hour before sundown, if you've a mind to eat with us. It's good honest fare, not the best in town, but it will fill the belly, and it don't taste bad, either."

"There is something you could help me with," Stephen said. "I'm looking for a couple of fellows."

"This isn't legal business, is it?"

"Not really."

"All right, then." She stood in the doorway, arms crossed, waiting for the question.

"I'm trying to find a certain Edmund Tomkys. I'm told he's a fletcher in town."

"He owe you money?"

"He owes me an explanation."

The woman smiled crookedly. "Arrows won't fly straight, eh? You're not the first to register a complaint about that. You'll find him in the Castle Foregate. On the right, down from the Peacock Tavern. And the other?"

"A fellow named Bill Sharp."

The woman laughed. "There's dozens of Sharps around here, and that's only counting the grown ups, and half of 'em 're named Bill! You'll have to do better than that."


The prospect of rest and a full belly tempted Stephen to fall upon the bed and wait until tomorrow to make further inquiries. It had been a long ride from Ludlow, which he and Gilbert had made alone rather than with a traveling party because he did not want to be confined to the leisurely pace preferred by most people. There was nothing like a thumping trot that went on for hours to put a cramp into the small of your back and an ache in your head. They had done so well on the road that there was still time left in the day. He could not see wasting it over a tankard of ale in the inn, so he went down to the hall.

Gilbert was still at his place on the bench, not having moved any more than to turn around so that he was now facing the table bent over a quarter round of white cheese. He paused in carving a slice from the quarter round and said with a mouth full of cheese, "Want some?"

Stephen sat down beside him and accepted the sliver. It was quite good cheese, to his surprise, with a sharp and salty flavor. "This is good."

"Best cheese I ever had in my life," Gilbert said, forcing another sliver into an already full mouth.

"Careful there," Stephen said. "You'll choke."

"Then I will die of pleasure."

"I'm going into town," Stephen said. "Want to come?"

"I am not moving from this place."

"You could bring your cheese."

"No. I've had enough traveling. I want only supper and bed. You are an evil man to drive me so hard."

"You didn't want to sleep by the road, did you?"

There was nothing between Ludlow and Shrewsbury but little villages, which meant that if they could not find a place in the corner of someone's house or in their barn, they would have had to settle for a bed of leaves. And there was the prospect of robbers to contend with, not to mention the vile things that country legends said slipped through the forests at night. "There is that. What are you going to do? See the sights?"

"I want to find this Tomkys fellow."

"What about Sharp?"

"Apparently the town is full to the brim with Sharps, almost all of them named Bill."

Gilbert sighed. "That will make things difficult on that front, then."

"Yes, that's why I thought I'd leave that part of the work to you."

"You wouldn't! This is your inquiry! I'm only here to record the results."

Stephen patted him on the shoulder, then cut the remainder of the cheese round in half.

"Hey!" Gilbert protested as Stephen bit into a half.

"I'm paying for it, after all."

"Yes, well, then don't forget to pay the woman before you go out. I'm not sure she'll let me run a tab. Innkeepers are always so damned untrusting."

Stephen set out over the northern bridge off the island, which crossed above marshy ground rather than a proper stream that bled into a pond rimmed with ice on the right. The path of the innkeeper, who had fled across the pond, could be made out where the ice rim had been crushed.

He paused to admire the new stone tower on this side of the river guarding the bridge to town. To the east, the abbey church's blunt tower, just visible among the abbey outbuildings, glowed almost orange. He thought about going in. Gilbert would want to hear about it when he got back, as he walked across the stone span over the Severn leading to the town. He paid the toll to enter — no dispensations for a crown officer so far outside his jurisdiction — delayed only a short time by a shouting match between the two gate wardens and a prisoner in the little jail within the tower. He walked up Sub Wyle, a muddy street on flat ground with the low wooden houses of the poor on either side. At the first right, he turned onto a street called Wyle and began a climb up a steep hill past the houses and shops of a tailor, a dyer, a glover, and two furriers. Before the top of the hill, another, more narrow street came in from the right, Doggepol, the innkeeper's wife had called it. He turned here and continued to the top of the hill, where Saint Mary's Church occupied the summit in a square surrounded by houses of the deacons and a few of the more well-off inhabitants of the town.

Stephen entered the street on the south side of the church and paused three houses from the corner. A woman servant was airing a mattress over the sill of a window above him. She stopped to give him the eye and said something to someone behind her. Stephen could not see who it was, only a vague shape. He almost asked if the mistress was home, but he couldn't bring himself to speak. The thought that Margaret de Thottenham might actually be here, within those walls, smarted through the longing and desire that had driven him here against his better judgment. It was foolish to come. Although they had lain together, it had turned out to be strictly business on her part. She hadn't really cared for him, after all, and probably would not appreciate it if he called. Besides, it was unlikely that she was here anyway. The manor-born moved about from one property to another, so she was as likely to be in the country as here. He turned away before he embarrassed himself any further.

As he reached the castle, the street bent left and descended. Just beyond the north gate, the road forked, the left heading off toward the river and the right, the broader of the two, heading downhill toward the gray country beyond.

No signs gave away the location of Tomkys' shop and Stephen had to ask directions at the Peacock Tavern whose main customers appeared to be off-duty soldiers from the castle, and only got them after he bought a pint of ale he didn't want and tipped the serving girl.

It was strong ale, and, not one to waste a drop even if he hadn't desired it in the first place, Stephen was lightheaded as he emerged into the street, hugging the edge to avoid a collision with a fast-moving post rider, and then a cart pulled by a pair of oxen loaded with so much hay that a person in one of the windows above could have stepped into the summit of the mound.

"Careful there, sir!" the wagon driver called out to him, laughing at Stephen's narrow escape, unmindful of his own danger since the huge stack swayed ominously and could collapse upon him at any time.

Now that he could direct his attention down the street without the threat of being trampled, Stephen had no trouble identifying Tomkys' shop: while he had been in the tavern, a wagon had stopped in front of it and a half dozen men were clustered on or about the wagon. Someone was passing bundles of finished arrows through the shop window to two of the men who handed them up to another who stood in the bed. Most of the arrows were unpainted, but at least two of the bundles held yellow-painted arrows with red stripes, just like the arrow that Stephen had recovered from the murder site on the Shrewsbury road — well, not quite an exact match. Instead of three red stripes near the notch, these arrows had two. Nonetheless, Stephen's heart thumped against his ribs, not exactly with excitement, but something close to it: the same exhilaration he experienced on the hunt at the sight of the quarry, or at beginning of a fight.

Trying to appear casual and unconcerned, Stephen strolled down to the wagon. He paused to stroke the head of one of the horses, while at the same time examining the men as surreptitiously as possible for some hint of whence they had come. Nothing in particular marked them out as belonging to any lord, although they had to have had such an affiliation. These men were well-enough, but plainly dressed, with simple long tunics that hung almost to their knees: yellows and blues and reds; and good quality stockings also of varying colors that often clashed with the color of the tunic, and sound, well-made shoes. Yet no one but a lord bought a full wagon-load of arrows at once. They had the lean, wolfish look of soldiers, and all of them carried long daggers just like the one at the small of Stephen's back rather than the simple knives many peasants bore.

The fellow in charge of the horses suffered Stephen's attentions for a few moments, but soon lost his patience. "Lay off there, you," he snapped.

"I am doing no harm," Stephen said mildly. "I have business here, same as you, and you are blocking my way to the shop."

"If she bites off your fingers, I don't want to hear you crying about it. She's got a temper."

"No more than I have," Stephen said, pushing the horse's muzzle away from his face.

The driver spat into a puddle to show how much regard he had for Stephen's temper. He said, "Mike — trouble."

The fellow addressed as Mike turned from the shop window. "See him off," he said.

"He ain't going off. Says he's got business here."

Mike frowned at Stephen, and for an instant, his eyes widened as if in surprise and recognition, although Stephen was at a loss to say if they had ever met before. His lips pursed as he weighed what to do next. "He's gentry, boys," he said to the other men, and then to Stephen: "We'll be out of the way in a few moments. Hope you don't mind waiting."

"Not at all," Stephen said.

Mike wasn't wrong about his estimate. A few more bundles came out of the window and found their way into the cart, and then the driver mounted the right lead horse, and the wagon lurched off up the hill toward the north gate, trailed by the men. Mike and the driver exchanged intense whispers as they drew away and cast glances back at Stephen.

The shop was like many others of its kind: a tall, narrow house with a large window in the front beside the door, distinguished by its green-painted timbers. Meanwhile, whoever occupied the shop had closed the window against the chill.

Stephen hesitated, knocked on the door, and when a gravely voice called, "Come in!" he pushed it open. A passage forward led to the hall of the house. He did not go there, but turned into the shop on the left, where a man was seated on a bench wrapping string about the end of an arrow shaft painted yellow with red stripes to secure three shaved goose feathers to one end. He was balding and bearded, the beard, streaked with gray, making his face appear square and broad, and older than he probably was. His fingers were short and blunt, and did not seem up to the delicate work in which they were engaged. The shop smelled of glue, dog, and a person needing a bath.

"What do you want?" the man asked, as if Stephen's appearance was an imposition rather than an opportunity. Like the Ludlow fletchers, the advent of war had increased his business beyond his capacity to meet it. Bundles of finished arrows, stacks of stems which were the raw material for shafts, and bags of feathers lay heaped about the little room. With so much to do and backed up orders, he had no interest in more business and so felt no need to be polite.

"Are you Tomkys?"

"That would be me." Tomkys regarded the painted arrow in Stephen's belt. "And that looks like one of mine."

"That's what I'm here about," Stephen said, drawing out the arrow and handing it to Tomkys. "Did you make it?"

Tomkys bounced the shaft lightly in one hand, as if assessing its weight. He bent it slightly, sighted along it, and examined the threads holding the fletches in place. "Are you satisfied with it? Do you want more?"

"I'm not in the market for arrows."

"What did you come for then, as it's all I have to sell?"

"Information."

"If it's gossip you want, you'll have to inquire elsewhere."

"Whom did you sell this arrow to?"

"I sell my work to many people. Everyone hereabout has brought from me at one time or another."

"This would have been to someone in the honor of Clun."

Tomkys chuckled. "Well, there is the earl. He bought two-thousand a year ago. And another thousand, just now."

Stephen had expected such an answer and he almost smiled with triumph. Then in his mind he heard Perceival FitzAllan's voice refuting the charge of murder at court, saying that, with so many arrows laying about his storerooms, available to all his retainers, the fact he had bought some proved nothing. The judge and the jury in this imaginary court nodded their agreement, and everyone shot glances of disapproval in the imaginary Stephen's direction for bringing such a foolish and unwarranted charge. He could feel himself shriveling with embarrassment in front of the crowd. I must be careful, Stephen reminded himself, I must be very careful. I must have rock-solid proof. "I noticed that the markings on this shaft are a little different than those that you sent out today."

Tomkys' eyes drooped as he cast another look at the arrow in Stephen's hand. "I had an apprentice until a few months ago who marked his arrows that way, three stripes instead of one."

"He's no longer with you?"

"He died in the troubles. Killed by the Welsh near Owestry."

"Ah. I'm sorry."

"Save your sorrows for his mother. He was a useless boy, always talking back and shirking his work when no one was looking."

"Did you sell arrows marked with three stripes to Earl Perceival?"

"Of course."

"Anyone else?"

"Probably. I cannot recall."

Tomkys went back to his work, unwilling to be distracted by what he regarded as a frivolous conversation, although from Stephen's perspective lives balanced upon it, not least of which was his own.

Yet he could not avoid the feeling that he had struck another dead end, and feeling the weight of failure, Stephen struggled to think of the one thing that would break the truth loose from its hiding place. But nothing occurred to him. He was not clever like Gilbert or Harry. He could only plod along until he reached whatever goal lay in the gloom ahead. He had gone as far as he could here, and it had come to nothing. Unless someone blurted out the truth while on a binge in some tavern or whispered it in a whore's ear and she happened to repeat it, there was no way he would solve the mystery of those sad deaths on the Shrewsbury road. He hated not knowing, and he hated his own inadequacy even more.

He was out in the little hallway about to exit to the street when Tomkys spoke up. "Well, there's two others I remember."

Stephen stuck his head back in the workshop. "Two?"

"In Clun honor."

"And?" Stephen asked cautiously, fearful of getting his hopes back up.

"Eudo Walcot for one. Warin Pentre was the other."

The names meant nothing to Stephen but he nodded, thankful that he had got this much.

"What's this about, anyway?" Tomkys asked.

"One of them lost this," Stephen said, indicating the arrow, which he had put back in his belt. "I fancy returning it to the rightful owner." Whoever that might be.

Tomkys shook his head as if he thought Stephen's good sense had slipped its tether. "I hope he'll be glad to see it again."

"Somehow I think not."

# Chapter 14

The cider the innkeeper's wife put before Stephen was on the brink of turning sour, but he had drunk worse — muddy water sipped from the remains of a pond in Grenada came to mind, as he nursed the cup. So he did not complain, as he hunched over the cup, the aroma of cabbage and beef wafting out of the kitchen in the rear of the inn.

Stephen heard the door to the street open behind him, but did not turn to see who it was. He assumed another traveler stopping for the night. But a boy of fourteen or so halted at his elbow, and asked, "Are you Stephen Attebrook, sir?"

"He certainly is," Gilbert answered for him. "Sir Stephen, to you."

"Yessir."

"And who might you be and what do you want of Sir Stephen?"

"I am directed to give him this." The boy held out a note. It was folded with no seal and nothing was written upon the outside that indicated it was for him.

To receive a letter at any time was momentous, but to get one at the place where no one could reasonably suspect you of being was extraordinary. Stephen unfolded the letter and recognized Margaret's handwriting, for as with her last note she had written it herself, not some clerk.

It read: "From Margaret to Sir Stephen, Greetings. I learned by chance that you have come to Shrewsbury. It would please me greatly if you would come to my house this evening for supper. The boy will conduct you."

"Good heavens," Gilbert said, leaning over the table to attempt a look at the note, which Stephen quickly folded. "Who could that be from, I wonder?" His tone said that he did not actually wonder much.

"Nobody."

"Nobody, my foot!"

"I am invited to supper."

"This can't be good. I shall come along. I'm not mentioned there, am I? No matter. I shall come anyway, even if I must languish in the kitchen. That woman is trouble. You will require protection."

"No, I think not."

"Stephen, please, reconsider. Look what happened last time. You were nearly killed."

"I don't think she has that in mind yet."

"But you cannot be sure. She is devious and crafty, far more so, I am afraid to say, than you are. At bottom, you are truly a simple soul."

"I'm going." Stephen stood up. "Enjoy your supper. That boiled cabbage smells wonderful. See if you can warm my side of the bed, too, later."

"That assumes you come back. I can think of several reasons why my work in bed may be wasted."

"Not all of them gruesome."

"No, regrettably."

"My lady said I am to show you the way," the boy said.

Stephen put the note in his belt pouch beside the picture of the girl in the ice, light headed, almost giddy. "Lead on."

Stephen followed the boy across the drawbridge at the town gate where no toll was demanded when the boy told the warden Stephen was with him, and uphill to Margaret's house across the street from Saint Mary's Church.

Someone inside must have been on the lookout for their appearance, for the front door opened as they approached. The fellow holding the door was Walter, the same soldier who, months back, had shot a crossbow at Stephen during his dispute with Margaret over possession of that valuable list. Walter grinned slightly as he said, "Good evening, sir," an indication perhaps that he wished there would be no hard feelings about the shot. "May I take your cloak and cap?"

Stephen handed them over. Walter, who must double as a butler, hung them on a peg by the door, and said, "My lady is in the hall, sir, anxiously awaiting your arrival."

"Waiting, but I doubt anxiously."

"Ah, well, sir, you shall have to gauge her feelings then for yourself."

During the climb up the hill, Stephen's giddiness had given way to wariness, and, when he reached the hall, he saw good reason why he should think that Margaret might have other motives than merely the desire of his company. There were four men there besides Margaret: all dressed in split-sleeve embroidered tunics that were the fashion among those who had wealth, two with knee boots of supple leather, their long hair neatly combed and oiled so that it almost shone in the light of the fire in the middle of the room. One of them Stephen recognized immediately: Arnold Bromptone of Wickley Manor, a man with the shoulders of a bear and brown hair and beard flecked with gray, especially at his temples.

Stephen had no idea who the others were, but they were lords, there was no doubt about that. He felt shabby just standing in the same room with them. He was manor born himself, which meant something socially, but he had not inherited and what little he possessed he had lost. So now he was a mere servant of a crown official, and a poorly paid one at that, a fact they were sure to know, and equally sure to look down upon him. In a world where status and pride were so bound up together, Stephen had little status and could therefore afford little pride, although he had come to find that often those with little wealth had more pride than the mighty above them.

Margaret glided across the room, and grasped his hands.

"Thank you for coming on such short notice, Stephen." Her voice was low and musical, every word sincere, but he was on his guard now. She was more beautiful than he remembered, almost white blonde hair artfully coiled under her wimple, which framed a face so smooth, so sweet, so innocent that no man would ever grow bored gazing at it, nor suspect the steely mind and inflexible purpose that operated behind those blue eyes. No doubt that face had deceived many, himself included.

"My pleasure," he replied dutifully.

"Is it really?" she laughed. "I hope so."

"You know that no one can resist you."

"You did well enough the last time."

"Only partly."

"In the most important part," she smiled. Such a broad smile had the capacity to melt a man's heart, but Stephen was ready for it and it dented his mental armor only a little.

Margaret guided him to the others, where she performed introductions. There was William de Farlegh, tall and thin-necked; Gilbertus Juste, with nervous hands that were constantly clutching and unclutching each other; John Gardeuille, as handsome a man you could want, although on close inspection his nose was veined and his jowls beginning to sag from perhaps too much devotion to the wine barrel; and last there was Bromptone. The men solemnly shook Stephen's hand and, surprisingly, without condensation. Bromptone especially seemed glad to see him, for he said heartily, "Good of you to come. We hope you can help."

Stephen wanted to asked, "Help how?" — his suspicions confirmed that something was up — but Margaret cut in. "Let's leave such unpleasantness until after supper. Please!"

Of course, no request by the lady of the house could be ignored by a gentleman, so they retired to their seats at the table, while from the rear of the house servants appeared with platters, trenchers, and bowls for a meal as elaborate as any dinner.

"My lady!" Gardeuille leaned back in his chair, as servants carried away the remains of supper. "You certainly know how to stuff a man to his gills!" He swirled his wine cup and held it out for a refill without glancing at the servant who hastened to replenish the cup.

"I am glad you enjoyed it," Margaret said.

"However, I for one have had enough talk of horses and who is bedding whom," Gardeuille said. "It's time we got to business."

"I suppose it is," Margaret sighed. "Such unpleasantness. So much death and waste." She shuddered. "I hate to think upon it." She shot Gardeuille a coquette's smile. "You are a cruel man to force me to do so, sir."

"My apologies," Gardeuille said. "I know our affairs wound your tender nature. But now that your man is here, I can see no reason why we should not discuss them, as there is need. Urgent need."

"He is not my man," Margaret said, "I merely said I knew him."

"I stand corrected," Gardeuille said.

"I know him as well," Bromptone said.

"Really?" Gardeuille asked.

"He's provided assistance to my family in the past."

"Of the sort of assistance we require now?"

"Something like it."

"You don't wish to share the particulars so that we may judge his worth ourselves?"

"It was a private matter," Bromptone said. "But I will vouch for him, if that is what is required here."

"I also have some knowledge of his ability," Margaret said, "otherwise, he would not be here. Sir Nigel would vouch for him as well, if called upon to do so."

Bromptone smiled. "I heard about that. Sir Stephen here bested FitzSimmons in single combat last fall. They had a falling out."

Gardeuille looked at Stephen as if in a new light, and the glare was not complimentary. "It is dangerous to fall out with FitzSimmons. Why should we engage him if he is FitzSimmons' enemy?"

"They have had their differences," Margaret said, "but they are mended. Aren't they Stephen?"

"For my part," Stephen said. FitzSimmons was a key supporter of the barons gathering around Simon de Montfort, King Henry's brother-in-law and the man scheming to supplant that weak and vacillating ruler who surrounded himself with avaricious men bent on using the country for their own profit and power. Stephen had killed FitzSimmons' cousin, and they had been in feud, which he hoped had been resolved by single combat between them.

"It is settled." A hard note crept into Margaret's voice. "And if they were not, as you know, I have FitzSimmons' warrant to do all that is necessary to resolve this desperate business. And if I think Stephen's help is necessary, that is enough."

"Help at what?" Stephen asked, dreading the answer.

Stephen expected Margaret to answer that question, but Bromptone spoke up instead. "Stephen, there is trouble in the March —"

"When is there not trouble?" Stephen asked.

"This is not the Welsh, but something more sinister."

"They can be sinister enough from what I've seen," Stephen said, remembering the smoke rising above the ruins of the border town of Clun, only a few miles southwest of Shrewsbury, which the Welsh had burned in November when he had been sent to the Augustine friary of Saint George just across the river. The friary had burned as well, though its people had been spared, having fled to the forests with their goods and animals.

"That is true." Bromptone said. "Many have suffered at their hands. But we, we four, have suffered as well, and we believe that the Welsh are not to blame, although many think them to be the culprits."

Stephen then remembered what Harry had told him. "Your barn was burned."

"It was more than my barn — my house and all its outbuildings were laid waste, not to mention my village. Nothing remains there but cinders."

"I am so sorry," Stephen murmured, who understood what it was like to lose everything you have better than most people.

"Save your sympathy," Gardeuille shorted, drinking long from his wine cup. "We know what side you're on."

"Sir!" Margaret spoke up. "Let us not quarrel. We are friends here."

"What friend could he be?" Gardeuille said. "He is a king's man."

"Yet I think you will find true sympathy there," she said. "Stephen, as you may suspect from Arnold's misfortune that similar things have happened to people in Shropshire — house burnings, barns destroyed, villages laid waste, the harvest carried off."

"A common problem in the March," Stephen said.

"Common enough," she replied, "but seldom does it happen to folk living east of the Shrewsbury-Ludlow road." She waved at the other men. "All have lands east of the road. Since the outbreak of the war with the Welsh, all have been ravaged."

"So?"

"So, all are supporters of the barons. You may recall having seen their names on Baynard's list."

Now that Stephen thought about, he remembered at least two, Bromptone and Farlegh. "What of it?"

"We do not think it is a coincidence. I have made inquiries. No one else has suffered so, none who has favored the king."

"And you suspect whom?"

"One could throw many names on the table," she said. "But we have no proof against anyone."

"King's men, of course," Stephen said.

"Damned right, it's king's men," Farlegh snapped.

"But you're certain it's not the Welsh," Stephen said.

"I was home," Farlegh said. "I defended my house and they could not burn that. But they burned my barn and village.

The Girl in the Ice

They weren't Welshmen. They were English. I could hear them talking plain as I hear you."

"That's what my people say," Bromptone said. "Englishmen, not Welsh."

Stephen swirled the tip of his finger in a puddle of wine spilled on the tabletop that had not soaked completely through the cloth covering. "There are quite a few king's men hereabout. It could have been practically anybody."

"It would have had to be a man capable of raising a good-sized force," Margaret said. "There were twenty to thirty men involved in each raid. Not an army, perhaps, but large enough for its purpose."

"Archers or men at arms?" Stephen asked.

"Archers, mainly," Farlegh said, "from what I saw. A couple of men at arms or three. But mostly archers."

"It's not hard to raise thirty archers in the March on the promise of plunder," Stephen said. "It could indeed have been anyone. Your close neighbors, in fact."

"This is not simple raiding," Juste spoke out for the first time. "They picked us out deliberately! They meant to ruin us! Because we have spoken out against the king!"

"The raiders passed by other manors fat with the harvest to get to us," Bromptone added.

"Guesses," Stephen said, who knew quite well the danger of making them, for he was prone to charge forward on them and that had led to mistakes. "What proof do you have?"

"Very little, I'm afraid," Bromptone said. "We, or I should say, our hostess has suggested you would find it, as we are not as skilled as one would hope for such an endeavor, I am afraid. It is great fortune that we should all find ourselves in Shrewsbury at once, but good will come of it, I hope."

"What do you want from me?" Stephen asked. "To name your attacker — even if it leads to a king's man?"

"I told you he could not be relied upon!" Gardeuille slapped the table.

"I think that Stephen cares more about truth and the law than he has let on to you," Margaret said. "And we have law on our side."

"Fat lot of good the law does in war," Farlegh said. "And that's where we are now, at war."

"It is true that law and war have nothing to do with each other," Margaret said. "But war has not yet broken out. We are dealing with simple pillage and murder. And murder is Stephen's trade, not the doing of it, but the solving of it. Am I right?"

"This is not my jurisdiction," Stephen said. "You should go to the sheriff."

"He is a king's man!" Gardeuille said. "He will look the other way out of sympathy for our assailants, if he's not already been paid to do so."

Margaret folded her hands on the table, playing with an opal ring on an index finger. "Stephen, we must know who was behind these attacks. There are sure to be others. Please help us. If we have a name, at least there is a chance we can put a stop to the terror before more harm comes to other innocent people."

She made her plea so sweetly that Stephen thought she had some hidden motive. If he agreed, he could step deeply into the conflict that was coming between King Henry and Montfort. Although war offered opportunities for men of his position, his maimed foot rendered him incapable of taking advantage of them. No one wanted a warrior who couldn't properly fight from a horse. Better judgment said he should decline. He had other business that need tending. He couldn't just go off on this errand.

Then Farlegh said to no one in particular, rubbing his face, "I shall not soon forget the sight of all those arrows sticking out of my people, as if they were pincushions. They even shot down the dogs."

"Arrows?" Stephen asked.

"Oh, yes, they left quite a lot of them behind," Farlegh said.

"What did you do with them?"

"We pulled them out of the dead and burned them," Juste said. "What else were we to do with them?"

"What did they look like, these arrows?" Stephen asked.

"What has that got to do with anything?" Gardeuille asked.

Stephen asked, "Were any painted?"

"Now that I think on it," Farlegh said, "they were yellow, most of them."

"Is that all?" Stephen asked.

"No," Farlegh replied. "They were red as well."

"Striped?" Stephen asked.

"Indeed, I believe they were. By the nock."

Stephen looked at the others. "The same for you as well?"

About the table, brows furrowed as memories were consulted. Bromptone and Gardeuille nodded. "I think so," Bromptone said, "although I must admit, this was one detail I paid little attention to. Most were cleared away by the time I returned home"

"Is this important?" Margaret said.

"It is all you have to go on," Stephen said. "No one bothered to track them, I suppose, to see where they had gone."

Heads wagged around the table.

Yellow arrows with red stripes, Stephen thought. It could be coincidence. But he thought not.

"If you find us the proof that will name a culprit," Margaret said, "we can take the matter to law, and obtain some recompense, little as it is compared to what was lost."

Stephen knew he should refuse. If he was connected with their inquiry, as was sure to happen, what then? He had never seen Sir Geoffrey Randall enraged, but this would set him off and Stephen's livelihood, meager as it was, would be lost. But then the memory of the dead Saltehuses, naked and surrounded by flies, especially the slack face of the little child, floated into his mind. Yellow arrows with red stripes: really, did it mean anything, anything at all?

Against his better judgment, his mouth said the words, "I will accept your commission. Here are my terms."

The others had gone, and Stephen was alone with her by the fire in the center of the hall. The moment brought back the longing he had felt while he stood outside on the street, but she was unobtainable: interested in him only for what she could use to her benefit. He smiled wryly, wishing it were not so. But the world did not conform to your expectations or desires.

She was quiet, gazing into the fire, its orange light playing on her lovely face. He wondered what thoughts, what plans were churning within.

"You think you know," Stephen said.

"What?" she asked.

"You think you know who it is."

She shook her head, frowning into the flames. The expression hardened her face with a steely purpose that he was sure few ever got to witness. "There are several possibilities — Earl Bertram Montgomery, your friend Perceival FitzAllan, even," she added lightly, "your cousin."

"You'd have me betray my cousin?" One of Stephen's cousins was also a Marcher earl, though a lesser one than the other men she had named. The March had more earls than anywhere else in England, many of them men who elsewhere would be counted as mere barons.

She smiled. "Well, I don't really think he's the one. His lands lie too far to the south. But you asked for names. Do you have anyone in mind?"

He realized she had mentioned his cousin only to needle him. "I know a place where I might make fruitful inquiries. There are a few things I will need, besides what we've already agreed on."

"Oh? And what are those?"

"A horse with full tack, a new set of clothes that would look well on an archer, a longbow, and arrows."

"At my expense?"

"Naturally. This is your project."

"And you will keep the horse? They are expensive."

"You can have it back when I'm done."

Margaret placed her hand upon his. "Stephen, what are you up to?"

Stephen withdrew his hand and stood up. "It's better if no one knows."

"You don't trust me?"

"Oh, I've already seen how far I can trust you. It's the others I'm worried about. Good night."

## Chapter 15

The curfew bell had rung more than an hour before, and the streets were quiet under a night of scattered cloud, sharp stars, and a half moon, which made almost unnecessary the lantern carried by the boy who'd fetched him to Margaret's house and now was to escort him back.

Stephen turned toward Doggepol Street, but the boy said, "Sir, the drawbridge will be up. They let it down for no one at night. We'll have to go by the east quay. We shall hire a boat there to take you back."

"After you, then," Stephen said, pulling up the hood of his cloak against the cold. Although it had been a warm day, the night had brought with it a teeth-chattering chill that crept over the town while he had warmed by Margaret's fire. Already, the mud was beginning to freeze, turning the rutted street into a corrugated surface that made walking difficult, puddles rimed with ice between the ridges.

"This way, sir," the boy said, stumbling the other way toward the corner of Saint Mary's, holding the lantern high upon its pole to light their way.

Stephen followed as best he could, hopping from one ridge to another. The ridges were not always fully frozen yet, so sometimes he slipped into a puddle with a splash and a repressed curse. He thought he heard similar splashes in the distance as if another curfew-breaker was making his way along Doggepol by the front of the church, but when he looked behind he saw nothing but empty street and dark houses, bathed in pale moonlight.

As Stephen and the boy reached the northern side of the church, a figure came round the far corner and stopped before them in the middle of the street. There was light enough to make out that he held a cudgel in one hand. An instinct for ambushes told Stephen that he couldn't be the only one: he was meant to hold his victim's attention while the real threat approached from another direction. He looked quickly backward, and, sure enough, there were two more men emerging from the shadows, also armed with cudgels.

"Sir?" the boy called as he pulled up short at the sight of the man ahead, smart enough to know trouble when it reared its head. He bravely pulled his knife, but Stephen said, "Put that up and get out of the way. This isn't your quarrel."

From the light thrown down by the lantern, Stephen recognized the man ahead as the fellow called Mike from earlier in the day outside Tomkys' shop.

"Hello, Mike," Stephen called. "It's a bit cold for a stroll in the dark. But then, I suppose you're looking for me."

"That we are," Mike said, slapping his palm with the cudgel.

"Is there a price on my head? I hope FitzAllan's made it a good one."

"He's made it rich enough."

"Better have, because you're going to have to earn it."

"That's big talk," Mike said as the three FitzAllan men closed in.

"No talk's too big for the man who broke out of that pig sty you called a jail," Stephen said. "While it was on fire, no less. A fat bastard like you couldn't do it. You'd have roasted like the rat you are. What did you do when the Welsh came to Clun? Hide in the cellar?"

Mike spat and came toward him.

Stephen stepped in Mike's direction as if about to attack, then spun about and ran at one of those behind, the man on his left. The object of Stephen's attention raised his cudgel and, as he struck a mighty blow with all his strength, Stephen slipped to the left so that the stick flew just past his head. Stephen kicked the fellow in the stomach, and seized his cudgel as he bent over. Stephen stepped around the fallen man, keeping the casualty between him and Mike, as he launched a savage horizontal blow at the third assailant followed immediately by another from the other side. The man drew back, avoiding the blows, stumbling in a rut. Stephen grasped the stick with a hand in the middle and rammed one end into the fellow's throat, and he fell over backwards making an awful throttling sound.

Now Stephen turned to face Mike, who had pulled up.

They stood in their guards, ready for each other in the moonlight, the jets from their labored breathing filling the air about them like smoke.

"Call for the watch, why don't you?" Stephen asked.

"I ought to," Mike said. "You've done murder."

"And I'm about to do another."

But if Mike thought Stephen intended him to be the target, he was mistaken. Stephen swung the cudgel down on the head of the first fellow he had knocked down, who was just then struggling to his knees. That fellow collapsed face down in a puddle and did not move.

"There," Stephen said. "Now it's your turn."

Mike held his cudgel over his right shoulder as if he was ready to fight. Then he turned and ran.

On flat ground and in daylight he would have got away, but it was dark and the street was full of ruts. Mike stumbled on one, which slowed him enough that, even with a bad foot, Stephen caught up with him by the church's far corner. He extended the cudgel between Mike's pumping legs. Mike fell heavily on the half frozen ground. He rolled on his back and thrust upward with his cudgel. Stephen batted it out of the way, put a foot on his arm and planted a knee on Mike's chest. He drew his dagger and set the point under Mike's chin.

Mike grimaced and closed his eyes.

"We're not done yet," Stephen said. "I've some questions I want answered first. If you answer me true, I'll let you live."

Mike's eyes fluttered, then opened so wide that the whites were visible all around. He looked at the dagger, eyes almost crossing. The swagger had gone out of him. Pinned to the ground with the dagger at his throat, having seen how far Stephen would go, he had no doubt Stephen was not bluffing. "Get off my chest," he gasped.

"No," Stephen said, although he removed some of the pressure.

"What do you want?"

"There've been some village burnings, barn burnings east of the Ludlow road. It's FitzAllan's doing, isn't it?"

"I don't know nothing about no burnings! Other than what the Welsh have done!"

"Neither you nor your friends have been out in the night for Lord Percy, with torches?"

"No! I swear!"

Stephen hesitated. He had been so certain. It *had* to be FitzAllan. Mike must be lying. Uncertainly, he looked up. The boy with the lantern had not run away. Drawn to the tableaux in the street, he had stumbled over and was gawking at the two men. Stephen spotted a small silver cross slip out of the boys shirt.

"Give me that!" he barked to the boy.

"What?"

"Your cross! I won't keep it. I just want to borrow it."

The boy drew the chain over his head and handed the cross to Stephen.

He held it to Mike's lips. "Kiss it," Stephen said, "and swear to God what you say is true."

Lips trembling, Mike kissed the cross in Stephen's fingers. "I swear," he stammered.

"Did FitzAllan or any of his men have anything to do with the burnings?"

"We didn't have nothing to do with no burnings."

"You'd know if anyone on Clun manor was involved."

"I'd know. I'm the second in command of the lord's archers."

"Shit," Stephen said.

"Are you done? Will you get off my chest now and let me up?"

Stephen held out the cross again. "There're been robberies on the Ludlow road, murders. In November six people and a child carrying a load of salt north of Onibury."

"I don't know nothing about that."

"You swear on the cross?"

"I-I-I swear, for God's sake!"

"No one in Clun?"

"No one's said a thing about robberies or murders, and I ain't had anything to do with any!"

"And no one you know."

"No one I know," Mike wheezed.

"Are you going to let him go?" the boy asked.

Stephen hesitated. He shouldn't. It was not the prudent thing to do. If he released Mike, he'd return to Clun, tell FitzAllan what had happened, and the next thing FitzAllan would appeal against him for murder. But the heat that had consumed Stephen had cooled. And he had given his promise; while not exactly an oath it was close enough. Against his better judgment, he stood up and backed away.

Mike got to his feet and shambled away without another word.

Stephen held out the little cross to the boy. "Go home. Say nothing about this."

"I'm not to call the watch?"

"No. Tell no one."

"Not even to my lady?"

"Yes, she'll need to know. But otherwise, no one. Understand?"

"Yessir."

"Do you? Your life may depend on your silence. If Perceival FitzAllan connects you with this incident, he's as liable to kill you as a stray dog."

The boy gulped and nodded vigorously.

Stephen sheathed his dagger. "Which way to the quay?"

The boy pointed north, in the direction of the castle. "There is a gap in the wall not far from here. A corridor leads down to the river. Knock on the gate." He fumbled in his purse and held out a few coins. "These are to get you through the gate and should be enough to hire a boat this time of night."

"Thank you."

"Thank our lady."

"Thank you for saying nothing."

The boy ducked his head and hurried off toward Margaret's house in a wavering cone of candlelight.

## Chapter 16

Stephen did not mention to Gilbert what had happened until they woke in the morning.

"I told you that woman was trouble!" Gilbert wailed when Stephen finished with his story.

"She had nothing to do with it. It was FitzAllan's work. He still has hard feelings about our jailbreak and that thumping I gave his fellows at Clun."

"Have you given no thought how they found you there? Who's to say that her house is not being watched? You could be connected with . . . with . . . treason! Not to mention murder!"

"It was self-defense."

"You know that doesn't matter to the law. You'll be arrested — why, I could be arrested merely on suspicion because I am your companion. Then we'll have to petition for a pardon, and you know how hard those are to get. We'll be ruined. At best we'll have to abjure the realm if they don't find an excuse to hang us. I don't fancy becoming acquainted with a strip of rope, or having to live in foreign parts among foreigners. They are so *foreign*."

Gilbert climbed out of bed and raked his hands over the fringe of gray hair surrounding his bald dome in an unsuccessful effort to smooth it down. The first thing he put on was his cap, which helped, but not much. He looked very odd clad only his braies and cap. "We cannot remain here," he said urgently. "We must be away." He began throwing on his clothes while at the same time repacking his satchel. "What are you doing? Get moving!"

"I am moving," Stephen said, still under the covers. "Just a little more slowly than you."

"Damn it," Gilbert said, now almost fully dressed and fully packed, "think this through. Anyone outside in that district after dark will be suspect. This gatekeeper you had to bribe, he'll remember you. So will that ferryman. A few inquiries of the folk on this island will lead directly here. In any moment, the sheriff's men will be knocking on the door asking after you."

"I doubt they'll be here before breakfast," Stephen said, getting out of bed at last. There was sense in what Gilbert said. They could not remain here.

"Yes," Gilbert murmured. "Breakfast. We'll have to miss that, I'm afraid. A pity. I was so looking forward to it. More's the pity — we shall never find out now who the girl in the ice was."

It was a sign of Gilbert's agitation that he was willing to forgo breakfast, although he managed to secure a quarter loaf and cheese before they rode away from the inn.

They were munching on the bread when they reached the crossroads below the southern bridge off the island. The main road, the one that lead to Ludlow, was the left fork, but Stephen took the right one, which gave way to a path that ran along the river.

"Where are you going?" Gilbert called out. "Home's that way."

"We're not going home."

"What are we doing?" Gilbert asked as he came up beside Stephen, looking as uncomfortable as ever in the saddle.

"Changing residences."

"This is not wise."

"But necessary. We aren't giving up."

"Oh dear. And I thought I had brought you to your senses. Oh dear, oh dear, oh dear."

It was a slow, pleasant ride along the south bank of the Severn, despite the chill and the bare, leafless trees that lined the road and covered the steeply rising ground to the south. A few fishing boats were already out on the river, some with nets, others with poles, and the fishermen waved to them as they passed. As they reached the bend where the river turned north, a barge came into view, its goods covered by a tarp.

Boys sitting on top of the tarp waved until the steersman yelled at them to get down and mind the oars. It was almost possible to forget their troubles in this peace, but only just.

Presently, Gilbert pointed out with interest the low buildings of an Augustine friary, which consisted of only a collection of timber and thatch houses just outside the town's western wall, since they hadn't enough money yet to build a church. No one was about, but there were a few pigs in view, snuffling in the leaves.

Before long, they reached the village of Frankeville, which lay across the river northwest of Shrewsbury on the road to Wales.

Stephen found another inn among the shops of leatherworkers, which stank worse than the potters of Coleham, and lodged there. Unfortunately, they got no bed, even though it was morning, merely straw mattresses in a corner of a room they had to share with an apprentice glover and a draper's clerk.

The clerk found Stephen a boy to carry a letter to Margaret saying that it was not safe for him to come to her and that she should send the things she had promised to provide.

Margaret came herself, accompanied by her man James, without the horse and other goods. She sat in the inn's front room, which was too cramped to be called a hall, removed her gloves, and said with amusement and exasperation, "Stephen, how is it you manage to attract so much trouble?"

"It is not new trouble. It is old trouble."

"You have irritated Perceival FitzAllan? My boy said there was a price on your head. You've only been back a few months. How did you manage that?"

"You hadn't heard? I thought you were FitzSimmons' master spy."

"Please! Spies are little people we send out to hear rumors."

"Didn't hear that one, did they?"

Her eyes narrowed. He'd succeeded in angering her. For some reason, there was some satisfaction in that. "I cannot hear everything. Tell me the story. I must know. It affects my affairs, and I will not be left in the dark."

Briefly, Stephen told Margaret about having been sent to the friary at Clun to investigate the death of a monk, and of the bitter dispute between the prior and Earl Perceival, and how he had been drawn into it.

"So," Margaret said, "the earl dislikes you because you took sides against him?"

"I badly handled two of his men after they beat up Gilbert."

"Oh. I hope he's all right."

"He's fully mended, thank you."

"And," she asked slowly, "you haven't said anything to anyone about me?"

"Other than to wistfully remember how beautiful you are, no."

Her lips twitched as if they wanted to smile but she held them in check. "So Earl Perceival has no reason to think that your attendance at my house was any more than a romantic fancy?"

"If he does not hear about your other guests. Anyone with half a mind might connect you to the barons' party then."

"It was a risk I had to take."

"Better you should have met them in the country."

Margaret's lips tightened at the rebuke. It seemed she was not used to that from men. "What do you know about the business of intrigue?"

"I've been learning a lot lately."

"Now about this fellow last night," Margaret said, referring to Mike. "You believe him? FitzAllan is not our culprit?"

"So it would seem."

"Damn!" she said, the curse falling so naturally from her lips at that moment that Stephen was not startled by it, although for a highborn woman to swear in a man's company was almost unheard of unless they were married. "I had been sure it was him!"

"I was sure of it, too, if that's any comfort. But being sure doesn't mean being right, unfortunately."

"What do we do now?"

"Now? We go on."

"You suspect another?"

"I have some names. They could be the ones you seek. But they are small men. Where is my new horse and gear?"

"Walter is coming by a separate route. He'll be along shortly. What is it in your mind to do, Stephen? This smacks of some sort of disguise."

"It is. Since I have to go into Clun honor to ask your questions, it is better that I do not do so as myself."

She grasped both his hands and squeezed hard. Stephen almost started at the unexpected gesture. She said, "After last night, be careful. Come back to me safe and whole."

Margaret stood up abruptly and marched toward the door. Her man James held back a moment, regarding Stephen with hooded eyes, and followed her into the street.

## Chapter 17

Walter arrived not long afterward with the horse, the clothes, and the bow and arrows. Stephen had specified that the clothes must be well worn and of a kind owned by an itinerant soldier, and he was not disappointed, except there was no undershirt or braies, and he had to use his own. These were of good linen, though quite frayed in spots, and were a cut above what an ordinary soldier would wear, but since he could not do without them and they would be covered up by the tunic, coat, and stockings, he retained them.

Walter also supplied a bed roll. Stephen untied the roll to familiarize himself with the contents: two blankets, an extra tunic, and a small cook pot in the middle.

As he retied the roll, there was pounding at the door: the draper's clerk who wanted in.

"I'm busy!" Stephen said. "Go away!"

"It's my room too!" the clerk called through the door. "If you don't open the door right now, I'm going for the landlord!"

"Complain all you like. I won't be here long!"

Dissatisfied with the answer, the clerk could be heard retreating down the hallway.

"Is it all satisfactory?" Walter asked, pretending not to notice Stephen's left foot, which was missing from the arch forward, as Stephen put on his boots to complete his transformation from poor knight to poor archer.

"Well done," Stephen said, the bow in its cloth bag on his shoulder. "Do I look the part?"

"I wouldn't hire you," he grinned, "but those fools might. Are you sure you can shoot that thing?"

"Well enough to put food on the table."

Walter chuckled. "Well you won't be expected to do that."

"I'll say I fancy picking knights off their horses."

"That should impress them, if it's true."

"It's truer than your aim with a crossbow."

"You were moving. It's hard to hit a moving target."

"Yes, especially one only six feet away."

Stephen rolled up his own clothes and mail, which he put in a bag with his helmet. He handed the bag and shield to Walter. "Ask our lady to keep this safe until I return. Along with my horse."

"If you don't come back, can I have them?"

"That will be Lady Margaret's decision. But I have a son. He should benefit if I don't return."

"I think we'll see you again. I well remember the fight at Will Thumper's house — and the boy told me how you handled those three last night. You're hard to kill."

"I told him to keep his mouth shut. Speak to him for me again, will you? Before he blabs to the whole town."

"I'll see to it, my lord."

"Don't talk like that. I'm not a lord."

"I'll see to it, Sir Stephen."

They shook hands, and Walter departed.

Stephen slung the arrow bag and bedroll from his shoulders, and went down to the yard, passing the clerk and the innkeeper on the stairs. They gaped at his transformation and the fact that he was leaving without having spent the night.

Gilbert was waiting for him by Margaret's horse, bewildered as Walter led Stephen's mare and all his arms but for his sword out of the yard. "What's going on?"

"I have to go into Clun honor."

"Whatever for?" Gilbert gasped in horror. "Not that business at Onibury, surely!"

"Yes. Also Margaret has hired me to determine who burned Bromptone's barn. I believe there is a connection."

Gilbert took Stephen's face in his hands. "Your wits are addled, boy. Give this up. I thought we had agreed to stay as far away from Clun honor as possible. Besides, haven't you established that FitzAllan is not behind these troubles?"

"It may not be FitzAllan, but there are two others who may be involved."

"And what am I do to, wait and pine for you?"

"You might repair to the abbey church and light a candle for our inquiry. I know you want to visit there anyway. Oh, and you could find Bill Sharpe and the maid. Find the maid and we'll know who the girl in the ice was, and why she died. You can manage that alone, can't you? Or should we have brought Harry along to help?"

"I am more than enough for that chore, I assure you. Although I hope the sheriff's men don't catch up with me before I finish."

"I doubt anyone will be looking for you. In any case, I think we've covered our tracks enough that that won't happen."

"It's not me I'm worried about, you young fool. It's you." Gilbert sighed. He rummaged in this belt pouch and produced a small knife whose sheath dangled from a leather thong.

"What's this?" Stephen asked.

"I suspected you'd have some wild plan like this in mind. I bought you this." Gilbert extended the knife.

Stephen removed the knife from the sheath. The blade and tang were stout, thicker than usual.

"I thought it would be useful if you ever have to dig your way out of gaol again," Gilbert said. He motioned to his neck. "You wear it around your neck. I saw a Norwegian fellow carrying his knife that way once. It seemed odd, but practical."

"I see." Stephen lowered the thong over his head.

"You're supposed to keep it under your shirt out of sight. In case you get arrested again. No one will think to look for a knife there. It will certainly be more comfortable, not to mention useful, than hiding a knife in your shoe like last time."

Stephen was about to stuff the sheath inside his shirt when he had a sudden thought. He took the dandelion ring from his belt pouch, undid the thong, and fed the leather strip through the ring. He retied the thong. "This will keep both safe."

"There are cut purses everywhere," Gilbert said in a tone that suggested he thought this precaution was more than necessary, "even in the wilds of Clun, I'm sure. Well, off you go. I best get busy. Finding missing maids is hard work, and I want to get started early."

They said no more, nor even shook hands.

Stephen climbed aboard the replacement horse. He was about to turn the horse when he had a thought, something that he had neglected. He pulled the folded picture of the girl in the ice from his belt pouch. He had forgotten about it. He handed the drawing to Gilbert, along with the shard of wood with the dandelion sign, the fragment of one of the Saltehuses' salt barrels he had recovered at the site of the murders. "You'll need these more than I will."

Gilbert unfolded the picture and gazed at that immaculate face. "Ah, so I will. A lovely image. Truly lovely. Such a pity, such a waste." He shook a finger at Stephen. "Stay out of trouble, do you hear? Oh, what am I saying! You can no more stay out of trouble than any schoolboy! Be gone before I'm tempted to pull you off that horse, for your own good!"

"Find the maid," Stephen said, sorry that he had given away the picture.

He turned the gelding at last, and rode out of the yard.

Gilbert did not turn away until Stephen was lost from sight around the corner.

## Chapter 18

There were two good roads into Clun honor, but Stephen took the one through Bishop's Castle, which led close to Welsh lands. This hilly country might as well have been Wales itself, for it was full of Welsh people, distinguishable from the English by their bowl haircuts and the fashion of their tunics, which hung to the knees.

Being Welsh had not spared many of them from the ravages of the winter war. Here and there along the way, Stephen rode through villages that had been burned and pillaged by their Welsh neighbors to the west. Some villages were deserted, consisting only of piles of ashes capped with crusts of snow, the smell of smoke still in the air among charred timbers projecting skyward, stray dogs their only inhabitants. In a few, there were plenty of people living among the ruins in shanties and tents, some of the shelters just heaps of branches leaning against a horizontal pole with a fire in front for warmth. While in others, so much rebuilding was already underway that it was hard to tell that war had washed over the place.

Everywhere, the folk regarded him with suspicious eyes. Even in the best times, strangers — especially armed ones — were not to be trusted. But the hostility seemed more acute than usual, and Stephen spoke to none of them, glad not to have to share their misery and fear for the future.

Stephen reached Bishop's Castle late in the afternoon after a long, slow ride. He was happy to see that the town was intact, not a window smashed or roof stove in. It was odd how the Welsh picked their targets: one prosperous village might be destroyed while those only a mile or two away escaped unhurt, and so it was with towns. Clun had been burned, but Bishop's Castle only six or so miles away looked completely normal, as if there had been no war at all.

He found lodgings at an inn just below the castle's main gate. The charge made a significant dent in his funds since he had left most of Harry's money with Gilbert, who would need it more. But Stephen was not enthusiastic about sleeping in the cold and wet if he did not absolutely have to.

After Stephen had stabled, groomed, and fed the horse, he went up the hill to the castle. The gate warden asked his business and admitted him when he said he was an archer looking for work.

"The deputy constable's name is Martin Picot," the warden said. "You'll find him in the hall. We're full up, though, so I don't think there's a place for you."

"Well, perhaps he knows of someone else who's hiring."

"I doubt it, though it'll be better in the spring. I hear that Prince Edward's been given command of a force to punish the Welsh for the harm they've done."

"I've heard that rumor as well. It's a long time 'til spring, though."

The warden grinned. "True. You could starve to death before then."

"I've no intention of starving. There's always folk on the highway who are ready to be charitable with the proper persuasion."

The warden looked stern. "I'll take that as an attempt at humor. We've no patience for criminality around here."

"I meant nothing by it."

"You'd better not, if you don't want to end up decorating an oak tree. Now, don't flap your jaws and waste my time, and hand over that sword of yours, if you're going in. I'm a busy man."

"And an important one," Stephen said.

In many castles, the hall was in a great square stone tower that dominated the bailey, but not so with Bishop's Castle. There was no great tower; the biggest eminence in the fortress was the main gate tower. The hall was a timber building on the far side of the bailey beyond the well. Except for the high table, the other tables in the hall had been stacked away, and Picot sat on a cushioned chair watching some of the garrison wrestling dangerously close to the hearth in the center of the floor. He was spare man with black hair and a weak chin, a member of one of the many lesser branches of the powerful and rich Pico family.

He eyed Stephen with a bored expression. "What do you want?"

"I'm looking for work, sir."

"What kind of work?"

"I'm a good archer and decent with a sword and shield."

"What's your name?"

"Wistwode, Orm Wistwode."

"Orm? What kind of name is that?"

"Danish. My mum was from Yorkshire and they had lots of Danes in the family."

"Well, we're full up. We won't be taking on anybody 'til the spring, when there will be more than enough work for anybody who can pull a bow."

"So the gate ward said, sir."

"Then what are you bothering me for?"

"Well, sir, I thought that even if you aren't hiring, you might know somebody who was. I heard that Eudo Walcot might be in the market."

Picot laughed. "Walcot! If he's in the market for anything it's a new house."

"Sir?"

"The Welsh burnt his village and manor last November. He's gone off. No one's seen him in months, though since the trouble we've had more than our usual share of traffic from Lydbury."

"Lydbury?"

"His village," Picot said impatiently. "A wide spot in the road with a church and a few hovels about four miles off. They come here now to market because Clun has burned."

"The whole town?" Stephen asked innocently, although he already knew the answer, having seen the smoldering heap that the Welsh had left behind them.

"Every stick. Part of FitzAllan's castle, too," Picot said with a hint of malicious satisfaction.

"You don't get along with FitzAllan?"

"Why do you want to know?"

"So I don't step on anyone's toes."

"If you must know, our sympathies lie with the barons. FitzAllan would put his head up the king's ass, if our sovereign would let him, though that's not all our trouble. He's always pissing over where his boundary lies with us, hunting on our land, clearing our forests. That bastard."

"I've heard he was difficult."

"Difficult! That's a tender word for a son-of-a-bitch."

"So, sir, you can't help me?"

"Not now. Come back in March when the weather breaks and the campaign season starts."

"I'll keep that in mind if I find nothing else."

"Just keep out of Clun honor. It's a den of snakes down there."


While Stephen had no doubt that Picot told the truth as he knew it, he still had to see Lydbury for himself, so he rode out there early the next morning. The village lay to the east and south of Bishop's Castle on a muddy, churned-up road that gave evidence it had been traveled rather heavily, but he did not meet a soul or see anyone in the fields until he reached the village, which was identified by its little stone church and a dozen timber-and-wattle houses which were in various stages of construction. It did not take people long to throw up a house if they had the time and access to the materials.

The church lay on the north side of the road behind a wicker fence and a graveyard, which held a half dozen recently dug graves. Stephen turned up the side road across the western front of the church to a large, new house that lay across the street. An elderly fellow in a peasant's long tunic but sporting a tonsured head was cutting wood in the yard. Three other men were painting the timbers of the house a dignified black and a fourth was mixing plaster to cover some wattled fillings between the timbers.

All the men stopped what they were doing when Stephen entered the yard. They regarded him with suspicion, eyes wandering over his sword, bundle of arrows, and bow, which hung in its canvas bag from his shoulder.

"And what will you be wanting, my good fellow?" the tonsured man asked. "You're quite a bit off the beaten path."

"Nice house," Stephen said.

"It will serve," the tonsured man replied.

"Hey," one of the other men said, "you said it was better than the old one, Bertie."

"It will be when it's finished," Bertie said. He redirected his attention to Stephen. "I asked your business, fellow."

"Looking for your lord."

"Walcot? What do you want with him?"

"That's our business. Where can I find him?" Stephen had a good view of the village, and there was no structure grand enough to pass for a decent manor house among the hovels under construction, nor even what looked to be remains.

Bertie smiled. "You'll find his place back toward Bishop's Castle. First left after you leave the village, then across the bridge. Can't miss it."

"Thanks," Stephen said, turning the gelding.

"Say hello to him for us, will you?" shouted one of the men working on the house at Stephen's back.

The others got a good laugh out of that.

Walcot Manor lay across a small river. What had been the house sat at the foot of a wooded hill separated from the river by a sloping field. It must have been a rather grand house once, tall, broad, and long, with elaborate carvings around the doorway, but now it was a burned out stone shell, roofless, windows vacant, and one wall collapsed. Even the stairway leading up to the first floor was gone, leaving behind a cinder smear on the stone wall. The remains of a sizeable timber barn sat at an angle to the house, and an intact kitchen, smithy, chicken coop, pig sty, and laundry that no one apparently thought worth burning clustered opposite the barn. A small house had been newly built by the kitchen, but no one answered Stephen's knock. He called out, but there was no reply. It was very quiet; not even the cackle of chickens or the rooting of pigs disturbed the gloom.

It was an unlikely haunt of outlaws, and certainly not Margaret's barn-burners.

Stephen remounted the gelding and pulled his head around toward the bridge to the village. He had to pass close by the ruined barn and a flash of white caught his eye. It could have been mistaken for snow, but it was not on top of the burned timbers as snow should be, but beneath a layer of cinders at a disturbed place where it looked as though someone had been digging. He slipped off the horse and clambered across a burnt section of wall to the white spot. It was not snow. He licked a finger, pressed it into the white pile, and tasted the residue on the finger: salt. The charred slats of a barrel lay mingled with the pile of salt. Some of the slats were burned so badly that they fell apart in his hands, but he dug deeper and came upon several slats that gave little sign of the fire. He turned over one of those and found the Saltehus dandelion mark staring up at him.

"Just what the hell do you think you're doing?" an angry voice said behind him.

Stephen stood up and turned around. A gray-haired man of about forty faced him beyond the wall. Several hares dangled from his belt, and he held a bow with a nocked arrow. "Looking for a thief," Stephen said.

"You're trespassing."

This was true, of course. Trespassing was a serious matter.

"Send for the sheriff, then, and you can explain how you came by this." Stephen held up the slat bearing the dandelion.

The fellow's brows curled in a dismissive expression as Stephen clambered across the wall and fallen timbers to come within arms reach. The fellow said, "How we came by it is none of your business."

"I have made it my business," Stephen said, gauging the distance between them and wondering if the man could draw and shoot in the time it would take him to cover it.

The bowman turned his head to shout to someone out of sight. This was Stephen's only chance. He launched himself to the left, kicking at the fellow's groin. The blow struck on the thigh, but generated enough of a distraction that Stephen was able to grasp the bow and punch him on the chin. The man let go of the bow and fell on his back. He tried drawing his dagger, but Stephen stepped on his elbow, pinning the arm to the ground.

"I'll ask once more, politely. Where did you get the salt?"

"We bought it. In Clun."

"From whom?"

"I have no idea. I'm the steward here. I send people to do my buying, and if they get a good price, I don't ask questions."

"Who bought, then, for you?"

"Wouldn't do you any good if I told you. He's dead."

"Killed when the Welsh came?"

The steward nodded.

"And he didn't give you a name?"

"What name would that be?"

"Of the person he bought it from."

"Of course not. Why would he?"

Stephen took his foot off the steward's arm. He picked up the discarded bow and mounted the gelding.

"Hey," the steward said. "Give that back."

Spurring the gelding toward the wooden hill behind the wreck of the manor house, Stephen called back, "You'll find it just ahead!"

## Chapter 19

Stephen leaned the stolen bow against a beech tree at the edge of the wood where it could be seen by the steward and two of his fellows, who were following on foot. He waved at them, but doubted they appreciated the friendly gesture from the indignant noises they threw his way. Reflecting on how people were often so impolite these days, he continued uphill into the forest.

He swerved northwest as the forest obscured the pursuit's view, riding at an easy trot. It was a young forest with most trees no bigger round than his thigh, so there were lots of branches, which meant he spent a great deal of time bobbing in the saddle like some lovesick bird or waving his arms about to avoid a constant whipping.

Presently, he broke out of the forest. Ahead was a broad valley, empty pasture from the look of it, with gentle rising ground in the distance. He kept to the edge of the forest, heading southwestward. Only a few yards on, he passed a stone shepherd's hut; the trash piled outside the door smelled fresh, and it had not yet achieved that gagging aroma it acquired in warm weather. It was unusual it should be occupied this time of year, but he smelled no smoke and no one emerged to wonder what he was doing so far from any road.

Once he was away and the possibility of capture diminished, Stephen had plenty of time to contemplate his stupidity at Walcot Manor. He had not handled it well, blurting out the truth in his shock at being surprised. The venture depended on secrecy, stealth, and lies, and at the first test he had failed. Only luck had enabled him to get away. He was always blundering from one thing to another, especially in this finding business. He wished he had another way to make a living. Maybe with the war coming in the spring his prospects would change. Someone had to stay and guard the castles while everyone else was away winning glory and plunder. He could do that with a bum foot. But the thought did not make him feel any better.

The pasture gave way to cultivated fields a bit farther on, where winter wheat poked above the crust of snow. These fields must have belonged to the village he could see to the north, a handful of gray thatched rooms wreathed in smoke from the fires that people were at pains to keep burning in all weather.

Stephen skirted the fields — to ride across a cultivated field was a great crime not far beneath robbery or assault — by keeping to the edge of the wooded hills to the south, hoping that he would attract no attention.

He came around the shoulder of another hill where before him lay a pasture of flattened grass. Hoping that he was not under the eyes of any watcher who might call out at his trespass, he rode across the field to the hedge that was its far boundary. It was a hedge so tall that he could not tell even from the back of the gelding what lay beyond it, and was so thick that he could not see a way through. But by riding along its length for a short way, he found a break where carts came and went, and crossed through to what proved to be a wide and well traveled road.

All the villages in England were connected with their neighbors by a spider's web of footpaths and cart tracks that were often so narrow that even a cart might find them a challenge. It was possible to travel from Chester to Dover upon them if you were fortunate enough to know the way, not that anyone might, of course. But your better chance of getting about was on the king's roads which by royal edict were maintained along their length by the lords whose lands they passed through, and this had to be such a road: wide enough for two carts side-by-side and even with ditches to carry off the rain, although here they were shallow and weed filled. It could only be the road from Bishop's Castle to Clun.

A pack train was plodding north a short distance away when Stephen burst onto the road. The man in the lead pulled up and shouted an alarm, causing consternation and confusion along the length of the train, which was quite long, as many as thirty horses so laden that it was a wonder they could stand up beneath their packs.

A couple of hefty fellows clad in brigantines and wearing swords jogged forwards at the call of the leader. They drew their swords at the sight of Stephen, for it was not polite to go bursting out in front of people from the shrubbery and usually meant no good.

Stephen showed his hands as he ambled the gelding toward the pack train. "Good day!" he called when he had got close enough to speak to them.

"What are you up to?" the leader called back, apparently not convinced it was a good day.

"Taking a shit is all," Stephen replied, which was a reasonably plausible explanation as, while it was permissible to pee in the road even if there were women about, it was bad form to crap there like a dog where anyone could step in it. "You coming from Clun?"

"We might be. What's your business?"

"Everybody seems to want to know that today, for some reason. People are so touchy hereabout."

"We've got good reason to wonder about people who jump out of bushes."

"I didn't jump. As you can see, I am on a horse and we are moving slow."

"Well, keep on, then, and make no trouble."

"Trouble is not my intention. How is Clun these days? It has been a while since I've been there."

"It's still there, barely."

"I heard it was roughly handled."

"Yeah, Welsh burnt the town, but they're rebuilding. You're looking for work?"

"I am, but not of that sort. Is FitzAllan in residence?"

"No, he's gone off south. Westminster, I heard, to suck up to the King and Prince Edward."

"That's how his kind make their money."

"His kind would die if they had to make their way by honest labor," the leader spat into the road.

"Give him his due. Sucking up can be hard work," Stephen said. "Not that I mean to defend the earl."

"You would know. You don't look like a working man yourself."

"I just labor in a different field. Sometimes we are useful." Stephen inclined his head toward the two men with swords, who had begun to relax when the only threat appeared to be bad conversation rather than sudden assault.

The leader smiled. "I'll give you that, though your kind didn't do much good at Clun."

"Had I been there, the Welsh would have been too frightened to show their faces."

That was so absurd a boast that everyone laughed.

"I think they'd have been more afraid if you showed your ass," one of the soldiers said.

"I doubt that," Stephen said, accepting the jibe with good grace. "Say, you wouldn't know a fellow in Clun by the name of Blasingame, would you?"

"I've heard of him," the pack leader said. "Wool merchant. Why?"

"Thought he might be good for a few pence, to tide me over 'til I get employment."

"You're that friendly?"

"He's a cousin."

"He's doing all right, I suppose. Got his house burnt like everybody else, but now he's got a new one. Pretty grand one, too. How close a cousin?"

"Rather distant, actually."

"Well, he's got enough pennies to spare for the likes of you, though I don't know why he'd bother, seeing as you're probably the black sheep of the family."

The pack leader laughed at his little jest, and the soldiers chuckled with him.

"Well, you're right about the black sheep part. I've so disappointed my mother. She expected a priest and look what she got. Anyway, is his house still where it used to be on . . ." Stephen left that part hanging, hoping that the pack leader will fill the void.

He was not disappointed. The pack leader nodded. "Yeah, right there on High Street and Kid Lane where it always was."

Stephen touched his cap. "Well, I won't detain you any longer, seeing as you're such busy men. Good day to you."

To a chorus of polite "Good days," he turned the gelding south toward Clun.


Stephen did not look forward to slipping into Clun. He had done it once before in the autumn, but he had been recognized and nearly caught by the townspeople, who knew of the hatred the earl held for him. That hatred could only have got worse, if the events in Shrewsbury were any guide. For all he knew, even Blasingame might turn him over for the reward, although Blasingame owed him the debt of his life, since Stephen had saved him from burning to death in FitzAllan's gaol.

As he rode south, up hills and down, he closed his eyes and tried to remember the layout of the town. Prior Philip of the Saint Augustine priory across the river from Clun had drawn him a map of the town and named all its streets for his last excursion. While Stephen's memory wasn't that good, after some effort he was able to conjure up the drawing and even recall Philip's words, so that he had a firm idea where Blasingame's house could be found. Clun was shaped like a box that had been sat upon so the angles were not properly square, the main streets running on the edges of the box along the lines of the town wall, with three small lanes running north-to-south through the middle. He recalled Kid Lane quite well, since he had visited a tailor's shop at the top end of it in the autumn. A prosperous man's house at the bottom of Kid Lane should be easy to find without having to ask for directions.

# The Girl in the Ice

His approach to Clun was on a road he had never traveled, so it was a bit of a surprise when he rounded a bend and there it was, the castle on its motte and the roofs of houses showing above the palisade.

The day was only half gone, and he could not just ride up and ask to be admitted. So he turned back for a short distance to be out of sight of any watchman in the castle, and climbed the hill to the east of the road, where a dense stand of trees capped the summit. He would wait there for dark.

Stephen descended the hill after the last light of dusk had faded. He could hear the bells of Clun ringing the curfew, which meant that the only people allowed on the street were the watchmen. Anyone else out after dark would be regarded as a criminal and treated like one until the appropriate bribes were paid.

He had entered the town surreptitiously the last time by climbing the wall, and he figured he would have to do the same again this time. This worried him, since the watch in peacetime tended to be lax, but with the recent hostilities, he might expect a greater chance of detection. But he saw no other way in. Certainly, he could not just go up and knock on the gate and beg admittance, assuming there still was a postern gate.

As he came close to the town, houses reared out of the dark on either side of the road. If they had been burned, a most likely prospect, they had been quickly rebuilt, a fact Stephen confirmed as some smelled of fresh paint and sawdust. It had always amazed Stephen how you could knock down people in the lower orders and they would just pick themselves up, repair the damage, and keep going, no matter how bad things had been.

The rows of houses paused at the town ditch and the wooden bridge over it. Stephen stopped to look things over. The two wooden towers that had flanked the gate were gone, and in their place was a makeshift gate and for some distance on either side, planks had hastily been thrown up to repair portions of the wall that had burned as well. No voice called out to ask his business, probably because no one was on the wall to watch for approaching dangers. A rivulet of smoke on the left dribbled into the sky, visible as a smudge against the stars: no doubt that was the hut where the watch sheltered from the cold, for despite the warm days, the night were freezing, and nobody liked to be out in that. Perhaps the watch would not be so dutiful after all.

Stephen turned into the ditch and rode eastward along the north wall toward the spot where he had climbed the last time. Although he was not normally a creature of habit, he thought that since he had got over there the last time, it was as good a place as any do to the deed again. But then, he caught a glimpse of starlight through the palisade above. He went to investigate and found a gap in the planks where some of the boards had rotted, leaving a space just big enough for him to slip through. He was glad to find this gap, since the last time he'd scaled Clun's wall, he'd had to stand upon Gilbert's shoulders to reach the top.

He tied the gelding behind a nearby shrub where it should be out of sight of anyone on the top of the wall, and returned to the gap. It was a tighter fit than he thought it would be and he had to take off his sword belt to get through, but by diligent worming, he managed it.

The look of the street below had changed considerably from his last visit, but Stephen recognized the very spot. Just across the street at the top of what had to be Kid Lane was the tailor's shop he had come to visit a few months ago in order to question a witness to murder. Only the shop was gone, leaving an empty lot behind as if it had never been there. There were other empty lots as well where there should have been houses.

He lay prone on the top of the embankment for several minutes, breathing shallowly and listening for the sounds of the watch. There were faint voices of two men talking, and those of man and a woman locked in argument not far down the street. Otherwise, the night was quiet.

The impulse just to lay there and go no farther almost rooted Stephen to the ground. It had not seemed such a risk worming through the wall, but now that he had to stand up and step into the town proper, he could hardly move. Taking a deep breath, he got up and slid down the embankment to the street. The ground rose rather sharply to the left, where a house sat on the crest, seemingly all alone until he made out the shapes of tents in the field behind it where cows or goats ordinarily should be. The ground fell to the right toward the gate so that if anyone was on guard at the gate all they had to do was step out of their little hut and there he'd be, right under their eyes.

He entered Kid Lane. He stumbled on the ridges of a deep rut and nearly fell, the noise of the scuff seeming to echo through the darkness, announcing his presence to anyone outside. He froze in place, cringing at the prospect of a challenge, but none came and he continued up the sloping lane, walking carefully so as to make as little noise as possible, alert for any hiding place in case someone came along. Kid Lane was little more than an alley running across back gardens of the burgage lots on the right, where some houses had already been rebuilt. A field lay on the left, shielded from the road by a wattle fence. Where the alley bent left at the top of the rise, there was a partly built barn, fully framed and roofed but lacking fillings between the timbers of one wall, and beside it on the downhill side there was a tent where a candle cast the silhouette of a woman as she undressed. A man in the tent said something to her. She laughed and tossed her dress aside, and for a moment the outline of her naked body could be seen. He continued down the lane, envying the man in the tent.

The lane led downhill after the barn and tent, curving gently rightward. The roof of a house built smack on the lane loomed ahead, marking an end to the field that covered the highest ground. He was almost there.

A goat bleated in the field no more than thirty feet away, followed immediately by one voice uttering a faint curse and a second telling the first voice to keep it down. There was no mistaking the furtive nature of the whispers.

Stephen froze in place. His half baked plan had been to vault the fence and lay beside it to avoid being seen in the event he encountered anyone. He hadn't expected the chance of discovery to come from the field.

The grass rustled as the two men and the goat approached the fence not ten feet from where he stood. One man clambered over the fence and the other handed the goat across to him. Apparently the goat did not appreciate being taken wherever they were going, because it squirmed so much that the fellow could not keep it in his arms, but the boys had tied a rope to its neck so that it could not run away.

"Goddamn it," the second fellow hissed as he jumped the fence to join his companion and the goat. "I said, keep it down! You'll wake the whole fookin' town! Cadwick is a light sleeper. That racket will wake him!"

"I told you we should have cut its throat first," the other man said as he struggled to control the goat, which was attempting to flee.

"Makes too much mess. We want him to think the damn thing just got out."

At that point, the fellow interested in quiet noticed Stephen. He froze and held up his hand for the other. The pair, one on his knees clutching the goat possessively and stroking it almost like a dog to calm it down, stared at him.

"What the fook do you want?" the one not holding the goat demanded. He stepped toward Stephen aggressively and pulled a knife.

Stephen drew his sword and even in the dark it was possible to see the fellow's eyes grow large. "What are you boys up to?" Stephen asked.

"Nothing," the man with the knife said. "None of your business."

"I can see that."

"What are *you* up to, wandering about like this after dark?"

"None of *your* business. I suggest you take your goat away from here before she wakes the neighborhood and someone finds out you've stolen her."

"We ain't stealing nothing."

"Right. Shall we ask Cadwick about that?"

The thief had no good answer for that, and while he was thinking about what to say, Stephen edged by them, the sword point still between them.

"There now," Stephen said as he stepped backward down the lane, hoping there were no ruts or holes to trip over. Not only would that be undignified, it might also be fatal if the thief was the murdering kind, which he could well be since goat theft was a crime only a tad less serious than manslaughter. "Off you go."

The two gathered up the goat and disappeared in the other direction.

Stephen did not linger either, and hurried away with more haste that he might otherwise have done, in case this Cadwick had been aroused by the noise and discovered his goat was missing.

At the foot of Kid Lane where it ended at the road circumventing the town, there were two houses on either corner. Stephen realized he had not asked which one belonged to Blasingame. But one of them was only half finished and the other, newly built, had a large shed behind it. On a guess that the fully built house with the shed belonged to Master Blasingame, Stephen sucked a breath to calm his rapidly beating heart, and knocked on the front door.

He had to knock for some time before there was any sound of activity within, but after a while the door cracked open and Blasingame himself asked, "What the devil do you want at this hour?"

"Hello, Reggie," Stephen said. "I was in the neighborhood and I thought it would be rude not to pay a call."

"Good God!" Blasingame said, widening the crack so he could stick his head more closely to Stephen's. Satisfied that it was indeed Stephen, he grasped Stephen shirt and pulled him into the house. "Get off the street before someone sees you!"

Although it was very rude for Blasingame to tug on his shirt, Stephen made no protest because he shared Blasingame's sentiments about the danger and was glad to be off the street.

"Are you mad?" Blasingame demanded as they stood in the dark of what had to be his shop from the smell of wool.

"I've been accused of that," Stephen said. "But no. I am quite sane. Just a little desperate."

"What are you doing here? If FitzAllan finds out . . ." Blasingame's voice trailed off but the anxiety in his tone lingered in the air like the smell of wool.

"I need a favor."

"What kind of favor?" Blasingame asked cautiously.

"Information."

"Ah," Blasingame said, somewhat relieved that apart from putting his life in danger, the visit would not cost him any money.

"Who is it, Reggie?" a woman's voice called from the back of the house.

"No one, dear!" Blasingame called. "Go back to bed!"

But the woman did not go back to bed. She entered the room and in the light of the candle Blasingame had left on the table, Stephen saw it was his wife, her hair down and free, the white widow's peak visible like a blaze.

"You've got a lot of nerve coming here," Anna Blasingame said.

"I was just telling him that," Blasingame said.

"Apparently not forcefully enough," Anna said. "He's still here."

"I can't just toss him out," Blasingame said.

"Why not?"

"Well, I just can't."

"I'll have to do it then."

"No, we can't yet. I'd be dead if it wasn't for him and his fat friend, and our fortune lost. We can at least hear what he wants."

Anna crossed her arms. "All right. What do you want?"

"He said information," Blasingame said.

"Even that's not cheap," Anna said. "Hurry up, what do you want?"

Where to start? Stephen reflected, trying to formulate his questions. "There've been many robberies on the Shrewsbury road and a number of barn burnings to the east of it. I've been asked to find out who's behind them."

"And you think there're connected?" Blasingame asked.

"Yes."

"Connected with someone here?" Anna asked.

"Yes."

"That's ridiculous," she said.

"Why?" Stephen asked.

"Because we'd know about it."

"I doubt that someone who makes his living in robbery would be prone to spread that about among good people such as yourselves. But I was hoping that you might have noticed someone doing much better than expected in these times. Someone with wealth, with goods, with wagons of grain, that you'd not ordinarily expect them to have."

"That's exactly why we would know about it," Anna said. "You can't keep that sort of thing secret in a little town like this. Come morning, everyone on the street will know that we've had a visitor in the night. That's exactly why you should be going right away."

"Wagons of grain," Blasingame reflected as if his wife had not spoken. "Wagons of grain, you say?"

"Yes," Stephen answered. "The raiders burned the barns and carried off the harvests, as much as they could, anyway, and burned what they could not take."

"Savagery," Blasingame muttered. "Pure savagery."

"It was," Stephen said.

"Those poor people," Blasingame said. "They could starve."

"Someone else facing starvation must be behind it," Anna said. "But we've seen no evidence of wagons full of grain, except for the priory. They've plenty of grain, and houses in Lower Clun are going up like toadstools. Why, you walk across the bridge and you'd almost never know the Welsh had burned everything. Yet all they got were the buildings, not their grain. Now the priory sells to us at exorbitant prices."

"Yes," Blasingame. "Perhaps you should look to the priory for help."

"I don't trust the prior," Stephen said. "He betrayed me to FitzAllan last time I visited there. I am not sure he might not do so again."

"Yes, so you said. So you said," Blasingame ruminated, recalling how they had shared FitzAllan's gaol together before the coming of the Welsh.

"So there is no one around here who fits the bill?" Stephen asked again.

"No," Blasingame said. "I'm afraid not. Although they have plenty of grain at the castle, without having to pay the prior's prices, too."

"Where are they getting it from?" Stephen asked.

"Frankly, I'm not really sure. The south somewhere. One of the manors in the honor, I believe."

"Do you know which one?"

"I cannot say I paid that much attention."

Stephen produced the ring he had found beneath the body of the girl in the ice, with its dandelion mark. "Have you ever seen the like?"

Blasingame turned the band over and over, then stared at the mark. "I've seen this before, yes."

"Where?"

"Here, of course. A fellow from the south had barrels of salt with this mark upon them. Gave some to the castle, in payment of rent, I believe, and sold the rest at market."

"Who might that have been?"

"Let me think a moment. Ah, yes. A retainer of one of the Pentre's."

"Pentre? Warin Pentre?"

"The very one. There are quite a few Pentres around the southern part of the honor. A bothersome, grasping family, if you ask me. Do you know him? Poor fellow. He just lost his wife."

"You don't happen to know where his manor lies?"

"It's at a village called Bucknell."

"How to I find it?"

"Take the road to Knighton. At the River Redlake — you'll know it by the crossroads just south of the stream — take the east fork. It's about eight miles altogether. A decent morning's walk. I've made it more than once myself."

"Thank you." Stephen touched his hat. "Mistress Blasingame, I won't trouble you any further."

"I wish you hadn't troubled us at all," she said.

He opened the front door and stepped back into the night.

## Chapter 20

Stephen hurried up Kid Lane, fearful that he might hear Blasingame's voice calling out for the watch. Despite the favor that Stephen had done the wool merchant in saving his life, he did not entirely trust him. But the night was silent except for the murmur of the wind over the rooftops and the muffled sounds of the man and woman in conversation in the tent by the barn. There was no sign of the fellows who had filched the goat, of course, and even better, no sign of an irate owner stumbling about in the dark leveling accusations at every silhouette in range.

Getting out of a walled town, particularly one having only timber and earth fortifications, was much easier than getting in. Stephen had only to dash across the street and mount the embankment, where he lay quietly for a time listening for any town wardens who might happen by. When none did, he unbuckled his sword belt and slipped over the wall, hanging for an instant before letting go to tumble down into the ditch.

He scrambled up the other side and retrieved the gelding, relieved that he was still tied to the bush, and rode back north to the little copse on the crown of the hill overlooking the town. There he unsaddled the horse, replaced the bridle with a rope and halter, and draped an oat bag on the horse's head. The horse was so eager for the oats that he nearly forced the bag from Stephen's hands and he had to struggle with the gelding to secure it. He tied the rope to a wrist, a trick learned in Spain: not only did it prevent the horse from wandering away, but he would awaken Stephen if startled by anyone's approach. He wrapped himself in his cloak and blanket, and lay down to sleep.

Sleep came fitfully, however. It was bad enough that the ground was hard, cold, and troubled with roots. Then the horse finished with his oats, and nuzzled Stephen's face until Stephen removed the bag so that he could graze on the clumps of brittle grass that survived among the roots. This involved tugging on the rope as the gelding moved from one clump to another throughout the night, so that by morning, Stephen awoke without having got much rest. Lacking sleep and his breakfast, he was in a very grumpy mood. He wished that Gilbert was here so that he could take out this mood on him. Or better yet, Harry. A little verbal fencing with Harry would either banish gloom or send a person running for shelter. Stephen could have snapped at the gelding, but he had been too well brought up to take his unhappiness out on the horse.

Wistfully recalling a certain tavern in lower Clun that had sold excellent sweet buns, Stephen headed eastward. The way led downhill. At the bottom, there was a cart track leading south-to-north, which he crossed, passed through a field, splashed across a stream, and climbed a gentle slope to a forest at the top of the further hill. Just before he entered the wood, he had a glimpse over his shoulder of the roofs of the town, and if he could see it, someone there could see him, but he doubted that anyone would notice at this distance. He had been this way once before the last time he had circumvented Clun, but the inside of a forest looks different when you are heading the other direction, just like a road.

He hoped to descend the hill to the same spot where he had crossed the River Clun the last time, but he came out of the wood a bit farther east. A train of laden carts and some people on foot bearing loads on their backs, and in one case balanced on his head, were all heading westward toward Clun. It must be a market day, and these people had got on the road early, as the sun was hardly up yet.

Stephen waited for them to pass, before he went down and crossed the road, worried that someone else might come along and see him. Fortunately, he made it over undetected, and passed through the stream. Some distance away and directly to the south was a high wooded hill with a smaller wooded hill closer and to the right. Beyond that, the big hill dropped to the west into what appeared to be a sort of cut. Stephen headed for the cut, certain that off in that direction lay the road to Knighton. All he had to do was go southwest and he'd stumble across it eventually.

He reached and followed the course of a stream that brought him within sight of an isolated farmhouse up the slope near the mouth of the gap in the hills, where you would not usually expect to find a house. A woman was scraping the hair from a deer hide that was stretched upon a wooden frame. He waved, but she did not return it, and she ran to the house. Stephen pushed the gelding into a trot in case she meant to raise an alarm, keeping to a faint footpath that now rose along the stream, little more than a depressed line in the leaf litter as if anyone hardly ever used it.

The stream ran down through the cut, which was steep on its left side and less so to the right, the ground covered with moss in spots, as he followed the path and stream upward toward its source in the forest. Deep into the cut where the stream forked, now hardly more than a dribble, there were old campfires in a clearing hacked out of the forest, a few shelters of tree branches fallen into ruin, piles of trash, and a latrine pit that no one had bothered to fill in — a place where people came to hide from the Welsh, Stephen surmised. It was quiet and pleasant here.

It was clear from the rising ground on all sides that he was in a cul-de-sac of sorts. There seemed to be no further advantage to pressing south, so gauging directions by the shadows and the moss at the base of the trees, he went to the right, where the ground gradually rose toward the top of a hill that could not be seen for the trees.

Presently the land leveled, indicating he had reached the top, and continued relatively level for more than a mile as he followed the hilltop to what he judged the southwest. After a mile, he was rewarded when abruptly he stumbled upon a good, wide road through the forest that had to be the road to Knighton, since as far as he knew there was only one good road anywhere about and that was where it went. As a stranger to a place, it was always easy to get lost and a great comfort to think you knew where you were.

The ride around Clun had taken a good bit of the morning, and the sun was almost three hours into the sky by the time he descended a gentle slope into a broad valley, where at the bottom flowed a stream that was larger than any of the others he had encountered so far. The road crossed a ford at the stream, which Stephen guessed must be the Redlake, for just beyond the ford another road branched to the left, running down the valley to the east, where Bucknell was supposed to be, if no one had moved it.

Stephen rested at the ford for a half an hour, hoping that someone might come along so he could ask directions, but when no one did, he finally mounted the gelding and took the branch road to the east, hoping that this was not a waste of time.

After about a mile, he heard the creaking of wagon wheels and the sound of men's voices up ahead. At a gentle bend, where a path led northward over a plank bridge across the stream, he met three carts coming the other way. The contents of the carts was covered with tarpaulins, so he could not tell what was in them, though from the lumpiness it looked as if it could have been bags of grain. It was not odd to encounter carts now and then on any road, but it was a bit odd that they would be escorted by five mounted men armed with bows and swords. The bows were in their cases and the flaps of their arrow bags were closed, however, and they were riding relaxed and easy.

"Expecting trouble?" Stephen asked, edging to the side of the road.

"No," said one of the riders, "we just enjoy a ride in the country, and you? You looking for trouble?" The man who had spoken glanced about as if he thought Stephen might be the decoy for an ambush, although this was an unlikely place for one, since the forest did not grow thickly enough by the road to conceal anyone, especially with the leaves gone.

"No," Stephen said, "I'm looking for work. Is that Bucknell up ahead? I've heard that the lord there has a need for archers."

"And where would you have heard that?"

"In Clun."

"From whom in Clun?"

"Just somebody at a tavern. A girl."

"What girl might that have been, who knows so much about our business?"

Stephen was not prepared for this keen interrogation and he wracked his memory for the name of a tavern in the town. A pretty girl in lower Clun, the English village below the Norman town, had once told him the name of one, but he couldn't recall it. He did remember the tavern where the girl had worked quite well, though. "Just a tavern in Lower Clun below the bridge. They were burned out in the troubles and were rebuilding. Her name was Aelflaed."

"People talk too much in Clun," one of the other riders remarked. "Especially Aelflaed."

The first rider asked, "Why didn't you ask at the castle?"

"Aelflaed said they weren't hiring and I should come back in the spring. Everybody seems to be saying that."

The first rider chuckled. "Yeah, there'll be plenty of work in the spring, that's true enough."

"But a man could starve to death before then."

"An honest man could." The first rider looked Stephen over as if making up his mind about something. "You an honest man?"

"Most of the time," Stephen said.

The rider pointed in the direction the train had come. "Bucknell's back there a ways. When you get there, go to the castle and ask for Edgar."

"Much obliged."

"I'm not promising anything. It's up to Edgar, and the lord. Come on, boys," he said to the others.

The drivers snapped their reins and the cart train moved off toward the road to Clun.

Stephen sat on the gelding for a few moments and watched them go. Then he turned the horse toward Bucknell.

Stephen knew he was near the village when the road crossed the stream not at another ford, but at a neat little wooden bridge. The road ran along the stream for some distance, then curved away, and within a few hundred yards, there it was, houses stretched along the road, a few clinging to a lane opening to the left and then a crossroads, with roads leading north, south, east, and west. It was too small a village to have a tavern, but there appeared to be an alehouse on the northeast corner, if the tables in the yard, beneath an oak that in summer would provide pleasant shade, were any indication.

Stephen was about to ask directions to the castle from a woman hanging laundry across a fence when he spied the castle's wooden tower through the branches of another oak growing in the very center of the crossroads. The street meandering eastward seemed to lead to the castle, so he took that. His suspicions were confirmed, for after only a short distance, the line of houses ended at the castle ditch, and the road led straight up the main gate.

It was a small wooden castle, typical of its kind, and Stephen had seen so many in his life that he found it utterly unremarkable. At another time, he would not have given it any more thought than a peasant's hut, but now he examined it with a critical eye. It was a motte-and-bailey, of course, one bailey from the look of things, and a rather small motte at the south end of the bailey, its top about twice the height of a man sitting on horseback, the sort of fortress that was cheap to throw up, which was why England was full of them — many magnates could afford one, though it might strain the finances of a single manor. There was the V-sided ditch, nice and deep, the grass long and in need of mowing, rising to a steep rampart higher than Stephen's head. It had only a single tower beside the gate, unusual in that it had a stone base about seven or eight feet high; the rest was wood that was square on the first story and round on the second, with a peaked roof. Much of the wall walk was roofed over so that for a good bit along its length there were no crenelations; instead shuttered windows from which a crossbowman could shoot opened at regular intervals. The roofs of interior buildings, covered with wooden slats rather than slate or thatch, projected above the walk, and watching over it all was the tower on the motte. Not for the first time did such a tower remind Stephen of a wooden church belfry, and it occurred to him that perhaps such towers were built using the same methods, for it was about the same height as a belfry, three stories, and its corner posts all leaned slightly toward the center, giving the tower, although straight-sided, a conical appearance that the peaked, round roof accentuated.

A single gate ward sat on a stool within the open gate, unhelmeted and unarmored, but with a sword, and a spear leaning against a gate panel.

The guard rose at Stephen's approach. "And what do you want here?"

"Is Edgar about?"

"Why?"

"Fellow on the road told me to ask for him. Said he might be able to give me work."

The guard's eyes ran over the bow stave in its canvas case and the arrow bag hanging from Stephen's saddle. "That wouldn't be his decision. It's up to the lord."

"Of course it is."

"Can I see him, then?"

"Who?"

"The lord," Stephen said.

"I doubt he's in a talkative mood."

"Is he ill tempered? Out of sorts today?"

"He's out of sorts every day. But go ahead, see for yourself." The guard waved toward a large timber and clay building across the bailey that must be the hall.

"Much obliged," Stephen said as he led the horse through the gate.

The guard hawked, spat, and returned to his stool.

Stephen left the gelding in the hands of a stable boy, and carried his bedroll, satchel, bow and arrows across the bailey to the hall.

Two great hunting dogs lay by the hall entrance, gray and brown, of an indeterminate mixed breed, but having the leanness that suggested greyhounds in their parentage. They rose and sniffed Stephen, who paused and made no threatening moves. A grown man would be hard pressed to defend himself against a single such animal, for their shoulders were almost as high as Stephen's hips, and one was more than enough to bring a man down if they had a mind for it. Curiosity satisfied, the dogs returned to their places by the door.

The hall was like most of its kind, a large room with a central hearth on the dirt floor and support posts running up either side which created an impression of three aisles not unlike many country churches. A woman near the door pointed Edgar out. He was a stocky man with a broad, friendly face, a cleft chin, and light hair cropped short in a fashion that had long gone out of style. He was superintending two others, one of them an archer by the simplicity of his shirt and hose, and the other a boy of twelve or thirteen, who were fencing with singlesticks and bucklers while others watched from benches nearby, shouting encouragement and advice to the boy, who was trying hard not to be hit and was doing very little hitting himself.

Stephen put his sword and belt against a wall with his possessions, since it was bad manners to go armed in a hall, and leaned against a post to watch and wait to be noticed.

A well-dressed man with graying hair came up to watch as well. When the archer clouted the boy on the shoulder, the man called, "Edmund! For God's sake! Fight back!"

The boy Edmund snarled and swung his stick. The archer easily deflected it with his buckler and launched a counter blow at Edmund's legs, which the boy barely avoided.

162

The man saw the frown on Stephen's face, and said, "I know. He needs work." He sipped from his cup. "I haven't seen you before."

"I'm must passing through, m'lord," Stephen replied, for it was clear from the man's clothes and his accent that he was gentry. "Are you the lord here?"

"No. My name's Walcot, Eudo Walcot. My honor is north of here. And you are?"

"Orm Wistwode, lord."

Walcot examined Stephen with a critical eye. "You look like a fighting man, Wistwode."

"I've done my share, lord."

The archer clouted Edmund on the arm and the boy cried out. Walcot grimaced.

"Your son?" Stephen asked, guessing that was the reason for Walcot's interest in the fight and his embarrassment at the outcome.

"Yes."

"I could help him."

"Could you? Better than those here?"

"Yes. Some men need to be brought along slowly. It doesn't help them to be thrown in the pit right away."

"Edgar!" Walcot called. "Enough. This fellow here claims he can fence. I'd like to see what he can do."

"Very good, lord," Edgar said, waving at the archer and the boy to clear the space between the pillars that was their fighting ring. "Shall I do the honors?"

"You're the best we've got. Try not to hurt him too much."

Edgar smiled, and took the archer's singlestick and buckler.

"If you don't mind." Stephen held out a hand to the boy for his singlestick, but did not take the buckler.

He stepped back to put space between him and Edgar.

"No buckler?" Edgar asked.

"I don't think I'll need it."

"Suit yourself. You don't mind if I keep mine?"

"Not at all. Shall we say the head is not a target?"

"What's the matter, afraid of messing up that pretty face of yours?"

Stephen shrugged. "If that's the way you want to play." He saluted Edgar as if this was a formal duel.

Edgar spat in the dirt and took up his guard, left foot forward, the buckler held out straight, the stick at his right hip. Stephen dropped his point so that the stick lay beside his right leg, and waited to see what Edgar would do.

They began to move about in the open space in a sort of dance, Edgar moving through one guard to another: the high guard, the tail on the left and then the right, the underarm, until at last he came to the half shield. He paused there for an instant, and then attacked, a cut at the head with a twirl of the wrist.

Stephen had no doubt that this cut was a feint, but it didn't matter. He drew his stick up the left Ox guard and, stepping out to his left, cut around at Edgar's shoulder. The blow landed with a solid crack, but to Edgar's credit, he neither winced nor cried out, but acted as if there had been no blow at all, and struck backhanded at Stephen's head. Stephen took the blow with a hanging point and struck around to the same place he had just hit, but this time Edgar was ready and slipped backward out of the way so that Stephen's stick swept through empty space which Edgar then filled with another cut to the head. Stephen answered with the inside guard and a thrust intended for Edgar's face but struck his chest instead over a buckler put in the way to deflect the blow.

They stepped back to regard each other, Edgar breathing hard, Stephen, who was trying to conserve himself, less so.

"Lucky," Edgar said.

"Of course," Stephen said.

The spectators had shouted encouragement to Edgar during the first exchange, but they fell silent as the two men came together again. The only sounds in the hall now were the scraping of their feet in the dirt, the clatter of the sticks when they came together, and the occasional clang when Edgar set aside a blow with the buckler. Even the household staff had paused in their work to watch, and the ring of bodies was a solid wall around the duelers, with people standing on the benches to get a look over the heads of those in front of them.

The fighters paused now and then after an exchange only to come forward again, the air filled with feints and false blows, followed by good ones that sometimes were parried and sometimes not. Stephen collected bruises on his forearm, collarbone, and knee, but he gave back better than he got, a fact that frustrated Edgar and made him more aggressive.

Then, one cut to the head led to a furious exchange of head blows which each man parried with a hanging point before returning with another cut, until Edgar broke the rhythm by striking with his buckler at Stephen's elbow. The blow turned Stephen and opened him to a cut to the head, but he dived and rolled out of the way. Edgar rushed after him, stick raised above his head. Stephen slipped underneath the blow and wound his left arm around Edgar's right, trapping it, and throwing him to the ground. Stephen prodded Edgar's chest with the point of his stick. Then he backed away and tossed the stick to the boy Edmund.

"I think that's enough," Stephen said to Walcot. "Don't you?"

"You know what you're doing, I'll give you that. You looking for a position?"

"I wouldn't mind if I found one."

"I can promise you the usual, a shilling a week. I can't pay regularly — we're short of cash. But when we're flush, which happens from time to time, I'll make the amount good."

"As long as I get hot meals and a warm place to sleep, I would be honored to enter your service, sir."

Walcot nodded. "Good." He waved toward the hearth, where a man, obviously another lord, sat in a high-backed chair, staring into the fire. Of all the people in the hall, he alone had paid no attention to the duel. "Come meet Sir

Warin. This is his house. We are guests here for the time being."

## Chapter 21

"So," Warin Pentre said, "you're a swordsman. That's an odd thing for a common man to be." Had he not been flushed, he would have been handsome, his mouth framed by a trimmed goatee.

"My father was a sergeant," Stephen lied. "He raised me to be one too."

"But you haven't managed it," Pentre replied, eyes returning to the fire. The cup made a journey from his lap to his lips, where it lingered for a considerable while, then fell back to his lap.

"I am the victim of misfortune," Stephen said.

"Aren't we all. It's everywhere, misfortune. The priests all say He is a loving God, but I wonder."

"Now, there," Walcot worried.

"Our chaplain's gone to his reward," Pentre said. "I can say what I think."

"It's not him I'm worried about."

"I know who you're worried about. I don't care if He hears." Pentre's face screwed up momentarily. "He's got it in for me anyway."

"You must buck up, man," Walcot said. "You'll find another wife."

"Not like her," Pentre said, draining his cup and holding it up for a servant to refill. "There's no one like her."

"That may be, but there are plenty who are serviceable. Many with fortunes."

"You keep saying that. I'm tired of hearing it." Pentre turned his attention back to Stephen. "So, can you shoot as well as you fence?"

"No," Stephen said. "But well enough."

"An honest answer," Pentre said with some amazement.

"You'd probably find out soon enough. Or your man Edgar there would have."

"He doesn't miss much," Pentre said. "He's a good judge of men. And you can ride as well?"

"As I said, my father meant me to be a man-at-arms."

"Well, stick with us for a while and you may well make it, if you don't piss away your share like the others at gambling and whores."

"Share?"

"You didn't tell him?" Pentre asked Walcot.

"Not yet."

Pentre said, "Of the loot. You get wages and a share of what we take."

"From whom?" Stephen asked, the hair on his head tingling. "The Welsh?"

"There will be that come the spring, but meanwhile, we've other work to do."

"I don't understand."

"We're at war, man. It's a small war right now, but it will be a big one soon."

"I don't follow."

"Have you been asleep these past years? Simon de Monfort's back and that means the barons will rise. Prince Edward has commanded us to put them down. We've just started a little earlier than most people."

"Oh."

"Do you have a problem with that?"

"Fighting's fighting. Doesn't matter who as long as the pay's good."

"Precisely."


"There is one thing that puzzles me," Stephen said to Walcot as they left Pentre by the fire.

"What's that?"

"No offense, lord, but neither you nor Pentre seems high enough to get orders directly from the Prince."

Walcot smiled. "We hardly are. But FitzAllan is his friend, and he is our lord. So if he says that the Prince wants something done, we do it."

"What is that, exactly?"

"You'll see soon enough."

There was nothing for Stephen to do for the rest of the day but sit by the fire, and as it grew cold and blustery, threatening either rain or snow depending on whose opinion was being aired, it was crowded there with every man who appeared to be a soldier. There were quite many of them, too; twenty-one at Stephen's count, too many for him to remember all their names after the introductions, and that didn't include the poor fellows pulling guard duty. This complement was far more than needed for even a castle as large as the one at Clun in peace-time. Walcot and Pentre soon went off somewhere, Pentre a little wobbly from all the wine he had drunk, and with their departure, the talk grew more liberated, dominated by expressions of discontent, especially about money.

"They make big promises," one of the archers grumbled, "but they pay slow."

"We'll see something when Ralph gets back," another said.

"Ralph?" Stephen asked.

"He and a few of the fellows took a load of corn to Clun." The fellow who answered smirked. "We're grain merchants."

"How is that?" Stephen asked. He had forgotten about Ralph and the wagon train. That pushed the number in the garrison close to thirty.

"Why, we buy and sell just like it's always done."

"Only we don't pay in coin," said a third archer.

"No, we pay in arrows!" the first archer said.

"It's cheaper and saves a lot of time in the haggling," the second archer said.

"Sounds like robbery," Stephen said.

"Robbery – do we look like thieves? It's just business. Stuff just happens to get lost in war."

"Pentre mentioned there's a war. Though it doesn't seem to be against the Welsh."

"Well, there is that one, too, but they've hardly got anything worth taking. Our enemies, though, they're rich and fat. War's good business all round. We got whores in the village. Didn't have none before. The alewife loves us. And there's even a stonecutter.

"He won't be here long," said another man. "He don't count."

"A stonecutter?" Stephen murmured. "You building a stone castle now?"

"Hell, no. He's here for the marker. For the lady."

There was quiet.

The fellow who had spoken finally said, "She was a beauty, the lady."

"Pentre's not got over her yet and it's been almost two months."

"Since what?" Stephen asked.

"Since she ran away, fool."

"She ran away? I thought she died."

"That's only the story that Pentre's put out. He can't stand the fact that she didn't fancy him."

"How'd she manage to run off?" Creeping out of the castle would be hard enough for Stephen to manage when the time came. A lord's wife had even less freedom to move about.

"She just slipped out one day with that bitch of a maid of hers, and off she went without a word of goodbye. It's the curse."

"What curse?"

"Don't matter now. She took it with her."

"When did this happen?"

"Before the Welsh came. End of November. The lord would have gone after her but he couldn't. We knew the

Welsh were coming. The earl would've had his head if he found out Pentre had deserted his post over a wife he couldn't control."

"It doesn't look like the Welsh came here," Stephen said.

"Well, they didn't, but they burned a village not two miles away, including the castle. Killed everybody."

"We'd have given them more of a fight if they'd come here," somebody else said.

"That's probably why they didn't come. The Welsh aren't as stupid as you."

There was a chorus of "ayes." It was not clear which statement everyone agreed to.


Those who had predicted rain were proved right when in the late afternoon, just before supper, a drizzle began to fall which added to the cold and damp, and made spots by the fire even more desirable. Servants brought in armloads of wood, creating a large pile by the hearth, which people fed constantly so that it was a roaring blaze hot enough that you could feel deliciously seared even sitting against the wall if there hadn't been people in the way, well the part of you facing the fire, anyway; the part away from the fire was chilled, the normal thing with fires. But it was enough to make for a merry atmosphere, especially as the men finished their rations of ale and hard cider. Pentre and Walcot allowed the men enough to feel happy, but not enough to get drunk, which just led to disagreements, fights, and hard feelings that often lingered to poison the air.

As the new man, Stephen did not engage in conversation much, and was on the lookout whenever anyone engaged him for the customary leg-pulling, lies, and deceptions that were the lot of the new.

After Walcot and Pentre retired, Edgar sought out Stephen. "You've the middle watch tonight. Best get what rest you can."

# The Girl in the Ice

Stephen had expected something like this. The middle watch was the least popular, since it meant that you got a bit of sleep, were awakened in the middle of the night for your watch, and then got what sleep you could in what remained. The next day you were expected to do the same work as everyone else, even if you had to drag your ass around to do it, and you were not expected to complain.

As he went for his belongings, which were still in a heap by the door, he saw that the men had begun to file out of the hall, leaving it to the servants. Edgar waved and said, "This way."

Stephen gathered his things and followed Edgar into the yard. The men headed to the right to another large, though one-storied, building, where a fire burned in a central hearth — a barracks for the soldiers. Everyone seemed to have their own place on the floor here and even their own straw mattress, for a couple of the men were at the mattress pile distributing the pads, calling out men's names which they knew from marks made upon the mattress sacks. Stephen was last to get one, a spare that had barely enough straw in it to separate him from the ground.

The others had all seized their places, and were throwing cloaks and blankets over themselves while one of the men laid a few more logs on the fire as Stephen looked about for a good space to claim for himself. He settled on a spot by an interior support post and put down the mattress. He put half his blanket on the mattress and was about to lay down when he noticed that an unlit candle sat upon a little shelf on the post just above his head. Marking the candle's presence, he lay down, pulled on his knit cap before draping the other half of the blanket over him, pulled his woolen cloak over that, and settled down to sleep, hoping that the rain would continue and get worse.

172

Someone shook Stephen awake deep in the night. "Your turn," the man said, without waiting to see if Stephen would rise.

Stephen did not tarry. He rose, grasping a handful of straw from the rushes on the floor, which he stuffed under his shirt, pulled on his coat, and hung his cloak upon his shoulders. Then, before the fellow who had roused him reached the door where two other men were waiting, he snatched the candle from its ledge.

"You coming or not?" the fellow asked at the door.

"I'm coming," Stephen said as he stepped around the sleeping bodies, careful not to stumble on anyone, for waking someone in the night without cause was a good way to start a fight.

The four of them crossed the bailey, slipping in the mud forming there to the single gate tower. A wooden stairway climbed to the first floor, as the stone base proved to be solid. All four men entered, where another four were waiting around a candle burning on the table beside an hour glass in which the sand had run out. It was cold enough to see everyone's breath.

"All right, then," said the fellow who had awakened Stephen. "We're here."

"Took you damned long enough," said one of those who had been waiting for them.

"The new man wanted to sleep late."

"I'm sure that's it." The other fellow, who had to be the earlier watch commander, glanced at the four spears leaning against the door. "Be sure to dry off the heads this time. You forgot last night and they're getting rusty."

"I know what to do."

"Then act like it."

With that, the four men of the previous watch filed out the door.

"So," asked the man who had awakened Stephen and who, he now understood, was the watch commander, "who goes first? Oh, yeah, you."

"You" meant Stephen. He had expected this and pulled his hood over his head as the others settled onto the benches and the watch commander turned over the hour glass to start the sand running.

"Try not to get lost," the watch commander said as Stephen took up a spear and opened the door.

"I think I know the way," Stephen said as he went out into the rain. It had not picked up any, falling slow and steady, if lightly. But it would be good enough as long as it held.

Stephen had stood castle guard enough times in his life that he knew what to do. One of the four should have been sent to stand watch in the tower on the motte, but none of them had gone there, and since he had received no such instructions himself, he assumed the watch commander expected him to make a circuit of the walls. Circuiting the walls meant only walking around them, theoretically alert for any sign of trouble, but in reality lost in one's own thoughts and struggling to stay awake. Walking the circuit was not so bad here, since at least half the circuit was roofed over. He could have tarried in these shelters, but he had the feeling that the watch commander knew how long it took a man to make the circuit and would be waiting for him to report. This proved to be the case, for when he returned to the tower, the watch commander was seated at the table staring at the candle flame as if mesmerized. The other two men were asleep with their heads on the table. Ordinarily, it would now be another man's turn to make the circuit, but the watch commander did not rouse any of the others and said to Stephen, "Glad to see you made it without falling off. Keep going."

"Right," Stephen said, not surprised at the order. He had been through this before. In fact, he was counting on it.

It took almost an hour for the watch commander to finally fall asleep so that all three men in the gate tower now had their heads upon the table, even though the candle was still burning. Stephen closed the door softly soas he would not disturb their slumber.

He stood upon the walk and surveyed the bailey. All was quiet and dark; the fires in the hall and the barracks had burned down so low that no light from them showed in the cracks around the shutters. It was as if Stephen had the whole place to himself. If there ever would be a time to do what needed doing without provoking questions, it would be now.

Stephen climbed down the stairs, careful about falling, but even then his foot slipped in the wet — leather soles were notoriously dangerous on wet wood. He dropped the spear, which clattered to the ground, in order to catch himself. He paused, hoping that the racket didn't waken anyone, especially the fellows sleeping in the guard room, but no one stirred, and no dog barked at the commotion.

He crossed the yard to the large barn that stood to the right of the gate tower and jutted out into the bailey rather than having been built against the embankment as were the other buildings, as if the barn had been there first and the fortress thrown up around it.

Some lords kept their barns locked, but this was not one of them, probably because Pentre thought that his archers were keeping watch during the night, and the dogs could be counted on to raise the alarm if anyone wandered about the bailey who should not be there. Fortunately, the rain kept the dogs in their kennel. Even dogs avoid the cold and wet if they can. It was a small matter to lift the bar and slip inside.

It was as dark as the inside of a sack and smelled of dust, onions, hay, and, implausibly, mint and evergreens with a hint of pitch. He leaned the spear against the door, and knelt to feel the ground. It was dirt. He removed the straw from beneath his shirt, where it had rubbed scratches, and laid the little pile on the ground. Then he fumbled in his belt pouch for his flint, which was wrapped in a piece of leather. He struck the pommel of his dagger upon the flint to produce sparks, which landed on the straw. After several tries, the straw smoldered. He blew on it to kindle the flame, which he used to light the candle. When the candle came alive, he stamped out the straw. The odor of smoke lingered in the still air.

Now that he had light, Stephen saw that the barn was filled practically to bursting. The closest items were a half dozen carts and wagons jammed in together, the tackle for harnessing the horses thrown on their beds. To the left, great stacks of hay strained against railings to leave only a small passage down the middle. To right were barrels and sacks, each on one side. The sacks were marked with charcoal symbols to denote their contents: grain, mostly, but also peas and beans, and flour. The barrels also were marked and held wine (not many of those and right beside the door where it could quickly fetched so as not to try the lord's patience when the supply in the hall ran out), salted pork, fish most likely dried or salted, almonds, apples, and pears. Farther to the right were the small barrels of spices — pepper, cinnamon, a mislaid sack of raisins, dates, figs, sage, parsley, garlic, and fennel were among the marks he recognized.

But search as he might, Stephen did not find a single barrel of salt, nor any barrel marked by a dandelion. He had been sure he would find at least one — no, he had expected to find stacks of them jealously hoarded, for salt was an expensive and highly valued commodity, and not all of it would have been sold, but saved for use here or for sale in the future. He was bitterly disappointed.

He stooped at the door to collect the straw he had used to light the candle, which he blew out, and stepped into the rain.

It had taken a long time to search the barn, and he reckoned that the watch would be nearly over now. The night watches never lasted more than two hours. He could not be late to awaken the next watch; that would be received as a sign that everyone had fallen asleep, and there would be trouble then.

But there was one more place he could look, two if you counted the pantry in the hall.

He crossed the yard to the kitchen, a round building beside the hall, and the only one with stone walls, although like every other in the castle it had a roof of slatted wood. It was sure to have a small storeroom where the cooks put the things for which they had immediate use to spare folk from having to fetch items in bad weather.

The kitchen door was no more secure than the barn in that it was not padlocked, although it was latched from the inside. That should have been a warning, but Stephen was too eager to get inside to heed it, and he slid his dagger through the gap to flip up the latch. But he had only to crack the door to realize the danger, for he heard the rustling of a straw mattress and then the sound of someone pissing in a night jar. He couldn't properly bumble around the place with people sleeping inside; he would surely wake them. He eased the door closed, but not before someone said irritably, "Bloody hell. How'd that door get open!"

Stephen flattened against the wall, hoping that the inhabitant of the kitchen would not think to investigate the cause for the disobedient door. Fortunately, he did not, since Stephen would have no good explanation for why he was not on the wall, and merely re-latched it.

Stephen sighed with relief, and returned to the gate tower.

## Chapter 22

Stephen awoke in a surly mood from lack of good sleep and last night's failure, but he put aside those feelings and, fetching a pair of singlesticks from the rack in the hall, went looking for Edmund, since there was at least an hour before breakfast.

It took some time to find the boy, for he was nowhere about in the bailey, and finally a woman doing laundry in a bucket by the well told him she'd seem him going up the stairs to the tower on the motte.

Stephen found him on the ground floor, where the emergency stores and great bundles of arrows were kept. He noted with interest that these arrows were the same as the one he had found at the scene of the Saltehus' murders, not that this fact alone proved anything.

The boy was swinging a singlestick at a furry object dangling from an iron ring nailed to a post, and it took Stephen a moment in the dimness to realize that the object was a cat.

"What are you doing?" Stephen asked, shocked. He pushed the boy away from the dangling cat and cut it down.

"I'm practicing," Edmund said.

"You'll learn nothing by this," Stephen said. The cat was still alive, moving feebly, but it was clear it was too badly injured to survive. He killed it with his dagger. "Don't ever do this again, or I'll string you up and give you the same treatment."

"You can't tell me what to do," Edmund spat.

"I can and I will. I am here to teach you to use a sword properly, and while you're under my instruction you'll do what I say."

"My father will see about that."

"Will your father be pleased to know what you do with cats?"

"He won't care." But Edmund's tone suggested some doubt about this.

"We'll speak to him about this when we're done." Stephen pushed open the doors so they had better light, and turned to Edmund. "Be on your guard."

Stephen resisted the urge to give Edmund a beating, which fight-masters often did to their pupils, as nothing encourages learning how to fence better than good cracks to the head and body. Instead, he confined his blows to touches, but Edmund flinched even at these caresses as if he had been struck hard. The boy's parries and counters were slow and clumsy, and it was immediately apparent that he had no aptitude for swordplay, nor it seemed any great interest, for he was gasping for breath and demanded a halt after a mere quarter hour. Stephen had known many boys like him, or rather the men they became: rich fellows who wore their armor well but who had hardly any notion which end of a sword to grasp, and who did their best to avoid fighting, the sort who rode into battle only when there was no way they could avoid it, who usually hung back and let others do the real work while putting up a show so that everyone would think they were brave and skillful. Stephen did not let him have his break, but kept him going until the bell sounded for breakfast. Edmund threw down his singlestick and raced out of the tower and down the stairs as if he could not get away fast enough.

Had this been any other manor, Edmund would have been sent for lessons in reading and speaking French after breakfast, but there was no one to teach him. However, he was also Pentre's squire, and Pentre had decided to go hunting, so Edmund spent the remainder of the morning gathering the lord's equipment, saddling and tacking horses, as they prepared to depart.

The keepers, meanwhile, had let the dogs out of their kennel, and although there were only five of them, they created more noise and confusion than three times that number, some jumping the fences where the goats and pigs were kept so that people had to dash about keeping them out of trouble.

Eventually, Pentre and Walcot emerged from the hall as the grooms brought their horses. The dogs knew what this meant and they crowded about the horses without any slackening of their loud enthusiasm; if anything, the clamor grew in volume. But the horses and dogs seemed to know each other very well, for none of the horses shied away, as they often did when dogs were about, for not all dogs were friends of horses, and no dog got stepped on or kicked.

As the hunting party of a dozen mounted men rode out the gate, Edmund showed Stephen his finger.

Stephen looked forward to an afternoon of leisure once the hunters departed, which he intended to use to solve the riddle of how to get a look inside the kitchen storeroom and the pantry without arousing anyone's interest or suspicions. However, Edgar called the remaining archers together and led them out to the field east of the castle, where archery butts had been set up.

"You first, Wistwode," Edgar said. "Let's see if you're as good with a bow as you are with a stick."

"Better, even," Stephen said with bravado he did not feel. He had not expected to have to prove his skill with the bow, though he should have seen this coming.

"That farthest one," Edgar said. "See if you can hit it."

That particular butt, which was hard to distinguish from a sheaf of corn, was at least two-hundred yards away. Several pigs, their winter fur thick and black, could be seen rooting among the stubble and patches of snow not far from it.

"If I miss and hit a pig, what happens?" Stephen asked.

"You better miss the pigs. They belong to the lord."

"I'll do my best."

"See that you do."

At this distance, the object was to see how close you got to the butt, since pin-point accuracy was hard to achieve. Archery obtained its effect by the fall of massed shot in a small location, although the really good men could put an arrow through a circle as round as a man's head at a hundred yards.

"Right," Stephen said, nocking his arrow, mindful to slide it under the string and over the stave from the rear rather that lay them over both as many amateurs were prone to do.

He fixed his eyes on the butt. A pig wandered within yards of it, then around behind it. He felt wind on his cheeks, and glanced down at a few of the surviving stalks of grass to gauge its direction. He would have to correct for the windage, which always threw off long shots, but it was hard to tell how much. He took a deep breath, held it, and raised the bow as he drew the string under his ear. The strain was so great that he wanted to groan, the string dug into his fingers so that he could barely hold on, and his arms threatened to shake, which surely would have betrayed him as a fake. As the arrowhead pointed to the place in the clouds which he hoped would send it true, he released the string, taking the vicious slap on his forearm without flinching, for even with the leather cover it still hurt.

The arrow bolted away and sailed upward, seeming to slow down as it receded. There had always been something about the flight of an arrow that stirred Stephen's heart: the joy and hope when they were your own sailing at the enemy as they flew upward, hung in midair, and then sank like birds of prey toward the enemy line; dread as they soared upward from enemy archers and then plunged toward you so that you watched them fall, praying, keeping your eyes on them until the last moment, when you ducked behind your shield for what protection it could provide. Although this was an outgoing arrow, Stephen watched it with dread, fearful that it would sail wide. It reached its greatest height and fell to earth, slowly at first and then gaining speed, the yellow and red on the shaft nearly lost to sight against the gray cloud and barren gray hills beyond.

The arrow struck some distance short of the butt.

Edgar grunted. "At least you missed the pigs."

Stephen shot again five times, the arrows falling around the butt, but by no more than ten feet or so. "Is that good enough for you?"

"You're already hired. It will have to," Edgar said. "At least that fool Walcot is paying you, not our lord. Go fetch your arrows and run off those pigs."

"Hey!" said a Walcot man. "Watch what you say about him."

"You're the one told me he was a fool," Edgar said, as Stephen set out across the field.


"Our lord is a fool?" Stephen asked the man who had protested as the group headed back toward the castle.

The fellow looked glum and shrugged. "He's no fool, but he's made, well, mistakes."

"Oh." Stephen was curious about what those might be, as well as anything the soldiers might say about the robberies and barn burnings. But he could not ask outright about such things for fear of igniting suspicions. He could only let the men talk, as soldiers could be depended on to do. "Not any that got someone killed, I hope."

"Worse. Lost our homes because of it."

"That's pretty bad." Losing your home was a disaster, because it meant losing everything you owned. "How'd that happen?"

The fellow walked on a few paces. "FitzAllen ordered Walcot down here to help Pentre. We came in November just before the trouble. When it broke out, he decided to stay here. Said it would violate his orders if we went home. The Welsh came and burned our village."

"Why'd FitzAllen send you here?" Stephen asked.

"You haven't figured that out?"

They walked on again for a few more paces. Stephen said, "I don't suppose there's anything you could have done anyway."

"There weren't but ten or so of the bastards," the man said bitterly. "We could have shown them off." The soldier added, "And we're stuck here. Can't even get back to rebuild."

"But you're being paid."

"We're supposed to. It's been a while. For all the work we do, you'd think it'd come more regularly."

When they got back to the castle, Edgar put Stephen on gate ward. Many castle gates had a niche built into the gate tower with a bench for the ward, but this castle had nothing of the kind, except a stool, which he was expected to occupy. It was a job almost as boring as night guard, although it offered the chance of conversation to anyone who came through. Nobody did, though, except the village vicar, and he wasn't disposed to talk, not even a "Good day" as he came, and later, went. The sight of the vicar gave Stephen an idea. Vicars knew everything that went on in a village.

The hunting party returned shortly before sundown with two red deer stags and a wild boar, a young sow by the small size of it, although even young sows could be quite large. Edmund was excited because they had flushed a bear, but Pentre had had enough by then and had called off the dogs. It was too late in the day to do anything but send the carcasses to the kitchen for dressing, and Pentre announced they would feast tomorrow, everyone, including the archers and the servants, who ordinarily were not entitled to eat wild game.

"Ralph should be back from Clun with our share of the takings tomorrow," Pentre said, "and we'll make it a celebration! Now get this game to the kitchen!"

In the excitement, nobody protested that tomorrow would be a Friday, which was reserved for fish, seasoned with lots of prayers, perhaps because they would have been left to eat salted haddock, while the rest got steaks, liver, kidneys, and tongues. Even the gristle of wild game was seen as a delicacy by those who hardly ever got any, legally anyway; salt and a good boiling made anything edible.

Pentre, Walcot, and Edmund went into the hall, where supper was being set out for them, followed by those soldiers and servants not engaged in that task, for nobody liked to miss a meal if it could be helped, while the cook's boys fetched the game into the kitchen for butchering.

No one came to relieve Stephen, as even the ward in the tower above him came down and crossed the bailey.

Although it was tempting to follow, Stephen had the feeling this was a test, which he would fail if he abandoned the gate. At this time of day, it was doubtful there would be any visitors, so he closed the gate, and climbed to the tower's guardroom, where he pushed open all the shutters so that he could keep an eye on the approaches to the castle.

Edgar sent out the night watch, which relieved Stephen at sundown. The guard commander told him that he could get some scraps in the kitchen if he didn't tarry so long that the servants ate them.

The only folk in the kitchen were a couple of boys washing pots and wooden trenchers under the eye of an assistant cook.

"What do you want?" the cook asked.

"I missed supper."

"What were you up to, chasing the girls in the village?"

"I was on guard. The watch commander said you'd feed me."

"He's pretty generous with the lord's fare."

"Come on, some bread, a bit of cheese, and whatever scraps you have left. If my growling stomach keeps the boys awake tonight, I'll make sure you're the one to pay for the trouble."

The assistant cook, a beefy man with two chins, was not the least intimidated. "Too fucking bad for you. There's nothing left." He waved at the two boys toiling over the buckets. "The boys there got hold of the remainder. Polished it right off, didn't you, boys?"

"There's some bread left," one of the boys said. "In the pantry."

"I'll take it," Stephen said, snatching up the single candle on the table and moving around the pair to the pantry doors before either of them could volunteer to help.

The assistant cook followed him and stood in the doorway so that he could keep an eye on Stephen and the boys at the same time.

Stephen found the leftover bread in a sack on the top of a barrel of dried apples. He opened the sack slowly, taking the opportunity to look around as well as he could, and removed a quarter loaf of black rye.

"Hurry up, there," the assistant cook said, not liking an unauthorized person in his pantry.

"Are you sure I can't have one of those?" Stephen asked pointing to three sausages dangling from a beam overhead besides bags of plums and onions.

"No," the cook said.

"Well, what about some butter, then?" Stephen asked. "This crust is hard as a rock."

"Butter won't soften it any, but there's some over there." The cook indicated a clay pot by the fire.

"How about some salt for the butter?"

"You are a picky eater," the cook said.

"There's salt on the shelf just below the butter," one of the boys said. "That little barrel there."

Stephen crossed to the shelves and knelt by the barrel the boy had indicated. He could have just removed the top to get at the salt, but he set the barrel down on the ground, turning it as he did so, holding his breath about what he hoped to see.

And it was there: the dandelion mark burned into one of the slats.

"Pretty little mark," he said as off-handedly as he could.

"What of it?" The cook had followed to stand over Stephen, apparently suspicious that he might try pilfering a handful of salt.

"I think I've seen this mark before. Down south."

"Take your pinch and close it up," the cook said.

Stephen broke the quarter loaf in half, spread butter on both halves with his finger, and sprinkled a pinch on the butter under the cook's watchful eye. He closed up the barrel and returned it to the shelf.

He stood up, leaned against a table, and bit into the bread. It was stale, but if he held it in his mouth, it softened enough to be edible. He wanted to keep this conversation going to find out what the cook might say about where the barrel came from, but he couldn't think of anything that didn't sound out of place or like prying.

"What about that cheese?" Stephen asked.

"Over there," one of the boys at the tubs said, drying his hands on a rag.

The indicated cheese, just a bit bigger than his fist, probably wasn't one served in the hall, for there was a good bit of mold on it, but Stephen scraped that off with his utility knife. "Can I have the lot?"

"I suppose," the cook said, apparently unhappy that Stephen had even got his bread, but now that his hands were on the cheese and he'd even taken a bite out of it as if it were an apple, further resistance did not seem profitable. "Get on now. Can't you see we're busy here? It's late."

Stephen did not move from his place by the table. He bit into the bread again. "Tastes like sea salt," he said. Some salt was mined, some came from the sea. Some people reckoned that they could tell the difference.

"Only the best for our lord," the cook said.

"Where'd he buy it?"

"You dimwit, he didn't *buy* it. Now get the hell out of here. We've still got a lot of work to do."

Stephen had been certain that the cook's revelation Pentre hadn't bought the barrel of salt was as good as a confession that he'd stolen it, but as he waited for Edmund to come out of the hall for his lesson, he realized that he had leaped to another conclusion. He needed more, and he could think of only two places where confirmation could be found.

Edmund was no more interested in this lesson than he had been in the last one. He was listless, responding to instructions and making his parries in a slump-shouldered, haphazard way, except for one time when they free-played and Stephen tapped him hard on the shoulder. Edmund took his singlestick in two hands and ferociously attacked, striking wildly and hard, forcing Stephen to backpedal, sidestep, and duck to avoid being hit. When Edmund at last ran out of energy, Stephen said, "That's enough for today."

Edmund threw down his singlestick and stalked out of the tower.

Stephen collected the sticks and put them up in the hall with the other practice weapons, and strolled toward the gate. Edgar wasn't in sight, so there was a good chance he might get away without being told to do something.

"Where you going?" the soldier on gate ward demanded as he passed through the main gate.

"I've a few farthings," Stephen said. "I've a fancy for a woman."

"They'll cost you more than a farthing!"

"What is this, London?"

"They charge like it is," the soldier said with some envy that Stephen could afford their prices and he could not.

Stephen came to the crossroads where the oak grew in the center and paused to look around. He had no idea which house held the village whores. The alehouse to his right and behind him was a good suspect. In warmer weather, unoccupied girls would be outside as much to advertise the business as to seek their leisure. But this was winter, so if they were there, the girls were probably huddled about the fire.

Also, many taverns and inns that offered whores with their ale had a yellow stripe painted above the door, although that was not always the case, and this alehouse lacked such a marking.

Anyway, it wasn't whores he wanted; it was the village priest. Whores were sure to talk about any unusual inquiries he might make, since they loved gossip as much as anyone, but a priest would not if handled right.

He already knew that the village church lay across the Redlake, so he took the road south. It curved to the left and after about fifty yards, crossed the brook at a wooden bridge where three small boys were throwing pebbles at a block of wood as it floated by. He could see the church, surrounded by a graveyard, before he reached the bridge. It was an old stone church that lacked a bell tower or steeple, and, covered with ivy that was climbing upon the roof, it looked as though it had been there for centuries. The entrance was on the south side rather than the west where a window stood between two projecting stone buttresses, and he had to pass down the road to reach the path to it, for the road was sunken below the level of the churchyard by as much as three feet, and it would have been undignified to clamber up that embankment and cut across the yard.

An awning had been set up beside the door, and beneath it a stone cutter was working on a cross, inscribing an exotic design, leaves of ivy scrolling up the sides. He wasn't chiseling as Stephen drew up, but studying the design as if deciding what to do next.

"Is the priest about?" Stephen asked.

"The house next door," the stone cutter said, twirling the chisel in his fingers.

"This for the lady?"

The stonecutter nodded.

"I don't see a grave here."

"It's just to remember her by. Now go away. I'm busy."

Stephen went round the church to a substantial house overlooking the brook and the path that ran along it. He knocked on the door and waited. A boy of about twelve answered.

"I'm looking for the priest."

"Papa!" the boy yelled over his shoulder. "Someone's here for ya!"

The boy shut the door, and Stephen heard some thumping around behind it. It opened for a man whose back was so bent that the top of his naturally bald head only came up to Stephen's armpit. The hair surrounding that dome was white as a summer cloud and wispy. The face was lined, with fans of wrinkles spreading from the corner of sharp green eyes. Stubby bare toes projected from beneath the hem of his habit. He grasped the doorjam, as if he might fall on his face without that support.

"He likes to call me papa," the old man said. "After the pope, you know. His little joke."

"Who?"

"My servant. Now, he isn't important. What's important is who you are."

"I'm new here."

"That's pretty plain. I know everyone for twenty miles around. What're you doing here?"

"I've just been hired on by Lord Eudo Walcot."

"Ah, you're one of those boys, are you? Yes, you have the look about you, I suppose. Terrible times, these are, terrible times. Wolves everywhere and not all of them walking on four legs."

"Father," Stephen said, "can you spare a few minutes to hear a confession?"

"A few moments? I've no doubt it will take most of the day, and I haven't a whole day to listen to a tale of woe. Nor the interest, if the truth be known. But all right. Wait a moment 'til I get something on my feet."

He came out, shut the door, and headed off toward the church, moving surprisingly fast, alabaster ankles almost a blur beneath the hem of his brown habit.

## The Girl in the Ice

At the church door, he said to the stonecutter, "Not done yet? You might get more accomplished if you actually, you know, chipped some stone."

"It's not all about chipping," the stonecutter said. "It's as much as about thinking how to chip."

"So you say, so you say. I know it's hard, especially when you're getting paid by the day," the priest said. "Just be sure to clean up after yourself."

"You said that yesterday."

"And you did nothing yesterday. One of my parishioners cut her toe on one of your shards. If she dies of it, I'll be after you."

"You're making that up."

"Just see that there's no debris." He turned to Stephen. "Quit your gawking. This way."

The priest entered the church with Stephen at his heels. As Stephen expected it was dark and cold inside, and deserted.

The priest led the way to the right toward an indentation that must be the church's nave, where there was a bench before the window. He sat down on the bench. Stephen hesitated, because the church was so small and the window open, that anyone could hear what he was going to say, and that included the stonecutter, who must be in earshot.

"What are you waiting for?" the priest asked.

"Nothing," Stephen said, settling onto the bench beside the priest.

The priest closed his eyes. "You can start any time you like."

"Forgive me, Father, for I have sinned."

"*Te absolvo.* Is that it?"

"No. There's more."

"Well, get on with it. I'm likely to fall asleep at this rate."

"A week ago, I killed two men."

That brought the priest's eyes open. "Only two?"

"Only two recently."

"Ah."

"They attacked me."

"I'm sure. Murder is never anyone's fault. Where did this happen, if you will pardon the question, as it's not strictly my business? Not anywhere in Clun honor, I hope."

"No."

"Good. The earl has little patience for lawbreakers in his lands."

"I also took this." Stephen held out the dandelion ring, which he had removed from the thong for this purpose. He watched the priest closely for any sign of recognition.

"A nice bauble. Did you kill anyone to get it?"

"No."

"And you stole it, I suppose."

"Not exactly."

"How does one not exactly steal?"

"I found it."

"Now we are getting somewhere. And it belongs to somebody else."

"Yes."

"And you know who that someone is, of course."

"Not exactly."

"Is this a confession or a game of riddles?"

"I found it under the body of a young woman."

The priest was quiet now. He stroked his lips. "There was a young woman who had a ring like that one," he said finally.

"Who was she?"

"Why do you want to know?"

"So that I can return it to her family."

The priest slapped his spindly thighs. "That is one of the worse lies I've ever heard."

"I will return it to its rightful owners. I swore an oath to do so."

"Really? A strange thing to swear an oath about. Where did you find this ring?"

"In Ludlow."

The priest bowed his head and nodded, muttering to himself, "It could be. It really could be." He raised his head. "And you think she came from here?"

"I thought she might."

"I wonder what made you think that." The priest took the ring and examined in the light from the window. "The boys at the castle said this ring was cursed." He handed it back. "You best find its rightful owner before the curse gets you."

"And the girl's name?"

The priest sighed. "Her name was Marjory Sharp. A pretty girl. A pity to hear that she is dead."

"She was," the priest said, having forgotten that they were in confession, "the maid to Lady Rosamond, Pentre's unfortunate wife. The pair of them disappeared in November. Said they were coming here, but they never showed their faces at my doorstep."

"You're sure it was Marjory Sharp?"

"She showed me the ring herself. Said that Pentre had given it to her after his wife spurned it when she found out how it was acquired." He held his hand to his mouth, which held far more teeth than you'd expect for a man of his advanced age. "That was a secret. I've said too much. I'm near to breaking my vows. You are a clever one!"

"How did Pentre get it, I wonder?"

"Oh, that's easy. He stole it, though if you want me to get into the wheres and hows of that I'll have to break my vows, and I can't do that. I've heard a week's worth of confessions on that one!" He added, "It's not something they like to talk about, though. Terrible business, sad business. Do you have anything more you want to tell me? I've done far too much talking when I should be listening."

Ralph returned just before midday. Stephen recognized him as the man he'd spoken to on the way in who, with several other bowmen, had escorted the wagons to Clun. The wagons were not so heavily laden now, holding only a few casks of wine, bolts of cloth, and stacks of leather — and a chest. Nonetheless, there was a lot of shouting and excitement when Ralph and his wagons arrived, and the men crowded around the wagon with the chest so that Pentre and his steward had to force their way through. Pentre climbed on the bed of the wagon and opened the chest, confirming for everyone that it was filled with silver coins, more money than Stephen had seen since he had been assigned in Spain to escort an entire army's payment.

"You counted it yourself?" Pentre asked Ralph.

"Better count it again!" someone shouted. "Ralph has trouble when he runs out of fingers!"

"It's all there," Ralph said, ignoring the insult, since it was not meant seriously.

"It better be," Pentre said.

"He's probably hiding some up his ass!" another man shouted.

"I'll hide some up your ass, Humbert!" Ralph said to the man who'd spoken.

"Enough," Pentre said. He motioned to the steward, "Count our shares, then pay the men."

The steward counted out substantial stacks of silver pennies. He slid one stack across the truck bed to Walcot, who swept the pennies into a cloth bag, which he handed to Edmund. The steward put the other stack in a cloth bag which he'd brought with him, Pentre's share no doubt, and then began counting smaller stacks which he laid out one beside the other. He called out the names of the archers, who came forward, more orderly and quiet now, when they heard their names to claim their wages. The steward startled Stephen by calling his name as well, and handed him four pennies. "For two days," the steward said, in a tone that suggested he had not really earned it. "Don't look so disappointed. It's enough to get you laid, if you fancy that. You'll get the rest when you finish the week like everyone else."

When the steward had given out all the shares, Pentre said, "Now we eat! Unless there are some of you who'd rather visit our house of ladies. Not that we mind, there'll be more for the rest of us!"

No one budged toward the gate, unwilling to pass up the luxury of wild game.

"What a sad bunch," Pentre said. "You put your stomachs before your dicks." He jumped from the wagon and led the men into the hall.


The cooks had labored since before dawn to prepare supper, and it was everything everyone had anticipated: roasts, pies, soups, stuffed breads, pastries, and stews that servants carried into the hall on trays laid on boards, and they could not serve fast enough. There was even fish, not salted but baked, for those with reservations about meat, although from what Stephen could see, those few who took the fish mixed it with the other delicacies that were available. The aromas alone were enough to make a hungry man swoon, though if you did that, your neighbor would eat your portion before you opened your eyes again.

The hall was crowded and noisy, and almost choking with smoke from the hearth, its fumes prevented from escaping through the roof hole by a down draft. The haze formed slanting bright shafts of light from the windows.

Stephen could barely make out the people at the high table for the haze, but he noticed one man leave his place and kneel by Pentre and Walcot. The three glanced in Stephen's direction and the man who had gone to speak to the two knights even pointed in his direction.

"Who's that fellow?" Stephen asked the archer on his right.

"That's Hudd. He's our guide."

"Guide?"

"Shows us to the targets. We'll be going on a raid soon. More fun that lolling around here, that's for sure."

"He's not from around here, is he?"

"Na. From Clun. Only comes down when FitzAllan has decided where he wants us to go."

From Clun. The words rang an alarm in Stephen's head. He rose.

"Where you going?"

"I've got to take a piss."

"He can't hold his ale," the archer said to the man on the other side.

"Do you think he'll mind if I finish that soup?" the other man said, eying the bowl at Stephen's place.

Stephen was on the far side from the door and had to work his way around the low end of the hall to reach it. As he approached the door, however, he saw it was too late. Pentre and Walcot were coming toward him, backed by three archers they had collected along the way. They all had daggers drawn, and their faces were set and hard.

"Going somewhere?" Pentre asked as they met at the door.

"Got to take a piss."

"Your name's not Wistwode," Pentre said.

"What if it isn't?" Stephen said, hoping that he might still bluff his way, but with dread in his heart.

"It's Attebrook, Stephen Attebrook."

"Who says that?"

"Hudd here says so. He knows you."

"I've never met the man."

"We've never been introduced," Hudd said over Pentre's shoulder, "but I know you as well as my sweetheart."

"Let's hope not that well," Pentre said.

"You're Attebrook," Hudd said. "I saw you plain when we arrested you. Last autumn, it was. At the priory of Saint Augustine at Clun." He then asked Pentre earnestly, "I'll share in the reward, won't I, lord?"

"That's only fair," Pentre said.

## Chapter 23

The castle had no gaol, so they marched Stephen up to the tower, tied his hands and feet, and strung him from a rafter using the same iron ring that Edmund had used to suspend the cat, so that he could not sit down. This must be where Pentre liked to keep his prisoners, trussed to iron rungs, for there were half a dozen at various heights beside the door. They went away, and Stephen thought with relief that this would be the end of things, that they'd leave him here like this, which would be terribly uncomfortable in a while to be sure, until they bundled him off to Clun for eventual presentation to Earl Perceival.

Those hopes were dashed, when after a couple of hours, Pentre, Walcot, Edgar, the guide Hudd, and three archers came through the door, trailed by Edmund, who was finishing an apple.

"Leave the door open," Pentre said. "It's dark in here and I want to see the results of our work."

"Of course, lord," Edmund said. He bit on the apple core and tossed it at Stephen.

"Stop that nonsense, Edmund," Pentre said.

Pentre turned his attention now to Stephen. "What are you doing here, Attebrook?"

"Your man is mistaken."

"I am not — I saw you plain, close as this!" Hudd snapped.

"You're full of shit."

Pentre paced before Stephen, a finger to his mouth, looking like a pedagogue in deep thought before his pupils. He must have had a teacher like that when forced to learn his letters as a child. Pentre stopped pacing. "Whom to believe? This low fellow here, who has the manners of an ox? Or you, who fights too well with a sword? I've known common men who were good with a sword, but they never put on as good a show with the singlestick as you did the other day. It takes an uncommon amount of time to achieve that degree of skill, unless you are supernaturally gifted. As supernatural gifts are rare, it has to have come from practice. Which leads straight to the conclusion that you are not who you say you are. Which means you are lying. Why are you lying? To conceal your true identity." Pentre gestured at Hudd. "He says you are Attebrook. That's good enough for me. If you aren't Attebrook, I'm sure the earl will recognize the unfortunate mistake, and set you free. If not? Well, I've heard he has other uses for this Attebrook."

"And there's a reward, lord," Hudd said. "Don't forget the reward."

"How much is it?" Pentre asked.

"Five pounds, lord," Hudd said. "Five whole pounds."

"Ah, that is quite a lot of money. I could do quite a bit around here with five more pounds. Roofs need patching, armor needs repairing, a few more horses would be useful. Oh, Hudd," Pentre said at the sight of concern on Hudd's face, "you'll get a share of course. A generous share."

"Thank you, lord."

"You are quite welcome, Hudd. Edgar here will tell you that I do not neglect good service."

Edgar nodded. "He don't. He's good to us."

"I've heard that," Hudd said.

"It puzzles me," Pentre went on to Stephen, "why a deputy coroner is skulking here, pretending to be what you are not. It must be very important for you to put on such a masquerade. It's so demeaning to wear the clothes of a common man. I've heard of knights dressing up as women, but never knights dressing up as one of the little people. It's beyond my understanding. What are you up to?"

"Nothing," Stephen said.

"Attebrook, these denials are tiresome. You might as well tell me."

Stephen stayed silent.

"Very well," Pentre said. He motioned to Edgar and the archers, who had brought singlesticks. "Let him have a dozen or so. We'll see if that doesn't loosen his tongue. Just on the back, mind? And nothing to the head. We don't want to addle his wits. Just tickle him a bit."

"Right, sir," Edgar said. His face betrayed no expression as he moved behind Stephen with the others in his wake, no sense of enjoyment, as if this was just another job he had been asked to perform.

Edmund slipped off his barrel. "Can I do him too?"

Pentre glanced at Walcot, who nodded slightly. Pentre said, "You can take a turn. But mind my instructions."

"Yes, lord," Edmund said with a smile.

One might think that a blow from a singlestick, which was not much thicker than a man's thumb, was not to be dreaded, but only if one who had never been cracked with one. There were few things more suitable for delivering a beating than a singlestick. It produced a satisfying blow without breaking bone, and if given in sufficient quantity had a salutary disciplinary effect. Fathers, teachers, and masters all resorted to the wand when a child, pupil, or apprentice needed instruction, and Stephen had received this same attention from all three. None of those beatings, however, had been as furious as the one that now began.

Two men worked on Stephen at once, hewing at his back as if cutting a tree, the wands flying so fast and with such force that they whistled in the still air. The pain was shocking and intense, worse than anything he had ever suffered, worse even than the moment the Moor had cut off his foot — oddly, that had hardly hurt at all. The axe had gone through his foot as if through a pastry, and his main memory of the event was the ringing of the axe as it struck the stone on which he stood. It had only hurt badly afterward, when Taresa had bandaged him up and corruption had set in. That's the way it was when you lost a limb: if you didn't bleed to death it was the corruption that killed you. Yet even that pain was nothing to compare to this.

Stephen clenched his fists, closed his eyes, and gritted his teeth, determined not to cry out. He had nothing left but pride, and although he knew that torture broke all men in the end, he was determined to sell his pride dearly, and it would not go to these men in this place. If he was to whimper and snivel, it would be later, to a greater man. He thought of Taresa, but her face would not come to him, and this troubled him more than the beating. All he could recall was the great cascade of her black hair and how it had smelled of musk. He remembered how she had held him when he had been close to death, and the comfort he had drawn from it, and how he had held her when she had fallen sick, and how all his efforts to save her had been so weak and futile, and failed her in the end. I'm sorry, he thought. I'll see you soon, love. Not much longer now.

There was a pause as the men behind him tired and traded places.

"That's more than a dozen," Stephen said.

"Is it?" Pentre said. "I've not been keeping count."

"Should we keep going?" Edgar asked.

"Let Edmund have a turn. He can hardly hold still back there."

The blows that followed fell with longer intervals between them and with less force, but they came lower, on Stephen's buttocks and thighs, which were more sensitive than his back and so hurt more sharply. Edmund grunted with every swing, as if he was putting everything he had into them.

At last, Pentre said, "That's enough, Edmund."

One more blow landed. Edmund prodded Stephen in the buttocks.

"Enough, I said," Pentre said.

"I want to see him piss his drawers," Edmund said.

"You'll have to live with the disappointment," Pentre said. "Now step back." He put his face close to Stephen's. "Come, Attebrook. Tell me why you're here. Otherwise, I'll be forced to continue. Is it our business?"

"What business is that?"

"You know."

"I gathered that you're raiding your neighbors."

"There is that. Is that why?"

"No," Stephen lied, forgetting that with this answer he had admitted his identity. "Your victims are Montfort's men. Why should I care about them?"

"I hope that's true." Pentre looked over Stephen's shoulder at Edgar. "Let him have some more."

It was hard to tell how long the beating went on. It seemed like hours, but must have been far less than that. Yet in that time, Edgar and the archers grew weary, and Stephen's shirt was soaked with blood where the sticks had cut his skin as if he had received the lash. Only Edmund had any enthusiasm left.

At last, Pentre waved for the men to stop. He said to Stephen, "It was our work, wasn't it?"

"No."

"It must be important, whatever it was."

For Stephen each breath was torture. He whispered, "There was murder on the Shrewsbury road. Near Onibury."

"I've heard that the road is dangerous. What is your interest?"

"The family asked me to find out who was responsible."

"And you think I am?"

"I found an arrow where they died. Like those over there." Stephen turned his head in the direction of the barrels containing arrows.

Pentre looked thoughtful, then chuckled. "That's a thin connection."

"I had to be sure."

Pentre stepped back. "Well, it wasn't us. A pity to sacrifice yourself for nothing, isn't it?" He motioned to Edgar. "You can let him down. We're finished here. We'll let the earl have him tomorrow."

The men filed out, but Edmund lingered. He kicked Stephen in the back and laughed, then he too went out and shut the door, leaving Stephen in the cold and dark.

There was nothing Stephen could do until sundown but shiver in the dirt as the blood dried and stiffened on his shirt so that the fabric hardened, gouging his wounds whenever he moved. He was still tied hand and foot, and bound to a post, but at least he could lie down, small comfort that was. The bell for supper rang, but no one brought food or came to check on him, although a servant brought him a blanket.

"That's kind of you," Stephen managed to say.

"Lord Warin doesn't want you to freeze to death so there's nothing for the earl to play with. We don't get no reward if you're delivered dead."

Daylight dwindled to full dark. The air grew colder. Laughter and song came distantly from the hall. The dogs barked at something. Someone shouted for them to be quiet. He heard the murmur of voices that sounded like men crossing the bailey to the gate tower to mount the night guard.

At last quiet settled over the castle as the night deepened. Stephen sat up and fumbled under his shirt for the knife hanging on its thong. He cut the ropes binding his feet, rose, and pounded the point of the knife into a support timber. He tried sawing through the cords tying his hands. The knife fell out of the pillar several times and he had to drive it back in, finally holding it there with his chest pressing against the butt to saw through the cords.

Stephen eased the door open just far enough to slip through. He saw with dismay that the sky had cleared. The night was filled with hard stars and a full moon so bright that it was hard to look at rising above the trees to the southeast. With that moon, it might as well be full daylight. He couldn't cross the bailey in such light, even with all the shadows cast by the walls and buildings.

As he made up his mind to go around the tower and scale the walls on the far side, he heard the scrape and thump of footsteps on the stairs leading up from the bailey. Someone was coming. He had only moments before that someone came through the gate of the wall surrounding the top of the motte.

His first impulse was to run around the tower, but he realized that the person approaching might be a night guard assigned to the top of the tower, in which case the fact he was missing would be immediately discovered and the alarm raised. They'd catch him quick. His second impulse was to hide by the gate and ambush the fellow when he entered. That moment of doubt ate up too much time and the gate swung open.

A guard armed with spear and sword entered the space at the top of the motte.

The guard brought down the spear, but Stephen brushed aside the point with his left hand and struck with the utility knife. Puny as it was, it could still kill. The guard, however, knew his business. He dropped the spear and parried the knife, pushing Stephen back to gain space and drawing his own dagger. He struck a return blow and opened his mouth to shout, a call that would be Stephen's undoing.

Stephen took the blow on his right forearm, hooking the enemy's arm with the blade of his utility knife, and jerked downward. The man came forward, off balance. Stephen grasped his shoulder and stabbed him in the back of the neck. The cry of alarm died as a wheeze rather than a shout.

Stephen knelt over the body, breathing hard, jets of air swirling around his head, back seething with pain, his whole body aching at the monumental effort he had just expended. It had taken everything out of him just to engage in this exchange. The thought of running away seemed beyond him. He just wanted to lie down and rest.

The fight had made noise, and a voice called from below, "What's happening up there?"

Not to answer could provoke an inquiry. Stephen called back, "Nothing. Slipped on the stairs."

"Clumsy ass," the voice from below replied. "Watch yourself."

Stephen took the dead man's cloak, sword, and spear, and went round to the other side of the motte. He clambered over the wall encircling the top of the mound, and slid down the slope to the bottom. There, he rested for a moment, trying to put out of his mind the thousand aches drumming against his consciousness. At last, he mounted the embankment. There was no stair here, and he had to pull himself up to the walk. He rested again, then slipped over the wall.

He took his bearings from the moon, which had risen far enough to throw down harsh silver light on the fields to the south and east of the castle, with black hills rising in the distance and a black line of trees where the stream should be. He had to cross this open space to get away.

He forced himself up and walked across the big field toward the east, hoping that no one on the watch would spot him.

## Chapter 24

After two hundred yards or so, Stephen came upon a road heading out of the village toward the northeast. He was temped to follow it. He could make better time. But he suspected that Pentre might expect him to do this, for it was the easy thing to do in the dark, and a patrol sent this way would surely catch him. So he struck eastward across more fields and through copses until he reached the forest, with the gurgle of the Redlake on his right as a guide.

Streams meander, which forced Stephen to cover more ground than if he used the moon as a guide and kept straight. But the presence of the stream was comforting. Even with the moon it was possible to veer off toward places you did not intend, and he remembered hearing somewhere that the Redlake ran into the River Clun north of Leintwardine. Beyond the Clun and above Leintwardine, there was a high road that led to Bromfield, which was only a few miles from Ludlow and safety. So he went that way, grimly, one miserable step at a time, running for intervals even though it hurt terribly, then walking to recover. It could not be far, he told himself; three maybe four miles. Not far, but it seemed forever.

Sometime later, he wasn't sure how long, he heard the baying of hounds.

Stephen had just leaped over a small rivet leading south toward the Redlake when he heard them, far away, a sound almost imagined so that at first, he wasn't sure he had heard anything. But the wind shifted slightly and the baying came plainly to him, though far away. He had been afraid many times in his life: waiting as the first man in line before a charge into enemy horse; at the slap of scaling ladders against the wall of the castle where he had lost his foot; at the last moments before the duel with Nigel FitzSimmons; when the Welsh fired the pig sty FitzAllan had used as a gaol at Clun. Nothing compared to the panic he experienced now. At all those other times, he'd had a shred of hope to see him through. Now he had none.

He could not outrun hounds, and the men who would follow them on horses. Yet, he ran anyway. There was nothing else to do.


The forest fell away to open ground, and the footing grew marshy, sucking at his feet as he stumbled on.

The baying had drawn closer. He didn't have much longer. The wet ground might mask his scent from the dogs, but he couldn't be sure. He turned south and splashed into the Redlake, which was only knee deep, and continued along it for a hundred yards, stubbing the toes of his good foot on the stones beneath the surface.

He left the stream on the south bank and struck due east away from it, for here the stream turned northeasterly. Maybe this would fool the dogs. Maybe, but not likely.


The baying grew uncertain, more yelps than eager bellows, which told Stephen that they had lost the scent. He slowed to catch his breath. The rest was only momentary, for the yelping resumed its eager confidence, and he knew they had found the trail again. He ran on.


The dogs were close now, no more than a hundred yards away, and Stephen could hear the voices of the men who accompanied them, when he came so abruptly upon a large stream that he fell off the bank and plunged full length into the water. He momentarily lost the cloak and the spear, but, fumbling, found them again in the waist-deep water which was so chill he could hardly breathe.

# The Girl in the Ice

He waded across to the far bank, pushed through a screen of over hanging branches, and climbed out just as the dogs reached the other side. The hounds milled about for several moments, reluctant to cross water as broad as this, for it had to be the Clun. They knew he was there, though, their prey; so first one, then the rest leaped off the bank, landing in the water with splashes that must be audible for miles. They swam across and climbed out as Stephen prepared to face them.

He retreated from the river into a clearing illuminated from above as if by a white lantern so that the world around him was a pattern of silvers and blacks. The hounds came into the clearing, howling that they had found him, for the baying of dogs changes in a subtle way when they have met the prey. Two of them occupied his front, snarling furiously while the other three circled around behind him. In moments they would charge to drag him down.

Stephen turned and flung the cape over one of the dogs while he swiped at a second, which danced back with such liquid grace that he missed it. The blow swung him around, however, so that his spear caught a third making his move. The impact broke the dog's leg. It howled in pain and limped away. Stephen kept whirling, for to stand still meant death, and struck another dog with the point, lifting it clear of the ground so that it sailed into the brush. The dog under the cloak shook itself free but was momentarily confused enough that Stephen was able to clout it on the head. It collapsed. The two remaining dogs hung back, waiting for the men.

Stephen saw the men now, two black shapes on the other side of the river. Their horses plunged down the bank and splashed across, rising on the opposite shore, swords gleaming in the moonlight.

Embolden by the hounds, the two men charged through the trees and burst into the clearing more rashly than they should have, for Stephen was ready for them. He threw the spear at the first rider. It caught the man in the chest and he hung precariously in the saddle, while his horse brushed by nearly knocking Stephen down. Stephen saw the man's face as he tried to pull the spear free: Edgar.

The other man, alerted to danger by what had happened to his companion, reined up. It was Warin Pentre.

Pentre moved his horse around the edges of the clearing, sword at the ready.

Stephen recovered the cloak, which he wrapped around his left arm, and waited to see what would happen next. He regretted throwing the spear. It would have been more use to him now than the sword.

"Here!" Pentre shouted. "Over here! I've found him!"

Stephen could not hear the sound of any other pursuit, and he wondered if this was not a bluff. Yet he could not gamble that it was. He had to do something now to beat Pentre, or he would die.

Edgar's horse had halted at the edge of the clearing. Edgar remained in the saddle, bent over from the weight of the spear. "I can't get it out," he muttered.

"Hold on, Edgar," Pentre said, as he maneuvered his horse in Edgar's direction.

But Stephen swung the sword at the animal's head, and Pentre reined it away, while striking back. Pentre's sword hissed in the air, and missed, coming down with such force that he just avoided cutting his own mount, turning the blade at the last instant so the flat struck rather than the edge. The horse leaped at the impact, as if whipped, and carried Pentre to the opposite side of the clearing before he regained control.

Stephen took this chance to step to Edgar's side. "Let me help," he said, as he pulled Edgar to the ground and drew out the spear.

"I'd say thanks," Edgar gasped, "but fuck you seems more appropriate."

"Fuck you will do well enough," Stephen said, turning to face Pentre. "Care to have a go?"

"No," Pentre said. "I think I'll wait."

"Afraid?"

Pentre's mouth twitched at the insult. But he could not be goaded. "The mark of a good leader is to do the prudent thing, not the rash thing, regardless of his personal feelings. Like I said, I'll wait."

"Well, then, while I have you here, tell me about what happened at Onibury. Surely you remember it. Last November. Seven dead, including a child. Hard to forget something like that."

"What do you want to know?"

"Why did you kill them?"

"We were told not to leave witnesses."

"Who told you that?"

"That, I'm afraid, is none of your business."

"But why the child? He wasn't old enough to identify you."

"I told the fellows that. But its crying was tiresome."

"So you killed him to shut him up?"

"Not I. Edmund did. He's rather good at that sort of thing, and enjoys it."

"Killing what doesn't fight back."

"Every man has his weaknesses. Edmund's is that he doesn't fight very well. I'm afraid he never will. A streak of cowardice, you know, to his father's shame. But he has his uses."

The sound of voices came distantly through the trees, drawn to the baying of the hounds, which had not stopped their clamor.

"It will be over soon," Pentre said. "I think I'll have you buried here. It's a nice spot."

"What? You're not preserving me for the earl?"

"Not after this," Pentre said, eyes on Edgar.

That was an unguarded moment, for Pentre looked upon Edgar with real affection and sadness, as he struggled for his last breaths, the wound making terrible sucking sounds.

Stephen took the moment to pull himself onto Edgar's horse.

"Go ahead," Pentre said. "You won't get far. We'll catch you in the end."

"I wasn't thinking of that yet," Stephen replied. He dug his heels into the horse's sides, wishing for spurs, but it responded well enough and bounded across the clearing directly at Pentre, as Stephen couched the spear under his arm and settled himself deep into the saddle fearful that an impact would throw him off the horse. Pentre brought his sword to his left shoulder, point in the air, ready to parry Stephen's thrust.

As Pentre's sword swept down to knock the blow aside, Stephen pulled the spear back and dropped the point to the horse's neck. The stab might not be fatal, but the horse shied violently away, sideways and out from under Pentre, who fell heavily.

Edgar's horse wanted to continue into the trees, but Stephen reined its head around, ducking low to avoid being swept off by a branch.

He slid off the horse and struck Pentre, who was just rising to one knee, on the head with the spear shaft. Pentre collapsed on his stomach, unconscious.

Glancing at the surviving dogs, which paced nervously on the opposite side of the clearing, Stephen retrieved Pentre's sword. It was small compensation for his trouble, seeing as he had lost his own, but would have to do.

"I suppose there is something to this curse," he murmured, thinking of the ring on the thong around his neck, as he mounted Edgar's horse. "It's brought you bad luck twice now." And me at least once, he considered, wondering if he should throw it into the forest. He resisted that impulse and looked around for Pentre's mount, but his horse had disappeared.

"Sorry about the horse!" Stephen called, as he took his directions from the moon, turning east, and continued through the forest upon gently rising ground. Somewhere ahead was a road, and he was eager to find it.

## Chapter 25

In under a quarter hour, Stephen came to a well-maintained road shining white in the moonlight. When you are a stranger to a place, it is hard to tell what roads go where, but this could only be the high road out of Leintwardine.

The road went north. After a short distance, it forked, one branch continuing northward, while the other bent to the east. To go north was to stay within the Honor of Clun. All the manors and villages along it belonged to the Earl of Arundel. He considered what to do for a moment. The baying of the dogs was still audible to the west. It was hard to tell if they were following him. The dogs surely could catch the horse if they had a mind to do it, but he felt much better mounted than on foot. Stephen went right.

Stephen did not know this country, having never been along this road, although he knew one connected Leintwardine and Bromfield, and he prayed as he trotted onward, moving as quickly as he dared push the horse, that this was the way. But how far he had to go, he had no idea. Not far, he thought, not far.

It was a punishing ride. He was miserably tired and cold despite the stolen cloak, for it was as dripping wet as his coat and stockings. His arm could barely hold the spear, but he lacked the courage to cast it away. He had known men who, in the desperation of the retreat, had thrown away their spears and shields, and who in the brief time remaining to them had surely come to regret it. But worst was the shrieking of his back. The wounds broke open from the jolting and the grinding of his shirt upon them, and he felt dribbles of blood running down to collect at his waist. Let it be over, he thought. Please, let it be over.

After no more than an hour, he reached the end of the road. It met another just above a wooden bridge, and even in the moonlight, he knew the place: Bromfield. A track just to the right led to the Benedictine priory and the Church of Saint

Mary. Even though it was the middle of the night, they would give him sanctuary and rest and tend to his back. They were used to travelers arriving late at night.

But he did not stop.

Nor did he turn south for Ludlow, even though his bed in the garret room which he shared with pigeons called to him. It was only four miles away; he could be there in under an hour. Yet he was not finished with his work. He turned the horse north toward Shrewsbury.

Stephen knew the exact distance to Shrewsbury almost down to the footstep — twenty-six and a half miles — and each step along the way was agony, each jolt of the saddle torture, his shirt a devilish device more cunning and terrible than any machine made by man, the cold due to the fact he was sopping from his dunking in that stream more penetrating than the most ferocious gale. Even his missing toes were not spared. Spikes of pain shot through them up his leg, leaving trails of red sparks across his field of vision. His teeth chattered so much that he thought they'd wake those in the dark houses he passed. He paused only once to wring the water out of his cloak and clothes. They were giving him such a chill that standing naked was almost warmer than being clad. The wrung clothes brought some relief when he got them back on, though the boots remained sodden and never dried out, and he hated wet boots almost as much as he hated a certain crown justice.

Familiar landmarks passed by unnoticed: the huddle of Onibury; the spot by the river where he and Gilbert had found the dead from the robbery, Stokesay somewhere off to the left beyond its fields; the crossroad where he and Gilbert had turned toward Clun during the autumn; villages whose names he couldn't remember lying as if deserted; passing under the old abandoned castle upon its hill south of Church Stretton , saplings sprouting out of the embankment; through Church Stretton's wide market, the ruts in the dirt etched as though in a drawing, a single light showing behind a shutter as if someone was up despite the hour; through the clusters of houses sealed against the night at Dorrington and Bayton. At last, the road descended and he smelled the stink of potters' works.

Coleham reared out of the dark, and he surprised a woman hurrying along the way. She was as equally startled and ran off between two houses, no doubt up to no good. But it was not his concern, and he turned onto the path along the river, grasping the pommel of the saddle now in an effort not to topple off, for it he fell, he would surely die there before morning.

He heard voices raised in what sounded like singing from the Augustine priory across the river. Was it that late — time for prime already? Dawn had not yet shown itself. Then he remembered that the monks often woke in the third hour before dawn for yet another of their devotions, Matins, he thought it was, glad that he was not a monk. At least you had to get up only once during the night for guard duty and didn't have to sing unless you needed it to keep you awake, although most sergeants of his acquaintance discouraged singing since it gave warning to any evildoers of the guard's presence.

He took a wrong turn in the dark where the path forked, and continued along the riverbank, where boats were drawn up on the shore like great beached animals to avoid the toll on the other side of the river. Someone in one of the boats called out, "Who's that?"

"Not the watch," Stephen replied, thinking that in fact this fellow was the watchman hired to keep an eye on the boats and any property they held. The stealing of boats was a popular sport along England's rivers, so they had to be minded as much as a man's horse. "Mind your own business."

"Anyone who passes is my business."

"Well, I'm gone now, so go back to sleep," Stephen called back over his shoulder.

Saint George Bridge, that impressive structure of red stone that looked better when the sunlight showed off its color, loomed ahead, glowing a dull gray under a moon that was now sinking to the west, throwing its last light into his face. Stephen came onto the road at the foot of the tower guarding this side of the bridge. The passage through the tower was a black maw, but there was enough light to see that the drawbridge within it was up, as it should be this time of night when no one was supposed to be about but felons and agents of the devil. There should have been a guard on watch, but no one called down to ask his business. He turned left, the aroma of urine and tannic acid in his nostrils. Despite the fact these scents had a tendency to make you gag, he was glad to smell them at last, for they meant he was almost there.

The street curved away to the left, lined with low houses except for the stone box that was Saint John's Hospital, smelling of latrines and the ash from fires that never went out. The horse, tired from its exertions, could barely plod up the modest rise from the river, so Stephen slid off and walked the rest of the way.

At last, he reached the inn. He recognized it not from its sign, but from the shape of the house, an L with the top end against the street and the stable next to it across its yard. As much as he wanted to curl up and sleep, he unsaddled and untacked the horse, and put him in a vacant stall with hay, oats, and a bucket of water as his reward for the night's work. He had been a good horse and had done more than anyone would expect of him on a night like this.

Then he crossed the yard to the front door. There was no use knocking. No one would be up, and the proprietor would be angry at being awakened. It was not unusual for innkeepers to find people sleeping in the yard come dawn.

Stephen, leaned the spear against a wall, crouched on the stoop, and wrapped the cloak around himself. His clothes had dried after a fashion, so the cold was not as punishing as it had been, but it was cold enough that his misery did not much abate.

Finally, he slept.

## Chapter 26

An innkeeper's boy woke Stephen with a push that sent him sprawling on his face.

"For God's sake, man, have a care!" Stephen groaned. "If you want my business, you'll be more polite."

"You are in the way," the boy said with some urgency. "Just be glad I don't give you a dousing." He descended to the yard and headed toward the road, bearing two chamber pots, which he poured into a tub, the sort of thing many people left out for the night soil workers to collect for the tanners and the farmers.

Stephen tried to stand, but could not and had to crawl to the door, where he managed to pull himself up, and even then he tottered if he let go of the wall. He ached in every fiber and his back screamed.

As the boy returned, Stephen asked, "Is there a Gilbert Wistwode staying here?"

"And I suppose you expect me to wake him?" the boy replied, heading deeper into the inn.

"I would expect that," Stephen said.

"Top of the stairs, to the right," the boy said as he climbed the stairs. "Wake him yourself, but mind the draper. He's got a temper and he was out late last night."

Stephen lurched from one table to the next. A women bent over the fire in the fireplace glanced his way with some alarm.

"You sick?" she asked. People were often afraid of the sick. No one really knew how disease passed from one person to another, but one common thought was it passed upon the air, so people liked to stay away from the ill in case they caught whatever ailed them by their mere scent or breath.

"No," Stephen said, "just beaten up."

"You look sick."

"I just need to lie down."

"Not in one of our beds!"

"That was the idea. Don't worry, I'm not about to die in it."

The woman did not seem convinced, but by this time, Stephen had reached the stair. The fact that he had to climb on all fours like a dog did not persuade the woman that he was well.

Stephen reached the top of the stairs and paused. He felt so wobbly that he feared he might fall. He couldn't remember which room he and Gilbert had occupied. He thought it was the second on the right, but when he reached it and raised his hand to knock, the boy collecting chamber pots emerged from a room down the hallway and said, "Not that one. The next one down."

"Thanks," Stephen murmured, and tottered as best he could to the next door.

He did not have to knock, for a small young man flung open the door and rushed into the hallway, sending Stephen reeling. Had another wall not been there, he would have fallen, but even then it was no sure thing.

"Out of the way, fool," the little man said. "I'm late."

In normal times, Stephen — or anyone else for that matter — would have taken offense at such deliberate discourtesy, but he was in no position to object. All he could think of was the bed that awaited beyond the door. Had the innkeeper demanded gold for it, he would gladly have pledged to pay whatever sum was demanded.

There was only one bed in the room, and Gilbert was sitting upon it, stark naked. It was not unusual for people to sleep naked, but when they had to share a bed with a stranger, it was not often done out of fear of accusations of immodesty.

Gilbert squinted at Stephen as he stumbled across the short distance that separated them and collapsed upon the bed beside him.

"At least you're alive," Gilbert said.

"What do you know about it?" Stephen muttered, face down on the blanket.

Gilbert patted him on the thigh. "Well, it's good to see you, even if you are in a state."

"That hurts too."

"I suppose at some point you'll tell me the story. A sad one of disappointment and tragedy, no doubt."

"And at some point you will tell me you told me so."

"I don't think I have to, from the look of you. You already know I was right. What did they do, by the way, although I don't want to spoil the story by jumping ahead."

"They beat me. With singlesticks."

"Ah. Well, those things can be dreadful. Let's have a look."

"I'm not moving. I've been up all night and I insist on rest."

"You can rest while I dress."

Stephen, who did not crack his eyes, heard moving around, and at last Gilbert knelt on the bed. He tugged at Stephen's coat and shirt. "Come on now, don't make me cut them off. I don't want to ruin this fine suit of clothes, cheap as they are."

"Go away."

"You're going to sleep like that, with your legs hanging off?"

"When you go to breakfast, I will command the entire bed and I will lie as my mother instructed me on the proper use of beds."

Coaxed by Gilbert's not always gentle tugging, Stephen sat up and allowed him to remove the coat and shirt. Gilbert sighed. "Oh, well. You shall have more scars to match those you already have. At least they didn't damage your face. A woman rarely looks at a man's back even after you're married."

Gilbert stood and deposited the shirt, which was crusty with dried blood, on the floor in a corner. "I don't think that's worth salvaging after all. Up now, let's see the rest of you." He pulled Stephen erect and drew down his hose, working them over his feet. "Not as bad on the legs," he said, "but bad enough. You came all the way from Clun last night on that?" Gilbert's finger poised inches away from Stephen's butt.

"From Bucknell."

"Where's that? I don't recall the place."

"It's farther than Clun."

"I see. A heroic accomplishment, though I don't think anyone will put it in a poem. 'The ride of the bloody arse.' Yes, it lacks something in the literary realm."

"Oh, shut up. Are you done now?"

"Yes, I think so. Just don't lie on your back. You'll soil the sheets. It will cost us extra to have them laundered. Meanwhile, I shall fetch a poultice. You'll need something if you're not to catch an infection. *That* could kill you."

Gilbert did not return for quite some time, but when he finally showed up, he brought bread and cheese for breakfast, a pot of some evil smelling mustard thing for the poultice, and Lady Margaret.

She was such an august person that the innkeeper himself rushed in with a stool and a cushion, which he placed beside the bed, and due to her presence registered no objections to Stephen's use of the bed. He might have stayed to watch the proceedings, but at her glare of dismissal, he went out and shut the door. Unmarried women were not supposed to be alone with men in the rooms of inns, for fear that the authorities would think them dens of prostitution that either had to be suitably taxed or put out of business should they refuse to pay. But in this instance, the innkeeper made an exception, since the lady could hardly be suspected of such low work.

"Well," she said as Gilbert drew down the sheets to expose his back and legs, "you've returned. Not altogether in one piece, I see. What have you learned?"

"Thank you for your concern."

She smoothed Stephen's temple. Her fingers were cool and left a waft of scent. "I'm glad you're alive."

"Does she look glad, Gilbert?"

"Oh, yes. She is positively beaming with joy," Gilbert said, applying a linen cloth soaked in that vile mustard poultice.

"If she has to smell that thing, I doubt she's beaming. It's worse than a chamber pot in the morning."

"She's beaming behind the grimace," Gilbert said.

"I wonder what that looks like," Stephen said. "Well, you might as well know right off, as I might die soon." Quickly, he told her what he had learned in Bucknell.

"That does not sound very certain," Margaret said when he finished.

"He does have a habit of leaping to conclusions," Gilbert said, having finished with the poultice and washing his hands in the basin.

"They're going to mount another raid?" she asked. "You're sure about that?"

"Within the next few days."

"Where?"

"That I didn't learn. Only that FitzAllan is behind it all. He picks the targets and sends a guide to Walcot and Pentre when he wants them to take action."

"That's not enough for us to stop them."

"It's enough for you to catch them on the way back."

Margaret sat still, a hand on Stephen's arm. She squeezed the arm. "That may have to do."

She rose and swept out of the room.


"Not even a word of thanks for all my work and suffering," Stephen muttered into the pillow when she had gone. "And I thought she cared for me."

"She is quite busy, saving the kingdom and all," Gilbert said. "Well, I suppose that depends on your point of view. Here, have some breakfast."

Despite the pain, general discomfort, and the nauseating odor of the poultice, the proffer of bread and cheese brought

Stephen's head up. Gilbert held the cheese so Stephen could take a bite.

"That is not bad," Stephen said. "Did you find the girl?"

Gilbert, who had taken command of the cushioned stool, folded his hands on his ample stomach. "Well, yes, I managed to. Finally, anyway. Who would have thought that the world needed so many Sharps. The town is bursting with them."

"And? And?" Stephen demanded, only now turning on his side so he could see Gilbert. "What did you learn?"

"There is a problem."

"What sort of problem?"

"The poor girl is mad, quite mad."

## Chapter 27

"Mad? How?" Stephen asked. "There are all sorts of madness. Some people see visions, some hear voices, some are harmless, some commit terrible crimes. Remember that fellow who climbed on the roof and had conversations with invisible people."

"Yes," Gilbert said, recalling the incident, which had ended in tragedy when the fellow had fallen off and broken his neck. "As to the girl, I don't know."

"What do you mean?"

"I mean I did not see her."

"Then how do you know she's mad?"

"Her family told me."

"Ah, and they have no reason to deceive you."

"Why should they have? They seemed truthful enough. Quite helpful and friendly. Though, I must admit, they were quite firm."

"Firm, no doubt, that she was not fit to have visitors."

"That's true. So you think I was fooled, this old man who's seen so much of the world?"

"We'll know that when we question the girl."

"That will have to wait, I'm afraid, if you've a mind to do it yourself, as I suppose you should since you indicate a lack of trust in my ability to inquire. You'll not be fit to rise out of that bed for some time."

Gilbert was right about that. It was a week before Stephen could do more than totter to the chamber pot without help. Even then, an old man with a cane could have beaten him in a race across the street.

His recovery was aided by the fact that in the evening of the first day, Walter and James arrived with servants and a litter, and removed him to Margaret's house in the town, where he got a clean room on a fine, soft bed, far superior to the rack that masqueraded as a bed at the inn, and the attentions of the town's best physician instead of Gilbert.

"I cannot have you die on me," Margaret said when they had settled him in. "My conscience would not abide it."

"I am glad to know you have one," Stephen said. "I was beginning to doubt it."

"Well, it is a hindrance to those with power and those who work for them, I admit, so I must often suppress it. Do you care for literature? I suppose that is a silly question, as you are a man, and worse, a soldier. Never mind. You shall have some anyway." She settled on a high-backed chair by the bed and opened a small book.

"Literature about what?" Stephen asked.

"Just be quiet and listen. Perhaps you might learn something useful. Your mind certainly could use a sharpening."

"Gilbert is right about her," Margaret said toward the end of the week. "She is mad."

"How would you know?" Stephen asked. He could lie on his back now if he wanted to, although that was still a bit painful, so he was on his side facing her. Margaret had been in the middle of reading from the *Historia Regum Britanniae*. They had reached the part in book four about Julius Caesar's invasions of Britain.

"I have made inquiries. You and Gilbert are not the only ones capable of that sort of thing."

"Ah."

"This is the point where you thank me, and compliment me on my cleverness."

"That would only fuel your self regard. What have you learned about her?"

"She was, as you said, the lady's maid to Rosamond Pentre. Her family is in trade here in town, cutlers, as the name Sharp suggests, but they are wealthy, and a good enough family for all that. Quite well off enough that Pentre would consider engaging her for that purpose."

Stephen nodded. It was not uncommon for tradespeople to put their children in service to the gentry. The daughters of wealthy men especially benefitted from the arrangement, for it helped the girls marry into the landed class. The infusion of money such a marriage could bring was often welcomed by debt-ridden men. "You're sure that the girl is Marjory?"

"Well, no one has seen her since she returned. You've no idea what she looks like?"

"Few spoke of her at Bucknell, much less discussed her appearance."

"Hardly surprising, I suppose. Who pays attention to servants, after all? A decent girl, apparently, from all accounts, pious, well behaved, naïve, mannerly — not the sort that anyone would notice."

"You say that as if you do not approve of her."

"The world is full of such people. They are put here so others can take advantage of them."

"So there was no sign of madness before the Pentres engaged her?"

"If there had been, I doubt they would have taken the risk. No, she came back from Ludlow in this state. Walked all the way alone, my informant said. In December, during the troubles and in the worse weather."

"Any idea why?"

"No, she apparently hasn't spoken a word since her return."

Stephen sat up and swung his legs over the side of the bed. "I suppose I should go and see her."

Margaret closed the book. "You should get dressed first."

"Yes, that would be appropriate. No point in frightening the girl more than she already has been — if she is Marjory and she is mad."

222

"She won't speak to you any more than she does anyone else, you know," Margaret said as they approached the corner at Saint Mary's Church at Doggepol Lane.

"I have to see for myself," Stephen said. Despite the speed of his recovery, he was having trouble keeping up with her. "I have to see, and then we can put this whole business to rest."

"And not know the answer?" she asked. "How can that be a rest?"

"I suppose you cannot always know the answer. Sometimes even if you know the answer, you cannot do anything about it," he said, thinking of the Saltehuses and what they might do with the knowledge he would give them about the deaths of their family and friends. Would they be satisfied just knowing? He wouldn't if it was him. He'd want revenge, however he could get it. "I wanted to know who she was," Stephen said about the girl in the ice. "I've put a name to her. That's all I intended."

"No, it isn't," Gilbert said from behind him. "You wanted to know how and why she died."

"And if we've reached a dead end? How can we force a mad girl to reveal her secrets, assuming that she has any."

"Yet she must know something," Gilbert said. "She must have seen something that drove her mad."

"Now who is jumping to conclusions," Stephen said.

"It's a reasonable conclusion. Admit it. You're just giving up. Why?"

Stephen did not answer for a few steps. "I'm tired. I just want to go home. I've had enough."

"You'll feel better in a few more weeks, and then you'll be sorry. Wait 'til Harry hears about this."

"Don't you bring up Harry."

"Who's Harry?" Margaret asked.

"No one," Stephen and Gilbert answered together.

"He must be important if you care about his good opinion."

"No one cares about Harry's opinion," Stephen said. "It was just a joke, wasn't it, Gilbert?"

"Hmm, yes."

"None of this is anything anyone should joke about. This is life and death," Margaret said.

"We never joke about such things," Stephen said. "We are serious, sober men. Aren't we, Gilbert?"

"Oh, yes, serious and sober. To a fault."

"Yet it seems you just did, or tried to," Margaret said, knowing when she was being deceived and not liking it any. "And it was a very lame joke, to my ears."

"I have no sense of humor, lady," Gilbert said.

"You can count on that," Stephen added.

Margaret was not convinced, but she did not press the point as they rounded the corner. To the right was Castle Street which led north to Shrewsbury Castle. They turned left onto what people called Le Cokerowe Street and headed downhill to their destination.

At the exact point where another lane emptied into Le Cokerowe Street, both Gilbert and Margaret halted before a shop whose sign contained a silver dagger resting on a barrel helmet and entwined with a grape vine.

"This is the place?" Stephen asked.

"It is," Gilbert said.

"Curious sign."

"It means they own that tavern there as well." Gilbert gestured toward steps which lead down to a cellar beneath the shop.

As with all the shops along the street, it had its shutters down for business, and Stephen could see rows not only of knives, the normal fare of a cutler, but daggers and shirts of mail along the far wall and helmets arrayed upon a table beneath them like so many severed heads. To one side were racks of swords, and a shelf of spearheads and axe blades. Noting Stephen's interest, a man in a billowing red coat called out, "We have the finest steel from Germany, sir! Come see!"

Stephen stepped toward the counter for a better look, but Margaret said, "Not now," tugged his sleeve, and led him to a passageway through the building. They came out into a courtyard with a well in the middle, and beyond it a large stone hall backing up against the town wall that any gentryman would have been proud to call home. It even had steps of stone rather than wood.

They climbed those steps to the first story, and knocked on the door.

Presently, a servant answered and asked their business.

"We've come to interview Marjory Sharp," Margaret said. "I am Margaret de Thottenham. This," she indicated Stephen, "is Sir Stephen Attebrook. He is deputy coroner for Herefordshire, and wishes to interview Mistress Sharp about a murder."

"Mistress Sharp is not seeing anyone," the servant said.

"If you do not produce her, you can answer for obstruction of justice to the sheriff."

"One moment," the servant said. He shut the door.

"If history is any guide," Gilbert said, "the door will stay shut."

"Oh?" Stephen asked.

"Yes, that how I was treated last time I was here."

"It better not stay shut," Margaret said.

This time, history did not repeat itself. The door opened and the servant stood aside so they could enter. Like the better gentry manors, the hall proper was separated from the entrance by wooden paneling with doors allowing admittance to the hall, and the pantry and buttery on the left. The servant beckoned them toward the hall and followed them in.

"Lady Margaret, and Sir Stephen Attebrook to see you, sir," the servant intoned.

The man spoken to rose from his chair behind the table, which was covered with papers that appeared to be business accounts. "Lady Margaret," the man said, "what's this about a murder? What could my poor Marjory possibly know such a terrible thing?"

Margaret did not answer this question. Instead, she introduced Stephen, neglected Gilbert, and identified the man as Buckwell Sharp, a fit-looking fellow but with the flesh sagging beneath his chin and thick gray hair. Yet Sharp's question still hung in the air afterward, so Stephen answered it, "We aren't sure. That's why we're here. To find out."

"Well, I'm afraid you'll find out very little. My daughter is," he paused, genuine regret and pain on his face as he seemed to struggle for the right words, "unable to speak."

"And why is that?"

"I don't know."

"Some terrible shock, perhaps?"

"I cannot say. I've had her examined by the finest physicians in Shrewsbury, but none has any explanation."

"It is said on the street that she has gone mad," Gilbert said.

"And who are you?" Sharp asked.

"Gilbert Wistwode."

Sharp glanced at Stephen and Margaret as if to ask who Gilbert was.

"My clerk," Stephen said.

"She is not mad," Sharp said sharply. "Disturbed perhaps. But not mad. It will pass, in time."

"You hope," Gilbert said.

"Must I talk with this man?" Sharp asked.

"He is useful," Stephen said. He thought he heard Gilbert mutter, "Thank you," under his breath, but he wasn't sure. He said, "I'm told that she was engaged as the lady's maid for Rosamond Pentre."

"That is true," Sharp said. "Who was murdered, if I may ask?"

"The lady."

Sharp looked stunned. "I had no idea! Surely you cannot think —"

"Of course not. But she may have witnessed it and can tell us about the men responsible."

Sharp shook his head. "This is hard to believe. When did this happen?"

"Early December. At the height of the great storm. It is our understanding that your daughter returned alone during the storm, that she walked the entire way from Ludlow. Alone."

Sharp was quiet for a long moment as if considering what to say. Finally, he nodded. "It's true. The wards found her in the morning shivering within the English gate. They brought her straight here. She hasn't uttered a single word since."

"You never wondered why she came back?"

Sharp's lips pressed together. "Of course I wondered."

"But you made no inquiry."

"The countryside is troubled. Commerce is at a standstill. It is not safe to venture far from town, and Bucknell is far away."

"Not that far. And FitzAllan's agents frequent the town. I saw some myself only a few weeks ago. You didn't think to ask them? I am sure that you do quite a bit of business with the earl."

"I saw no reason to ask them."

"It is a well-known fact that Lady Rosamond is dead. Pentre openly mourns her. They would know of this. I find it curious that, knowing your daughter was in service to the Pentres, none of them would mention her death to you."

"My employees conduct my day-to-day business. I have little need nor reason to speak with such people as come to the shop."

"Well, then," Stephen sighed, having hit a wall. "There is nothing for it but to see your daughter."

"I cannot allow that."

"No?"

"Her condition is delicate. Your questions would only upset her."

"I have no intention of upsetting her. I wish to see for myself that she cannot speak or give testimony."

"The indignity! Have you no respect!" Sharp burst out angrily. "She is ailing! Why can't you leave her alone? You say you are from Herefordshire? You have no jurisdiction here." He called for one of his servants, "Egbert! Please escort the lady and these men out. We have done our business for the day."

Back on the street, Stephen gazed up the lane opposite Sharp's shop at a tableau that often occurred on the public streets in certain quarters of towns. About fifty yards away a cow had been led out and a man stood at its head with a mallet in his hand. Stephen turned away before he could see the mallet used.

Gilbert, who had also turned away, murmured, "Quite protective, wasn't he? As any man would be with a daughter."

"He was," Stephen said. "No more than I suppose you would be, had it been you."

"I suppose not," Gilbert said. "Insanity in a family is an embarrassment."

Stephen noticed Margaret looked troubled. "Something bothering you?" he asked.

"I'm not sure," she replied. "He seemed a bit too indignant. What harm could have come had we just been allowed to peek through the door? But then, you wouldn't have been satisfied with that, would you?"

"No," Stephen said. "I wouldn't."

"I wonder if he sensed that," she said. "You are not good at dissembling."

"I am so."

"Pentre would not have caught on to if you'd been better."

"How would you know? You weren't there." Stephen gazed into the shop at the arms and armor. As much as he wanted to go in and inspect them, he pulled his mind away. "Where does that physician live who attended me?"

"Not far from here. Down the hill on Hundeswete Street."

"Show me the way."

"Are you feeling ill?"

"No, I'm fine, physically anyway. It's my disposition that needs attention. Gilbert, you stay here and keep watch on the house."

"Whatever for?" Gilbert asked.

"People coming and going. That's why people watch houses."

"You suspect something?"

"I'm not sure. I've a feeling." It was really more of a memory, something he had heard once and had forgotten, and could not yet recall it.

"Ah, yes, well, we've come to put so much trust in those, haven't we?"

"Gilbert!"

"I'm a clerk, a man of letters. I'm not the sort who's good at skulking in streets spying on people."

"You're all we have at the moment. So you'll have to rise to the occasion. Oh, and one more thing — the picture."

"Ah." Gibert produced it.

Stephen stuffed the paper in his belt pouch.

"Well, just don't be long," Gilbert said, moving off toward the lane where the men ahead had killed the cow and strung it up on a scaffold for butchering. Fortunately there was a tavern and bun shop not far away where Gilbert could shelter and keep watch.

"That physician, madam," Stephen said to Margaret.

"This way."


The physician's house was only thirty yards from the intersection with Mardefole Street, which led steeply down hill to Saint George's Bridge whose red towers they briefly glimpsed when crossing. It was a four-story timber building painted a dignified black and white; none of the yellows and blues and greens fancied by many shop keepers in an effort to make their establishments stand out. People did not trust flamboyant physicians, so black and white it was.

A servant admitted Stephen and Margaret to the hall, and hurried upstairs to fetch the physician, while they stood by the fire to wait. Presently, the physician bustled in, a tall slender man wearing a fox-trimmed, embroidered robe.

"Lady Margaret!" Helmo Pride exclaimed. "It is there some emergency?"

"No, Master Pride," Margaret said, "not one requiring application of your professional talents." She eyed Stephen. "At least as far as I've been led to believe."

"What can it be, then, that brings you here in person?"

"Sir Stephen has business with you. He has trouble finding his way around and needed a guide. I'll let him explain it, for he has not shared his mind with me."

"Your back is troubling you?" Pride asked Stephen.

"My back is fine. I wanted to ask you a few questions."

"What sort of questions?"

"Have you been summoned at any time recently to the home of Buckwell Sharp?"

"The cutler? Why, no."

"The physicians in Shrewsbury, do they have a guild?"

"Well, there are only four of us, but yes, we do."

"How often do you meet?"

"Once a month."

"When was your last meeting?"

"What does this have to do with anything?"

"Humor me."

"Two weeks ago."

"When you meet, do you speak about your patients?"

"Occasionally."

"I imagine that you would discuss difficult cases. Seek each other's opinions, that sort of thing."

"We do, yes, now and then."

"Had any of your fellow physicians been summoned to Sharp's house? To attend his daughter?"

"Why no, not that anyone has said."

"It's said that the girl has gone mad, that she's unable to speak. If any of your fellows had been called to the Sharp house for a case like that, do you think they would have mentioned it?"

Pride nodded. "Yes, I think they would have. The daughter of such a prominent man, yes." He added, "I have heard that she is addled."

"But not from one of your colleagues."

"No. Just a rumor, that's all."

"Thank you, Master Pride. You've been very helpful. Oh, there is one other thing."

"Yes?"

"I presume that you are familiar with Marjory Sharp."

"I have seen her many times."

Stephen fumbled in his pouch and produced the paper. He handed it to Pride. "Is this Marjory Sharp?"

Pride's eyes lingered on the drawing. "No. I have never seen her before. Such a beautiful girl. Enough to take your breath away. Who is she?"

"Rosamond Pentre?" Margaret asked.

"It would seem so, after all," Stephen said.

## Chapter 28

"Did you learn what you needed?" Margaret asked as they climbed up the hill toward the spot where they left Gilbert.

"I did," Stephen replied grimly.

"But what did he say that was significant?" Margaret walked on a few more steps, swerving to avoid a pile of trash thrown out a window. "Ah! I see. Sharp said physicians treated his daughter. Yet none had. He's lying!"

"It would seem so. About that, certainly."

"Marjory's not mad then?"

"I suspect not." Then the memory that he had been struggling to recover came to him as if out of the dark. "If she couldn't speak, how did this other Sharp person know where she stayed in Ludlow so as to recover her possessions?"

"I hadn't thought of that."

"Neither had I, until now."

"He's hiding her, then — protecting her!"

They reached the corner across from Sharp's shop and turned into the lane. Margaret's nose wrinkled at the stench of blood, mud, and shit that seemed a choking cloud. "I hate Butcher's Lane. Must we come here?"

"Only to fetch Gilbert."

Fortunately the tavern where Gilbert had found refuge was not far from the corner.

"You're not thinking of asking me to remain?" Gilbert asked when they entered.

"No," Stephen said. "I'll stay."

"Ah, thank God. Here." Gilbert thrust a leather tankard of ale into Stephen's hand. "This will complete your disguise. It's quite good, by the way. A pleasant surprise."

After Gilbert hurried out, Margaret asked, "Should I send to the sheriff?"

"You've already threatened that. He'll remember it."

"So there's no need?" she asked puzzled.

"Not yet."

"You are not a law unto yourself."

"That's a thing I should say to you, given your customary business."

Margaret smiled slightly at that, and went out.

Several hours passed before any activity outside the Sharp residence was of the sort that piqued Stephen's curiosity. An enclosed wagon pulled by four horses halted before the passageway to the courtyard. Men loaded two large trunks into the wagon. There was a long pause before two passengers, cloaked and hooded, boarded the wagon and drew the canopy all the way down on all sides so that they could not be seen. The driver, astride the lead left-hand horse, snapped his whip and the wagon struggled way up the hill, followed by two armed men on horses who gave every appearance of an escort meant for a journey through dangerous country.

Stephen left his tankard and a farthing coin on the window sill, and hurried after the wagon.

Four-horse wagons can outpace a man on foot when the road is good, but uphill in the mud the wagon's passage was slow and Stephen had nearly caught up by the time it reached Saint Mary's Street. He hung back, however, even though traffic increased as they neared the castle and the north gates, which slowed the wagon's progress to a crawl, and then to a halt within sight of the first gate. This sort of traffic jam was not unusual. The city gates were only wide enough to allow the passage of one wagon at a time, and as there were wagons coming in, the gate wards made them halt and pay the toll. This compelled those going out to wait until the wards had admitted several wagons and then allowed four or five to leave.

The wait was so long that Stephen began to feel exposed standing there in the street. Loiterers were suspected of having crime on their minds, and the escorts had already spotted him when one of them looked back for some reason.

If he stayed put, he'd attract attention and not necessarily theirs. So he passed down the line of carts and wagons. As he drew abreast of the enclosed wagon, a woman pulled up the curtain to see how much delay she might expect. She had to be more than forty, a jutting chin with lines around her mouth and eyes as if she scowled a lot. Judgmental blue eyes examined him as he trudged past pretending not to notice. At the sight of her, Stephen worried that he had made a mistake. Could this be some other business and the chase for nothing? He resisted the impulse to leap inside. If he tried this, the escorts would be on him in an instant. He had to find a way to distract them, but he could not think of a single thing to do. He considered following them to their destination. It was late in the day, with little more than an hour of daylight left, so they couldn't be going far, five or six miles at most, but the prospect of such a long walk and spending the night by the road did not appeal. And he preferred a public place for the inquiry, not someone's country house where he might not be able to get away if things went sour.

As he entered the gate arch, he spotted a small troop of urchins lingering about the Peacock Tavern on the other side of the street. They were throwing a leather ball about, but Stephen suspected that they had other motives. He'd seen gangs of cut-purses before, and this had all the signs of one. Late in the day was the best time for their activities, for this was when most marks were distracted with the satisfaction drink and a good meal afforded and the failing light offered the chance of an easy escape. Yet herein lay an opportunity.

He passed through the gate and approached the gang. They paused in their game and regarded him with suspicious eyes. Such a bold approach usually meant someone in authority and that meant trouble, and Stephen could see the urge to bolt taking hold in their minds.

He held up a hand and said, "Boys, I have a business proposition for you."

As the wagon with its escorts finally emerged from the gate, Stephen nodded to the leader of the boys, a child of no more than twelve or thirteen, but tall, strapping, and on the verge of manhood.

"Right, then," the boy said to his fellows. "That's the one."

The gang had already prepared a pile of mud clods, for there were no stones about, spheres of filth that they had molded with surprising care and enthusiasm.

They took up these disgusting missiles, formed not merely of mud but of the shit that people often dumped into the streets when they were too lazy to put it aside for the nightsoil workers, and gauged the distance and the aim. There was joy on their faces, since the chance to strike back at the upper classes and get paid for it was an opportunity that came only once in life.

When the wagon came abreast of the Peacock where Stephen waited and the escorts' backs were to them, the boys let fly.

The shower of mud clods struck the escorts in the back, and like anyone attacked suddenly from behind, they wheeled to get a look at their assailants, before charging to get their revenge, as the boys scattered in all directions.

That was Stephen's moment. He dashed forward, and leapt over the tailgate.

A sudden intrusion almost always meant robbers, and Stephen said to the two passengers seated in each other's arms on the forward bench, "Easy! I mean no harm!"

The older woman did not take him at his word, for Stephen had not even settled on the opposite bench when she whipped out a dagger and struck at him with devilish speed. The attack was so sudden, violent, and unexpected that Stephen barely had time to parry and swivel his body just enough to get out of the way. The woman dove at him with such force that the dagger stuck in the board behind him. Stephen pushed her back into her seat as he worked the dagger free.

"You can have this back after we've had a talk," he said.

"We've nothing to say to you," the older woman said.

Stephen turned his attention to her companion, who had watched these proceedings not with alarm, but with indifference. She was young and almost as pretty as the girl in the ice. Stephen had expected her to be collected and neat, but she was disheveled, her hair down and hanging about her face. The slump of her shoulders, the way she hung her head, her hands clasping together in her lap, and the cast of her eye — all spoke of a deep melancholy. Was she really mad?

"You're Marjory," he said to her.

"She is not!" the older woman said hotly.

The girl nodded.

"Do you know who I am?" Stephen asked.

"Don't say anything!" the older woman said.

Marjory shook her head.

"You have no idea why I've come to speak with you?" Stephen fumbled into his pouch for the dandelion ring. Marjory's eyes went wide at the sight of it.

"You've seen this before. You know what it means," Stephen said.

"Marjory, dear!" the older woman implored. "Please, girl, if you love me, say no more!"

"Nana, I'm so tired. I just want it over." Marjory's fingers twined and untwined in her lap. She asked, "What do you want to know?"

"I need to know how Rosamond Pentre died."

## Chapter 29

Warin Pentre came to her during the night. He and Rosamond had quarreled again. It had been so loud that everyone in the hall could not help hearing. It had been about the same thing that had sparked many of their other quarrels. He wanted his rights as a husband, and she refused him. He tried to take her again by force, but she had acquired a dagger — which Marjory had got for her — and she cut Pentre on the hands, only minor wounds, but he withdrew, cursing loudly, to have them tended. When he had been bandaged, he came to her.

"She tried to kill me!" he said to Marjory as he stood over her bed.

"Serves you right," Marjory said.

"She's my wife! She has no right!"

"You may have bought her body, like you do a swine or a horse, but you cannot buy her heart, nor beat your way into it."

Pentre sat on the edge of the bed and put his head in his hands. "I don't know what to do. She hates me, all because I do the bidding of my lord. You're supposed to obey those above you. Why doesn't she understand that?"

"Perhaps because you do so with too much enthusiasm."

"You think I enjoy it, the killing?"

"You do. Admit it. You and that little snake, Edmund. He's more your son that Walcot's."

"Edmund has his uses."

"But the child? Did you have to let him kill the child?"

"It was being noisy and bothersome."

"You had just killed his mother. What did you expect?"

Pentre put a hand on Marjory's throat. His grip was the same as if he intended to strangle her, though his touch was gentle. "And you, what do you think?"

"I think a man must obey his lord. Although, I think you have wide discretion in how you do so."

Pentre smiled. "So you disapprove of me too?" He reached in his pouch and came out with a ring. He held it out so she could see it in the candlelight. It had a polished green stone, the gold band consisting of a pair of dandelions. Rosamond had worn it until recently.

"What is this, lord?"

He hesitated. "She didn't want it. I thought you might like to have it."

"You are most kind." Marjory held the ring in her hand as if to admire it. She wanted to wear it no more than Rosamond, now that they knew how it had been acquired, but it would have been dangerous to refuse the gift. Besides, it was worth something. She put it on the table beside the bed. She drew aside the covers and he settled alongside her.

Marjory's hands went to his waistband as he lowered his head to kiss her.

Marjory did not wear the ring openly. She knew where it had come from and what Rosamond would say if she saw it. Yet because it was so valuable, she kept it on a chain around her neck beneath her shift.

A few days later, a rider came from Clun with the warning that they could expect a Welsh invasion despite the lateness of the season, and that they must send half the garrison to Clun immediately and should make ready with those who remained. As excited as the men were to mount what they called their expeditions, they greeted this news with apprehension and dismay. Pentre tried to make light of the men's fears. "The Welsh will have to take Clun before they bother us," he said. "And they'll never take Clun."

Nonetheless, after supper that day, Rosamond Pentre told Marjory, "We cannot stay here. It isn't safe. This place will easily be overrun."

"What should we do?"

"We must seek a place of safety."

"Shrewsbury," Marjory said, thinking of her home. It was a large town and would be hard for the Welsh to capture, should they be so rash as to try.

"No," Rosamond said, dabbing the lip Pentre had split. "It's too far and the road is not safe. How could you not know that from what you've seen here? I doubt he's the only one preying on the unwary. We shall go to Ludlow."

Marjory did not apprehend that when Rosamond declared her intentions, she meant to go without escorts or informing her husband. And in fact, Majory had no idea when this journey might take place. She assumed that all would be done as a reasonable person would expect, with preliminary discussions, permissions asked for and received, appropriate packing, and the selection of suitable men as escorts, because not all of them could be trusted out of the sight of their officers. So she was taken aback when, the next Wednesday, a ride to the village church for the daily communion turned into flight. For Rosamond did not turn as usual into the churchyard just beyond the bridge, but kept going south at a pace that quickened as soon as they left the last village hovel behind.

"My lady!" Marjory called with some alarm, as she began to have an inkling of what might be going on and not liking it at all. "Where are we going?"

"To safety, Marjory, what did you think?"

Marjory thought she heard Rosamond add, "And freedom," but wasn't sure, since Rosamond didn't turn around and Marjory was several horse-lengths back. She cried, "But it's so late! It will be dark by the time we reach Ludlow."

"Then we shall have to ride fast," Rosamond said. "It's only fifteen miles. We can make it."

"But, my lady! My child! The exertion could cause me to miscarry!"

"We shall just have to hope not, mustn't we?"

Marjory had first realized she was pregnant two weeks ago, when her time did not come. Some women were often late, but Marjory was as regular as the rising sun, so the fact she didn't bleed caused her serious alarm. She kept the matter to herself for several days before she shared it with Rosamond. Marjory thought that Rosamond would be upset, but she did not show any interest other than to say, "It's Warin's, I presume?"

Marjory nodded.

"Well, then, I'm sure he will be thrilled. He so wants a son. He will have to make do with yours. Have you told him yet?"

"No, my lady. I'm afraid to."

"Afraid of the repercussions?"

Marjory nodded again.

"You won't be the first girl a lord has got with child. It's not the end of the world. You can have it here. No one will be the wiser in your family or elsewhere. Keep your mouth shut about it, and you'll still be able to make a good marriage." Rosamond smiled slightly. "You'll need my help with that, you know. Warin could care less what happens to you in the end. You know that, don't you?"

Marjory nodded a third time. She knew that indeed. Pentre was a handsome, dashing man and she had been instantly attracted to him, and he to her. But she had learned that he cared only about himself, and everything he did was to secure his position and advantage even when it meant that other people got hurt. Even his marriage had been calculated to increase his own wealth, for Rosamond was the orphaned heiress to a sizeable estate, and it had cost a great deal to acquire her wardship. Then, once he had got her in his grip, he had forced her to marry him. This had been done without the king's permission, for which there would be another fine, but Pentre was prepared to pay that one too, even though the income from the manor was not up to the expense. He knew how to get the money, though. The only catch in the plan was that he had grown wildly infatuated with Rosamond, as he had with no other woman. The heart is such an odd thing; it goes where it wills and can cause all manner of trouble when not properly disciplined. As for Marjory herself, when Pentre had got all he wanted out of her, he would discard her like a worn-out shoe. She had never expected to be used this way, and should have seen it coming, but she had been too dazzled by the newness of her position and his looks. She regretted that she had been weak, yet even now when he came to her in the night, she could not send him away, for their moments together were the sweetest things she had ever known and she could not give them up.

"I know you care for him," Rosamond said, "but remember who will care for you. I shall need your help before long, and whatever I say must not be shared with him. Do you understand?"

"I understand, lady," Marjory said.


The ford of the River Teme lay just over half a mile south of Bucknell. They rode the whole distance at a canter, and by the time they reached it, Marjory was battered and gasping for breath. She was a poor rider unused to such exertion — who knew that riding was so much work? Good riders made it look so fluid and effortless. As a town girl, Marjory had hardly ever been on the back of a horse, while Rosamond could ride and hunt as well as any man.

The ford had been improved, which is to say that parallel lines of stones had been laid across the river like the edges of a road and the space between them cleared so that only sandy bottom and pebbles lay beneath the clear water. This made the crossing by wagons and horses easier because there were no stones for them to catch their wheels upon or cause them to stumble.

Marjory expected Rosamond to drive through the ford without slackening their speed, but she allowed her horse to drop to a walk as the animal entered the river.

On the other side, Rosamond turned at last to Marjory. Her face was flushed and happy for the first time Marjory could remember.

"We are away," Rosamond said, for the Teme marked the southern boundary of Clun honor.

"Indeed, we are," Marjory gasped, glad for the respite, however brief it might be.

Then Rosamond picked up a trot, and Marjory's rouncy broke into the same gait to keep up without having to be asked to do so.

Marjory clung to her saddle with dismay, for the trot was an even more punishing gait than the canter. Fifteen miles did not sound far, but it was going to be a long ride.


The remaining details of that ride were a blur in Marjory's memory. She recalled passing through Leintwardine only because of the surprise on people's faces when they saw two women traveling alone, but the rest she blotted out.

They arrived at Ludlow shortly after sundown, the light of a rising full moon obscured by gathering cloud so that it was only a pale glow, like a candle behind a curtain. The town gates were closed and there would be no admittance until the morning, but this did not seem to trouble Rosamond. They found an inn with a stable just down hill from the gate on Corve Street. There was no room at the inn: it was full up with refugees from lands to the west, and rumors of invasion were in the air. Marjory heard one man say that Earl Roger Mortimer and his army had been defeated and were surrounded somewhere in the west, and others said that Clun itself had been attacked along with Knighton and Presteigne, although no news of this had reached Bucknell before they had fled. Marjory expected Rosamond to make a scene when she brought her word in the yard that there were no beds in the inn, though they might sleep in the stables on beds of hay. But Rosamond merely nodded and said, "That's it, then," and turned on her heel for the stables.

In the morning, Rosamond sent Marjory into town to buy clothes while she remained at the inn, huddled in a corner so as not to be noticed. Rosamond was explicit about what Marjory should buy: simple garments of the kind ordinary people wore. Why Rosamond would want to appear like a serving girl, Marjory could not imagine, since the gentry were obsessed with status and loathed appearing low in the eyes of their fellows, each vying to seem better than anyone else. But she did as she was told.

After Rosamond and Marjory had changed to their more modest garb, they entered Ludlow. Rosamond kept her face cloaked and Marjory did all the talking and paid the toll to the gate wards.

They spent an exhausting morning going to every inn in town looking for a room. The town was choked to the brim with people who had fled the fighting and everywhere they went the word was the same as last night: full up. But finally they found space at a small inn called the Trumpet at the foot of Dinham Lane. It had a bright, appealing look with its blue-painted timber, and the innkeeper, Jacky Triplett, gave them space on the floor in a room occupied by a family and their servants from a manor outside Knighton. It was crowded and Marjory felt soiled at the prospect of having to sleep on the floor, but it was better than piles of hay in a stable surrounded by horses and mules. Unfortunately, the cost all but depleted the little money Rosamond had been able to steal away with her, and they had nothing left for food and any additional days' lodging.

The next day, Rosamond ordered her to sell the horses. Marjory was aghast at being given this task. She had never sold anything before, let alone a horse, and had no idea how to go about it nor how to avoid being cheated. She almost asked Rosamond how she should carry off this venture, but Rosamond came from a class which would never think to soil itself with commerce. Such people always gave the orders to others to see such things done and thought no more about the matter. "If they paid attention more," Marjory's father would grumble, "and spent a little less recklessly, they'd all be fabulously rich. But look at them. So many poor ones drowning in debt with patches on their elbows, yet going around pretending to better than the rest of us."

As much as Marjory wanted to marry into the gentry, an ambition that her father oddly shared given his opinions, she was her father's daughter and went about the task of selling the horses with measured deliberation. First, she had to find out what a horse was worth. She had a general idea, but general ideas were not good enough. So she spent a day chatting up men in taverns, inns, and stables to get a firmer idea of the going market rate in this town.

Fortified with this intelligence, she went round to all the inns and stables in town until she finally found a buyer at one of the fancier inns, the Broken Shield, who took the horses for one pound twelve for Rosamond's palfrey and nineteen shillings for her own.

"What shall we do with all this money?" Marjory asked Rosamond when she returned to the sale.

"Live on it for a while."

"A while? Aren't we going back soon?"

"I have no intention of going back."

Marjory was deeply shocked. She had heard of women leaving their husbands; such a thing happened now and then in the lower orders. But for a gentry woman to do so seemed unthinkable. She'd had no idea that this was Rosamond's intention all along, although she should have seen it.

"Now," Rosamond said, patting the box which held their money, "find a place to hide this so it won't get stolen, keeping out a goodly amount for our expenses for the next few days."

"Where will we go?" Marjory asked as she clutched the box under an arm.

"That is our next business. I need to send a letter."

"A letter," Marjory murmured.

"Yes. As soon as possible now that we have funds."

"To whom, lady?"

"A friend," Rosamond said, with a smile that softened her face, which of late had been set in severe lines of anxiety. "A dear friend. I cannot wait to see him again."


Marjory bought a sheet of parchment and rented a quill and ink, which she brought back to the Trumpet. Rosamond wrote the letter herself, seated at a corner table in the Trumpet's hall. She folded the parchment up and sealed the edges together with wax from a candle, pressing her signet ring into the daub. She wrote the recipient's name and location on it, which was how Marjory found out the man's name: Gregory de Mandeville, Webbly Manor, near Cambridge.

"Where's Cambridge?" Marjory asked.

"In Norfolk."

"That's such a long way away."

"It is, which is why we needed that money. It will take a month or more for him to get here."

"A month living in this place?"

"Yes, I know. The prospect does not appeal. But it's cheaper than many of the other inns in Ludlow, even as the innkeeper takes advantage of the crisis. Never fear, the ordeal will soon be over. Now off you go. I've heard they've a wagon train leaving for London tomorrow. We shall pay to have them deliver it part way, anyway."


After the letter had been sent on its way, Rosamond had one more chore for Marjory. "There are women who can make potions," Rosamond said cryptically that afternoon. "You know the kind I mean."

"I'm not sure I take your meaning."

"The kind that relieves a woman of the dangers of childbirth."

"My lady! You can't possibly mean that!"

"I do. There has to be someone here who can supply that want. Please find her right away."

"But, it's a sin to kill your child!"

"I don't care. I feel as though I have the devil's spawn in me. I want to be clean. For Gregory."

"My lady, do not make me complicit in this!"

"You are not complicit. It is my choice. I alone bear the responsibility. Now, go. Let it be done."


Marjory should have argued further, but the habit of obedience was strong. It took longer to find the potions woman than to sell the horses, but at last Marjory was directed to a hut outside Ludlow off the east road toward Titterdun Clee. She found the hut in the woods after a trek though ankle-deep snow, locating it only by the smoke plume of its fire. An old woman was seated outside the hut before the fire.

"What do you be needing, dearie?" the old woman asked. "You didn't come for my conversation, that much is plain. Hardly anyone does, except for a silly boy who pesters me with questions. But no matter."

"I need something for . . ." Marjory stammered, embarrassed.

"Something to get rid of an unwanted child, I reckon."

Marjory nodded.

"How far along are you?" the old woman asked.

"It isn't for me."

"Of course it isn't. But I'd still say that you're newly taken with child in any case. Well, just a moment." The old woman went into the hut and emerged with a clay vial. "A good swallow should do the trick. You might want to take it with ale or wine. The taste is not much to brag about, I'm afraid."

"Thank you," Marjory said as she passed over the price, a full penny.

"No, girl, thank *you*," the old woman said as she rubbed the penny in her palm.

Rosamond took the potion that afternoon, but even with a cup of wine, she gagged and was unable to keep it down. She threw up out the window, admitting a blast of cold air and a volley of snow driven by such a hard wind that the flakes stung Marjory's face when she pulled Rosamond back and slammed the shutters closed. When Rosamond had recovered from spasms of nausea, she tried again, with the same result. Too exhausted, she gave up for the time being.

When neither Rosamond nor Marjory appeared at supper, Pentre knew something was amiss. One of the servants said they had gone to the church, but a man dispatched there to ask after them returned with word that they had been seen riding on the south road out of the village at a good clip. Pentre could not believe they had gone for a ride in the country, but what he expected and hoped not to be true left a chilly, panicked feeling in his gut.

"Edgar," Pentre said, "take two of the dogs and four men. See what you can find."

"Right away, lord," Edgar said as he rushed out to the stable, calling the names of four archers.

Edgar returned close to midnight without the women, soaking and shivering from a cold rain that had began to fall after sundown. "The dogs lost the scene north of Leintwardine," he said. "The sleet and rain washed it out."

Pentre rested his head on a hand. "She's run away. I can't believe it."

Walcot patted his arm. "You'll get her back. She can't have gone far. Where can she go? She has no family."

"Leintwardine," Pentre said, thinking. "That would mean Ludlow. But she's a clever girl. What if she wants me to think that? I'll wager she's going to Marjory's family, in Shrewsbury

— and the abbey's there, and a small convent of nuns. She could take refuge there and then there's no way I can get her back. She just wants me to think she's going to Ludlow so I'll waste time looking for her there."

"But you can't be sure," Walcot said.

"No. I'll have to look in both places."

"You're not thinking of going yourself?" Walcot asked anxiously. If the Welsh came while Pentre was gone and FitzAllan found he had deserted his post, it would be the end of him. FitzAllan had no patience for men who failed in their duty, especially for what the earl was sure to view as such a frivolous reason. A man was expected to control his wife and he looked the fool when he failed.

"I'll have to send someone."

"We can ill afford to spare a man."

"We can make do with four less. That's two for Shrewsbury and two for Ludlow. I'll send them off at first light." He added, "To think I trusted that bitch."

"Rosamond?"

"No. Marjory. She could have warned me, but she said nothing. I'll kill her when I get my hands on her."

It was over a week before one of the men sent off to find Rosamond returned, and much happened in that time. The Welsh had attacked all along the March. Clun castle had been besieged and the town sacked and burned, Knighton Castle had fallen with the slaughter of every man within, Roger Mortimer and his army had escaped destruction only by a truce, and Walcot's house and village were destroyed by a raiding party. But no enemy came to Bucknell. It was quiet and life went on as if there was no war. And it snowed. No one liked the snow and the cold, but this time everyone welcomed it, for it had driven the Welsh away.

The archer, who returned from Ludow, told Pentre, "We found them at a little place called the Trumpet."

"I know that place," Walcot said. "It's just south of the castle by the wall."

"What in God's name is she doing in Ludlow?" Pentre said to no one in particular. "What's she up to? It doesn't make any sense."

The archer had returned at midday, and Pentre wasted no time in getting on the road. A fifteen mile ride ordinarily took only a little less than three hours, but with the falling snow, which had only grown heavier as time went on, it was after sundown before Pentre and his escort of three archers reached the town. The gates were shut, but he claimed to be a messenger to the constable of the castle, and the wards at Corve Gate admitted him without requiring the toll.

By the time Pentre turned onto High Street, the wind was driving the snow almost horizontally, where it eddied and swirled in the corners and the side streets, piling up drifts against the houses, so thick that he could not see ten yards. They groped their way along the edges of the buildings like blind men feeling their way. If they had not had the man sent ahead earlier, Pentre would have missed Dinham Lane, even though he thought he knew the town well. With the snow, nothing seemed to be where it was supposed to.

Dinham Lane was steep in the best weather, but seemed especially steep now, so treacherous that if he lost his footing he'd tumble down to the end and smack into the town wall at the bottom.

At last, the guide stopped at the foot of the street. Here, at the junction of the perimeter road, the town wall looming overhead, was the Trumpet. Pentre had to squint against the gale to make it out.

Firelight glowed dimly around the closed shutters and seeped through the cracks in the door. It would be warm and dry in there. Pentre was reaching for the latch when two hooded figures materialized as if out of the ground.

They were coming back from the Broken Shield Inn, where the food was better than the Trumpet, though more expensive, and the hall warmer and more comfortable. They had lingered far too long in that congenial atmosphere, enjoying the play of a band of minstrels stranded by the troubles and the storm, so that it was after curfew. Not that they had to worry about being caught out by the watch in this dreadful weather.

Marjory did not think anything about the men on the Trumpet's doorstep until the one who pushed open the door so that the firelight fell on his face barked, "You!" To her horror, she recognized Pentre, with Edgar behind him, distinguishable only because of the cleft in his chin.

"You bitch!" Pentre cried as he grasped Marjory's collar, and drew his dagger. "You betrayed me!"

"You leave her alone!" Rosamond shouted. "She was just doing as she was told!" She pushed him, but Pentre released Marjory only to deliver a backhanded blow to Rosamond's head, which sent her reeling against the Trumpet's wall.

Pentre turned his attention back to Marjory, regaining his grip. She saw death in his eyes, and her legs felt filled with water and she seemed almost to float above the ground. Then, as Pentre raised the dagger to kill her, Rosamond came off the wall and struck him on the hinge of the jaw with as good a punch as Marjory had ever seen. How a little gentry girl had learned to punch like that was a mystery. Caught by surprise, Pentre toppled over like a felled tree. The men with him were so startled at what had just happened that they stood there, looking at Pentre stretched out on the ground.

Rosamond grasped Marjory's arm. "Come on!"

They ran, slipping and stumbling, nearly falling, recovering, flailing to keep their balance, Rosamond fairly dragging Marjory behind her.

Rosamond turned the first corner they came to and the ground rose before them, making the going that much harder. Marjory looked back now and then, expecting to see the men right behind, their cruel hands outstretched to grab her again and bear her down beneath their crushing weight. Yet no one was there, although she could hear men's voices calling, the sound muffled by the rushing of the wind; they were pursuing, but out of sight.

They came to another corner, and Rosamond turned again.

"Can we stop?" Marjory gasped. "They aren't there."

"They'll be right behind us. We can't hide in this town. They'll find us if we don't keep moving." Relentless, Rosamond tugged at Marjory's cloak and forced her to continue.

"What about someone's back garden?"

"And be found in the morning, frozen solid? No, thank you."

"You've a better plan?"

"There's only one place we'll be safe. Saint Laurence Church."

Marjory remembered it only as a square stone tower jutting above the roofs of squatter houses around it at the east end of High Street. It was, in fact, the biggest thing in Ludlow besides the castle, but she had been so preoccupied as she hurried here and there on one chore or another that she had barely noticed it.

"There will be a priest, and an altar, and sanctuary," Rosamond puffed, pulling Marjory after her. "A town this size has to have a priest — several priests — not some damned deacon."

"I hope it's warm," Marjory said. "I do so hope it's warm."

"Since when have you ever known a warm church? At least it has a roof," Rosamond said. "Be glad for that. Warin won't dare bother us there, especially if we rouse the priest."

They reached another corner and Rosamond turned left. The street, narrow and steep, climbed the hill toward High Street, and Marjory recognized the place: the Broken Shield had been just ahead on Bell Lane, but the fury of the snow storm had concealed it.

They struggled up to High Street, which ran along the crest of the ridge occupied by the town. It was a broad street, wide open to the wind, which whipped through it with such force that Marjory thought she would be thrown down when they stepped into it.

Now that she knew where she was, she felt a little better, but only just. Saint Laurence's was not far off. She was glad of that, for she could hear men's voices calling to each other. She thought she recognized Pentre's voice and Edgar's. If she could hear them through the wracking of the wind, they had to be close. They ran on.

It could not have been more than a few hundred feet from Raven Lane to College Street, but it seemed like a mile, taking twice as long as the usual mile. But at last, Rosamond stumbled into College Lane, and they paused to catch their breath beside the stone wall separating the church from the street. It was quiet except for the howling of the wind, and they heard no voices now. Marjory hated that wind, for it cut through her clothing to the skin, but she saw there was some benefit to it: it had wiped out their footprints in the snow.

"I think we've lost them," she gasped.

"I hope so. Come on."

A snow drift had risen at the gate, which someone had neglected to close, or the wind had pushed it open before the worst of the snow fell. They waded through deepening snow to the east door. It formed a sort of cavern that offered some protection, the pavement stones oddly swept clear.

Rosamond put her hand on the door handle, but did not pull it open.

"Is it locked?" Marjory asked anxiously. The thought that they had run all this way to the only spot that might pose as a safe hiding place, yet to be denied it, struck terror in her heart.

"I don't know." Rosamond removed her hand from the handle and fumbled under her cloak. The hand emerged with the potion vial. "I can't go in yet. It isn't right."

"What are you talking about?"

"You have to help me."

"What do you mean?"

"You know what I mean. I can't keep it down. I have to keep it down. I have to. This time." She raised the little bottle to her lips. "You have to keep me from spitting up. Like this." Rosamond held her own hand over her mouth.

Marjory nodded.

"All right, then," Rosamond said and tossed back the entire contents of the vial.

She grimaced at the awful taste and immediately gagged. She struggled not to spit up, motioning Marjory to clamp her lips shut. Marjory put one hand over Rosamond's mouth and, to hold firmly, the other at the back of her head.

Rosamond's frail body shook with violent spasms as she struggled against the impulse to vomit, trying to swallow, yet obviously failing. It seemed as though for a time that only Marjory's strength held her up, but even that did not last, and the two sank together to the hard stones, Rosamond's hand over Marjory's so she could not let go.

In the end Marjory's will failed her and she withdrew her hands. She could not continue to be an accomplice to such terrible suffering.

Yet Rosamond's struggles did not cease. She did not vomit up the potion. Something seemed to have caught in her throat. She gagged and tried to breathe, but nothing came out. Her tongue protruded grotesquely, her mouth worked like a fish's, and her eyes bulged as she fought against whatever was blocking her breath.

Marjory grasped her shoulders and pulled her up to pound on her back. She had seen people choking on lumps of food, and this is what folks normally did at such times, but it brought Rosamond no relief. Rosamond looked up at Marjory with terror in her eyes as Marjory looked on helplessly.

Rosamond sank back and Marjory bent over her.

The dandelion ring on its chain had worked itself out of its hiding place and dangled in the air between them.

Rosamond clutched it; whether she knew what it was Marjory could not tell.

Rosamond's gasps grew shorter and shorter in duration, until they finally stopped, and she lay still, eyes half open as if gazing at a distant object. Snowflakes landed on her face and melted into tears. The hand grasping the ring hung in the air, refusing to let go, as if somehow Rosamond might pull Marjory down into the abyss. Marjory snapped the chain and the hand fell away.

She had gone and wasn't coming back.

Marjory was alone.

## Chapter 30

"I didn't mean to kill her," Marjory pleaded. "I really didn't. Please believe me."

Stephen had heard voices steeped in grief before, mothers who had lost their children, men their wives, his own sobs as he laid Taresa on the stony ground. This was genuine.

The wagon hit a deep rut in the road and it jolted and leaned precariously, throwing Stephen against the side while Nana held on with one hand and clutched Marjory with another. A wheel stuck momentarily in the rut. The driver cursed and applied the whip. The wagon lurched forward out of the hole. Marjory sobbed into her palms.

"Are you done?" Nana asked. "What more do you want from her?"

"No," Stephen said. "I'm not done yet."

"You are a cruel man."

"Marjory," Stephen asked, "am I to understand that you left her there where she died, on the doorstep of the church?"

Marjory raised her head, her eyes red and cheeks wet with tears. She nodded.

"You did not move her away, off the path?"

"No, I just ran away."

"What has this to do with anything?" Nana asked sharply.

"It is a detail not accounted for," Stephen said. "If Marjory's story is true, someone moved her after she died."

"Why would anyone do that?" Nana asked.

"A good question."

"And now what?" Nana growled. "The sheriff?"

Stephen had been thinking about this matter all along. Duty required that he report what he had learned and let justice run its terrible course. Yet would justice actually be done if he did so? What good would it do to punish this girl for what surely was an accident for which she had little responsibility, or to expose Rosamond as the sinner she was, when poor folk derived hope from her? In such a perilous world, hope was the only thing that kept people from despair. It occurred to him that perhaps there was more to the stories of the saints than put down in books and told in church, that they were more fallible men and women than the stories led you to believe, steeped in sin, their lives as filled with mistakes and misjudgments and even bad deeds as anyone else, and yet good still came from them. There were no perfect people in the world, and even many of the great hero warriors Stephen had known were men you might not admire, other than for their inspiring bravery. Who could understand why miracles flowed through some people and not others?

"It was an accident, no more than that," Stephen murmured. "It wasn't your fault." He leaned over the women's bench and parted the curtain so he could call to the driver. "You there! Stop the wagon!"

The driver's head swiveled around in surprise and alarm, as he had not had any inkling there was another passenger, particularly a male one. "What? What are you doing there?"

"Just do as he says," Nana said. "It's all right. He needs to get off."

The driver reined in the team, and the wagon shuddered to a halt.

Stephen climbed out onto the road. "Hello, boys," he said to the two escorts who were even more astonished and embarrassed than the driver. "Nice afternoon for a ride in the country."

Nana leaned over the side. "Thank you for this."

"Just make sure that she never speaks of it to anyone, ever. You understand the price she will have to pay."

Nana nodded. The curtain fell back into place. Taking his cue from that, the driver snapped his whip again and the wagon jolted forward. Stephen stepped to the side of the road as the escorts trotted by.

Stephen gazed back toward town, where the aged wooden tower on the castle's motte kept watch, an odd contrast with the brownstone walls about it.

As the wagon drew away, he trudged back up the hill to the town gates.

## Chapter 31

After supper, when they were seated around the fire with blankets on their laps for warmth, even the servants having gone so that they were alone in the cavernous space, Stephen told them what he had learned. It took a while, and when he was done, Gilbert and Margaret stared into the fire. Stephen had expected them to shower him questions and criticisms, but perhaps they were only gathering their thoughts.

"A bad business," Gilbert murmured at last. "A sad business. She left her on the doorstep of the church, you say?"

"Yes," Stephen said.

"And you believed her?"

"I did."

"There was no sign of deception?"

"None."

"You're easily fooled. Isn't that so, my lady?"

"What would I know about that?" Margaret asked coolly, sensing a rebuke.

"So, then," Gilbert continued, insensitive to the chill, "someone dragged her thirty feet away and left her in a snow drift."

"So it would seem," Stephen said.

"Some chance person who saw an opportunity for plunder?" Gilbert pondered, tapping his lips with a finger.

"You think so?" Stephen asked.

"One must consider every possibility, no matter how trivial or unlikely."

"That seems pretty unlikely," Margaret said, "given that you found the ring under her body, not in her hand. It was a valuable ring, wasn't it?"

"Gold," Stephen said. "At least the band. Here." He removed the ring from his belt pouch and held it out.

Margaret bent over to view it. "A pretty thing."

"So whoever found Rosamond's body removed the ring from her hand," Stephen said. "The only likely culprit is Pentre."

"You mentioned that he claimed she was dead, not merely a runaway," Gilbert said. "This would explain it."

"He could have worked out that the girls had fled to the church," Stephen said. "It would have been the best, even the only, sanctuary after curfew and in such a storm. He arrived there, most likely alone, and found her."

"Why move the body?" Margaret asked.

"So she wouldn't be found immediately," Gilbert said, following the trail that Stephen had set. "He would want to be gone before she was found. It would diminish the possibility he was a suspect. Which it did quite well."

"And the ring?" Margaret asked. "Why did he leave it?"

"Because of the curse," Stephen said. "Pentre's men believed it was cursed. After this, perhaps he had come to believe it himself."

"It is a pity you will never know for certain," Margaret said.

"What do you mean?" Stephen asked.

"I have some news of my own. This afternoon I received word from Arnold Bromptone," she said. "He failed to intercept Pentre on his return from the last raid — they sacked and burned a manor at Upper Hayton five days ago. However, he followed the trail back to Bucknell, and took the castle by surprise escalade during the night, with no small help from your description. Pentre, Walcot, and a few others sought refuge in the tower, but Bromptone managed to set it afire. The wood was old and dry, apparently. A little barrel of pitch was enough. It made a torch visible for miles, he wrote."

"All were killed?" Stephen asked.

"Some escaped, but not many."

"I hope he is happy with his revenge."

"I suspect he is for now, and happy that he has recovered some of what was lost."

"I hate not knowing," Stephen said.

"Suppositions are thin consolation for all our hard work," Gilbert agreed.

"Our work?" Stephen asked.

"I did find the maid, after all. That was hard work. I had to scour the entire town before I tracked her to her hiding place. What would you have done without that?"

"All you got out of that was sore feet."

"And I should be compensated for them, though there seems to be no possibility of that. Not even a 'Well done, Gilbert. You've found the key.'"

"Well," Margaret said, rising from her chair and taking the pitcher of Gascon wine that had rested on the ground beside it, "have some more wine."

Gilbert extended his cup. "Thank you, my lady. That is an excellent wine."

After she had filled his cup and set down the pitcher, she held out her hand to Stephen, who hesitated in doubt and uncertainty about what this meant before he took it.

As she drew Stephen to his feet, Margaret said, "Master Wistwode, I leave the pitcher to you. May it ease your suffering feet. Meanwhile, I hope you will excuse us. Stephen and I have some unfinished business that we must conduct before he falls asleep."

Gilbert managed not to gape in surprise or ask what business that was.

He reached for the pitcher as Margaret led Stephen across the hall to the stairway to her chambers.

# Epilog

Although rumors circulated about the March for some time, consensus settled around the notion that Bucknell had suffered a winter raid by the Welsh. Such raids were unusual, but the border had been dreadfully unsettled of late, with raiding parties penetrating twenty or even thirty miles into England. Only a few suspected the truth, and they kept their suspicions close, plotting their revenge.

In mid-February, the weather warmed almost to the point that the air was spring-like. People welcomed this turn, for it meant less discomfort, especially at night when they usually crouched around the fire for relief from chills and drafts before scampering off to bed, but those who had to take to the roads cursed it, for the wet turned the roads to ribbons of mud, halting virtually all traffic that rode on wheels. A single horse, however, could make good time on the verges, which were not as churned up, so Stephen took the opportunity to ride down to the Saltehus' home at Worlebury. It was farther south than he had expected — beyond Bristol on the shore by the bay of the Severn. There he returned the ring and informed them of how their family had died and who was responsible, and the fate that befell them.

On the way back, Stephen stopped at Gloucester, where he called on a certain draper named Peter Bromptone, a younger son of Arnold Bromptone with whom he had a short acquaintance, and his wife Alicia, who was noticeably with child. They were grateful at the news Stephen brought of Bromptone's home and father, and invited him to stay the night, the hard feelings that had arisen from their last encounter having dissipated to the point that they shared an odd affection born of shared hardship and nostalgia, but he declined. Bromptone did help by recommending a cutler across from Saint Mary's Church on Graselone Lane by the north gate to buy one of the swords Stephen had taken during his escape from Warin Pentre. He had neglected to sell it in

Shrewsbury, a decision he regretted, as he had much debt and the amount offered for it in Ludlow was not enough to cover what he owed. He thought he might get a better price for it in Gloucester, and he was right.

Stephen returned to Ludlow by a circuitous route that brought him to the Galdeford Gate on the east rather than Broad Gate to the south where the bridge on the Hereford Road crossed the Teme. He did not wish to confront Harry for he had not yet repaid him. Harry had said nothing, since no one was supposed to know that he had any possessions whatsoever, let alone four shillings in hard money that he had let out to loan. But Stephen wanted to avoid further accusatory looks and comments about his own pauper status.

As he was putting the mare up, Gilbert entered the stable, having been alerted by one of the boys to Stephen's arrival. "Have you got it?" he asked anxiously.

"Yes," Stephen said. "More than enough to shut his mouth."

"Thank goodness! He's been pestering me about it since you went away — as if I have some responsibility for it." Gilbert sighed, "You'd think that picture should have kept him satisfied, but he gave it back."

"Why?"

"He was afraid Jennifer would see it and think ill of him."

Stephen smiled. "Poor Harry."

They went out to the yard where Gilbert called to one of the house boys to take Stephen's belongings to his room. Stephen would have followed, but the sight of the little cart caught his eye, and he had an inspiration. "Fetch Mark!" he called to the house boy as he entered. "I've a chore for him!"

"Right away, sir!" the boy called back.

"What are you up to?" Gilbert asked, sensing something afoot in such uncustomary behavior. After a long journey, most people wanted to settle by the fire and relax.

"You'll see," Stephen said.

When Mark came out to the yard, Stephen tossed a farthing at him and told him to bring the cart.

He and Gilbert, followed unenthusiastically by Mark and the cart, went out to Bell Lane and down Broad Street to the gate.

Harry saw them coming from a long way off, nodding as they drew close. "Look who snuck into town," he said. "How long have you been back?"

"Long enough to put up my horse," Stephen said, stopping before Harry.

Harry eyed the saddlebag on Stephen's shoulder and threw a look at the nook where the gate ward took shelter. "Have you got it?"

"Got what?"

"You know what I mean."

"Ah, that. I have, and I think we should celebrate your good fortune."

"My good fortune. What the devil are you talking about?"

Stephen did not answer that. Instead, he said to Mark and Gilbert, "Gentlemen, if you would be so kind as to load this fellow on our cart."

Neither Mark nor Gilbert seemed happy at this request, but Gilbert grasped Harry under the arms, and Mark took what remained of his legs, and they lifted him to the bed of the cart. Gilbert grimaced from the exertion, as Harry was quite heavy even though there wasn't an ounce of fat on him.

"I think I've pulled out my back," Gilbert said as he staggered away from the cart.

"Serves you right," Harry said, "assaulting a man like this. What's going on?"

"We are taking a short journey," Stephen said.

Harry leaned over and hissed in a voice he hoped to would not carry far. "I want my money. I don't want any journey."

"Nevertheless, you're getting both. One before the other."

"This is an outrage," Harry said.

"We haven't even got to the best part yet," Stephen said.

He turned about and headed through the gate.

The mire was such on the street between the gate and the bridge, that it took the three of them to pull the cart through the mess. But finally, they reached the Wobley Kettle, a bathhouse that stood across the street from Saint John's Hospital.

"What are we doing at this den of vice?" Harry demanded.

"I said it was to celebrate," Stephen said. "Can you think of a better place?"

"My stall," Harry said. "I like my stall."

"You shall have your stall in good time." Stephen then called through the door for servants of the bathhouse to take Harry inside, as he could not mount the step himself, and Gilbert was not up to the effort. Carriage was not free of course, but he felt as though he was rolling in money from all he had got for the sword and the other half of the Saltehus' commission. Once Bromptone finally paid up, he'd be a rich man.

Several whores were waiting for customers in the hall when they entered, and they blew kisses at the sight of the new arrivals, anticipating their custom, although they looked at Harry as if someone had introduced a rat among them.

"Take him to the back," Stephen said, indicating the doorway that led to the tubs where people took their baths. "He'll need a smaller tub than most people, the one you use for children. He'll drown otherwise."

"Stop this," Harry said, as he began to thrash in protest so that the porters nearly dropped him. But they held on firmly, which wasn't easy, anticipating more money from Stephen for their efforts.

"You need a bath, Harry," Stephen said. "Be still."

"It's winter. I don't take my bath until July."

"Nonetheless, you're going to have one. You stink bad enough to kill a mule."

Despite his protests, Harry ceased thrashing, and allowed himself to be carried to the rear of the house, where the porters put him on a bench in the stall containing the small tub used for children.

Harry contemplated the bath, which other servants were filling with pails of hot water, with something approaching dread.

"Clothes off, Harry," Stephen said. "Or I cut them off."

"You are an evil man," Harry said.

Stephen sent Mark out and drew the curtain. He sat beside Harry and began counting out pennies from his saddlebag. It took a long time to count out eight shillings, but when he was done, there was quite a substantial stack of pennies between them.

"That's more than I gave you," Harry said.

"Yes, and you can have it all if you get in the bath."

Torn between his natural greed and his aversion to baths, Harry regarded the pennies. At last he said, "I can't climb in that thing by myself."

"Gilbert," Stephen said, rising, "give me a hand."

"I am injured!" Gilbert protested. But since it was only a short trip from the bench to the tub and did not require a great change in altitude, he suffered to lend a hand, and between the two of them, they managed to deposit Harry into the tub without spilling the contents.

"Oh, God," Harry muttered.

"Terrible, isn't it?" Stephen handed Harry a cake of soap.

"What's this?" Harry pretended ignorance.

"You know what it is. Get the worst off."

When Harry took the soap, Stephen pushed his head under water.

Harry came up spitting and cursing. "I'll never forgive you for this!"

"Oh, I think you will," Stephen said, scooping the pennies into the bag.

A couple of the house girls entered the stall, and Stephen and Gilbert withdrew so they could work their magic without the distraction of spectators.

They heard Harry say, "What the hell?" and "Oh!" before they reached the doorway to the hall.

"I wouldn't mind some of that," Gilbert said a bit wistfully.

"You're a married man!"

"Well, yes, but I'm allowed to dream. Just don't tell Edith."

The two girls came out and said they were done. Stephen and Gilbert returned to the stall with the barber who had a shop next to the Wobley Kettle so as to provide his services to its customers whom baths had softened up so they were less inclined to object to his prices.

"No! Not that!" Harry cried, recognizing the barber.

"Yes, that," Stephen said. "It's time to see what you've got hidden under there."

"I like my beard. It helps me keep warm."

"Have at him," Stephen said to the barber, who was regarding the wild mat of hair and beard as a professional challenge which he might not be able to handle.

"It's worse than I thought," the barber said, who knew Harry of course but had never pondered the problem of his beard up close. "It's going to cost you extra."

"Just try not to cut his throat," Stephen said.

"Can I at least cut out his tongue?"

"No, that's the best part of him."

"I don't think many people would agree with that," Gilbert murmured.

Harry looked set to resist further, but the warm water and the ministrations of the ladies had weakened him, and the barber set to work after Harry had been toweled off and dressed in fresh rags.

It took a full hour before Harry's hair had been shortened to civilized length and combed, and his beard shaved.

"Well, well," the barber said when he stood back to admire his masterpiece.

"I cannot believe this is the same person," Gilbert said in astonishment and awe. "No one will recognize this as Harry."

"What? What?" Harry said.

"Our work here is finished," Stephen said. "Let us get him back."


The return to the Broken Shield was a quiet business, marked only by the fact that the boy Mark had managed to get drunk during Harry's bath, and kept slipping in the muck and occasionally falling down. But with the three of them pulling the cart, they got it up the hill as far as Bell Lane without spilling their cargo and ruining the good work that had already been done.

Jennie Wistwode was stirring laundry in a tub over a fire in the yard when they entered. She gaped at the spectacle, and asked as they passed, "Who is that?"

"It's Harry," Stephen said. "He's had his bath. Could you bring him out some supper after we get him settled?"

"That can't be Harry," Jennie said. "He's . . . he's . . . handsome!" Normally, Jennie had to be badgered to fetch things for Harry, but now she rushed into the inn without further prompting.

"Did you hear what she said?" Harry asked, as Stephen and Gilbert set Harry on his board, since Mark was still having trouble holding himself up let alone anyone else.

"I heard," Gilbert said, not altogether happy about what was happening. "Don't let it go to your head. What you have of one, anyway."

"My head is worth two of yours," Harry said sharply.

"That's the old Harry," Stephen said.

Harry disappeared into the stable, and Gilbert and Stephen lingered in the yard, enjoying the last light of the day.

Jennie brushed by them carrying a tray and went into the stable.

"Harry?" they heard Jennie ask.

"Yes," Harry said. "Would you like to come in?"

"You really are Harry. It's so hard to believe."

"Do you like me better this way?"

"I do."

At that, Stephen took Gilbert by the elbow and turned toward the inn, where Edith was leaning out a window to call them to supper.

There are times when the world seems knocked out of kilter, where nothing goes right and all the best intentions end in disaster. But at this one moment, things felt good.

"I shall not get used to that," Gilbert said.

"It may not be so bad after all," Stephen said as they crossed the doorstep into the warmth and comfort of home.